The

Lawyer

Copyrighted Material

ISBN: 9781796771756

Chapter 1

Los Angeles, CA
1994

Robert Jameson had just come back from his jog when he told his wife that he wanted a divorce, like he had just said he wanted cereal for breakfast.

"What?" Trish asked.

"Please don't make me repeat it. It was hard enough to say the first time," he said as he sat down in the breakfast nook.

Patricia 'Trish' Truman Jameson's mouth dropped open. Her hands trembled as she stood at the white kitchen island.

"It hasn't been working for a while, now," Robert said as he rubbed his chocolate bald head.

"It hasn't? We just had sex last night. Believe me. There wasn't any hint that you weren't into it," she blurted and placed her hands on her hips.

"There's no need to be petulant. I meant mentally. We haven't been connecting. We've grown apart."

Trish kept her hands on her hips. "Who is she?"

He looked down at his tennis shoes.

She dropped her arms to her side and walked around the counter. She sat down with her husband. "We've been married for almost nine years. I think I deserve a better answer than, 'we just grew apart.'"

Robert looked up at her. "You're right. You do." He took a deep breath. "There is someone else."

"Who?"

"Trish-."

"I deserve to know the name of the woman you are leaving me for. I'm not going to do anything to her. I just want to know."

"Helen Daughtrey." Her name dropped in the room like Robert just dropped a glass.

"Your patient?"

"My ex-patient, now. Soon to be fiancé."

"She's sixty years old!" Trish shouted.

"She's fifty-five," he corrected. "And she doesn't look a day over forty-five."

Trish's dark brown eyes widened like a child who was just told her parents were getting a divorce. "I guess not thanks to your services."

Robert was going to speak again, but Trish interrupted. "Let me get this straight. You've been having an affair with your...former patient - who is old enough to be your mother - and you're leaving your wife for her. How long has this been going on?"

He mumbled something.

"I didn't hear you, Robert."

"About eighteen months," he said with a sad look.

Trish jumped up from the breakfast nook. She didn't know whether to be pissed or disgusted. "I...I don't know what to say," she said as she ran her hand through her long, dark hair.

"State your terms, and I'll do my best to meet them."

She just stared at him like he was an alien. "Is that it?"

"There's really nothing more to say," Robert said and stood up.

"It takes a while to process a divorce, Robert. What are we going to do until then?"

"You can stay here until I sell the house. I'm moving into Helen's estate. I already got some clothes there. You can use the money we have left in the joint account. I opened a separate one last week."

Shallow breaths escaped from Trish's throat. "Well…it seems like you've thought of everything."

Robert walked to the door that led to the garage. Turning around he added, "I have to say, you're not as upset as I thought you'd be."

Trish looked dead into her husband's brown eyes. "If you can come in here after a morning jog and just throw the words 'I want a divorce' at me after all we've been through to get where we are-." She stopped, exhaled, and then continued, "We've never had anything to begin with. Therefore, there's nothing to get upset about," she finished as she shook her head.

Robert turned and walked out the door that led to the garage.

Trish grabbed a glass of orange juice from the island and threw it at the door. The glass shattered as liquid dripped down the light yellow walls. She covered her mouth to conceal her anguished cries.

Chapter 2

Clary, PA
Six months later

Trish Truman sat in the back of a black minivan that was being driven by an old African-American man who, it turned out, was a real chatter bug. She patiently listened as he talked about his dead wife, his three sons, and his grandchildren for twenty minutes.

She sighed with relief as the driver pulled into the paved driveway. The Jacobs' two-story red brick house hadn't changed in twenty years.

"This looks like a nice neighborhood. I'll try to get your bags," he said, hinting that Trish had a lot of luggage.

"Don't worry. I'll help you," she said and got out of the van.

The driver pulled the latch to open the trunk and got out of the vehicle. As they walked to the back of the van, Darlene Jacobs jogged out of the front door. "There she is!" Darlene shouted as she ran to greet her childhood friend.

Darlene's short, sunshine-blonde hair shimmered in the sunlight, and her blue eyes sparkled with excitement. The ladies embraced.

Darlene pulled back and looked at Trish as she flashed a big smile. "It's going to be like old times."

Trish chuckled. "Not necessarily. Instead of us having a sleepover in your room, I'll be living in your basement."

"Apartment," she corrected. "Daddy had it done really nice. I helped, of course."

"Oh, of course," Trish said with a grin.

They walked to the back of the van with the driver.

"Holy cow," Darlene said as she looked in the packed down van. "You must have brought everything."

"I'm coming out here to live not visit. What I couldn't take on the plane is in a storage unit in L.A."

"We only have so much room, young lady," James Jacobs said as he approached them.

"I know, sir," Trish said with a smile.

"Is that a trunk?" Darlene asked.

"I got a hand truck in the garage. No way we are lifting that thing," Mr. Jacobs said and moseyed towards the garage.

Trish laughed. "It's good to be back."

****

Trish surveyed her new home. The basement apartment walls were beige, and the wood floors were a light brown. The living room was furnished with a sky blue couch with a love seat and recliner. The kitchenette had white appliances and beige cabinets, and the island was white with a sink. Four wood bar stools lined along the island. The wood burning fireplace had a slick gray finish. The basement apartment had a door that led to the backyard. Brown boxes were scattered around the room, filled with household items that Trish had sent ahead of her arrival.

"The bedroom and bathroom are back there." Mr. Jacobs pointed with his left hand. "We took the liberty of unpacking the two TVs. The cable man came before you got here."

"I also unpacked your towels and linens and washed them. I made the bed for you," Darlene added.

"Thank you. I can't tell you how much I appreciate it."

"Before you get settled, we need to go over the house rules," Mr. Jacobs said.

"Daddy," Darlene said flatly.

"His house, his rules. Lay it on me, Mr. Jacobs," Trish said as she took off her black fur-collared coat.

"No parties after midnight. No overnight guests of the opposite sex," he began.

"Oh God," Darlene moaned.

Trish chuckled. "I don't think you have to worry about that. Anything else?"

"Trash runs on Thursdays. I think that's it."

"Yes, that's it," Darlene confirmed and rolled her eyes.

"Oh no, I forgot," he said and reached into his pocket as he walked to Trish. He pulled out a black keychain that said, Jacobs Investments. "This is the key to the front door, and this is the key to your separate entrance," he said and dropped them in Trish's hand. "And one last thing."

"And that is?" Trish said with a big smile.

Mr. Jacobs cupped both sides of Trish's brown face and bent down to kiss her forehead. "Welcome home, sweetheart. I sure did miss that pretty smile of yours."

"Awe," Trish said.

Mr. Jacobs removed his hands from her face. "If I was born thirty years later…"

"Gross!" Darlene exclaimed.

Trish and Mr. Jacobs laughed. "Come on, Darlene. I haven't gotten a sincere compliment from a real man in ages and probably won't again. Let your father flatter me."

Darlene just stared at them with disgust.

Mr. Jacobs eased down into the recliner. "I doubt that. Yeah, your marriage broke up, but you're what, twenty-eight?"

"Twenty-seven, Daddy. Trish and I are the same age; we're only a month apart."

"That's right. Anyway, you're still young and beautiful. The men will come running in no time."

"I hope not. I don't think I can invest that much time and energy into a relationship again."

"You say that now, but give yourself time," Mr. Jacobs said as he leaned back.

"With that being said, how is the divorce coming along?" Darlene asked as she sat down on the couch.

"It's not really. I don't have an attorney. Robert's lawyer sent legal separation papers months ago, but-."

"Are you stalling on purpose?" Mr. Jacobs asked.

"No. I want it over with, but the attorneys in L.A.

are so expensive. I have to be mindful of my budget. I'm hoping to find an attorney here who won't cost too much."

"What about David Shaw? I heard he was both reasonable and good," Darlene said.

Trish looked at Darlene like she had recommended the devil. "No way. Are you nuts?"

"What's wrong with him? I heard the same thing," Mr. Jacobs said.

"He's an ass," Trish said and sat down next to Darlene, crossing her arms across her chest.

Mr. Jacobs face scrunched up with confusion.

"I know what this is about. Do you still hate his guts for that snake incident?" Darlene asked.

"Yes," Trish replied with more than a hint of anger.

"What snake incident?" Mr. Jacobs asked.

"Oh, you remember, Daddy. It was the fourth of July. You and Mom hosted a BBQ in the backyard. Trish and I were lounging on a blanket when all of us heard David yell out. His foot went into the air along with something black and long."

Trish was steaming. "It was a big black snake that he threw at me. It landed right in my lap."

Mr. Jacobs slapped his knee and bellowed with laughter. "Gosh darnit, I remember now. Oooh, once you got that thing off you, you really went after that boy." He stopped and shook his head. "I never seen a fourteen-year-old girl so mad in my life."

"Wouldn't you be?" Trish asked. "I was fourteen, and he was already in college. He was a tool then, and he's probably a tool now."

"It was an accident. He tried to explain that to your

mother back then," Darlene said.

"What do you mean?" Trish asked.

"Let me tell this part," Mr. Jacobs said. "After your daddy pulled you off that poor boy, your mother got in his face. Waging her finger and all, and he blubbered how he felt something crawling on his foot, and he looked down, and it was a snake. He was so shocked he just kicked the snake away from him. He didn't mean for it to land on you."

"If that was the case, why was he laughing?" Trish asked.

"Hell, we were all laughing as I recall, except your mother," Mr. Jacobs said. "I think."

"I wasn't laughing, and David wasn't laughing anymore when you caught up to him," Darlene said. "Didn't you ask Mr. Truman to beat him up?"

"Yes, and he wouldn't do it. Dad said I hit and pulled everything on David that wasn't nailed down, and Mom was reading him the riot act; he didn't think David deserved any more punishment. He also said it was over now and to calm down."

"Yeah, but I bet he gave you a big hug afterwards," Darlene said.

Trish gave a weak smile. "Yeah, but I never forgave David or bought that bull story about it being an accident. Why did he kick it my way? I tell you why. It was because he wanted it to land on me."

Mr. Jacobs scoffed. "I believed the boy. He never caused any trouble before or since that I know of."

Trish shook her head. "I disagree, and the last thing I want is for him to be involved in my personal business."

Chapter 3

Thirty-one-year-old David Shaw walked around the dilapidated interior of his office wondering what went wrong with his life. He had landed a job straight out of law school with Lakedale Associates in New York. Heather, his now ex-fiancé, there by his side until that fateful day he walked in on her having sex with his boss.

He resigned before he was fired for punching one of the partners in the face. He stopped pacing to look out the dirty window as he clenched and unclenched his chiseled jaw. A tapping at the door interrupted his thoughts. "Come in," he said.

Mrs. Hinkle, his sixty-five-year-old secretary, opened the door. "Mr. Shaw, your two o'clock is here."

"Good, send her in," he said. He stood waiting for Darlene to come in. She wouldn't tell Mrs. Hinkle why she had made the appointment. He figured it was an extremely confidential matter.

"Hi, David," Darlene cheerfully greeted.

"Hi. It's good to see you," he said and took Darlene's hand. "What can I do for you?"

Darlene shyly shifted her head to the side. "Well, it's

not for me – more for a friend of mine." Darlene looked back past the door that Mrs. Hinkle was holding open. "You may as well come in."

Trish slowly stepped into the room. Her lips were pressed together like she had just swallowed a lemon, her hair was pulled back in a bun, and her makeup was flawless. Trish's leather coat was open, revealing a tight red turtleneck and a black skirt that hugged everything below her waist. The black leather from her boots stopped under her knees.

Tension struck his body at the sight of her. David wasn't sure if it was from arousal or annoyance. He fought the urge to roll his eyes, and his upper lip turned up to his nostrils. "Darlene, why did you bring this prizefighter with you?"

"Pardon me?" Trish asked.

David ignored Trish's response and looked at Darlene. "Darlene, I thought this appointment was for you, but I can see that is not the case. Whatever trouble Trish has gotten herself into, I'm not getting involved." He walked away from Darlene to sit down behind his desk.

"That's it," Trish said through gritted teeth.

"Trish, wait," Darlene begged as Trish made her way to David's desk.

Trish looked dead into his smoldering dark eyes. "Considering that your reception area looks like the entrance of a crack house, the windows are so filthy dirty that you may as well paint over them, and the paint on your desk is chipping onto your stained carpet, I would think you would take all the clients you could get."

David opened his mouth to speak, but Trish

interrupted him. "Also, I do not appreciate being judged by an obviously struggling lawyer, when I let my friend convince me to give you a chance at making some real money."

David opened his mouth again, but was interrupted - again. "However, I don't want to continue insulting your precious ego with my presence. I'm sure I can find another attorney in Clary that I can do business with."

David shot up from his chair, his five-foot-nine frame casting a shadow over Trish's face.

"Are you done?" he asked in a deep voice.

Mrs. Hinkle continued to stand at the door with her mouth open. Darlene waited with baited breath.

With fire in her eyes, Trish responded. "I'm quite done, Mr. Shaw. Good day. Come on, Darlene." Trish turned to walk out.

"Wait," David said.

Trish stopped, but she kept her back to him.

"I apologize for my unprofessional behavior, Mrs. Jameson. Please sit down, and we'll discuss the purpose of your visit," David said with an unreadable expression.

Trish kept her back to David as she looked at Mrs. Hinkle whose faded eyebrows were raised in expectation.

She then turned her head to Darlene who had a pleading look on her face. "He said he was sorry. He really is a wonderful lawyer, Trish, I promise."

Trish turned her head to face the open door. "How long have you been practicing, Mr. Shaw?"

Once again, he fought the urge to roll his eyes. "Nine years," he answered.

"Win-loss record?" Trish asked.

"I've only lost five cases."

"Have you always had your own practice?"

"No. After I graduated law school, at the top of my class, I worked for Lakedale Associates in New York City. I decided to move back to Clary to be closer to family and friends two years ago. That's when I opened my own practice."

"Two years is a long time to have such a short client list," Trish replied.

"As you know, the economy is slow, and it takes time to establish a reputation."

Trish looked at Mrs. Hinkle again. Mrs. Hinkle mouthed the word, please. Trish's face softened slightly. She turned around to face David. "Thank you for the apology, Mr. Shaw."

"Is it accepted?" Darlene asked.

Trish glanced down at her boots before looking back up. "Yes. Thank you."

"Thank you, Mrs. Jameson. Please come and sit down," David said and gestured to one of the fake black leather chairs across from his desk.

Trish walked to the chair and sat down. She crossed her legs and placed the file folder she was carrying on her lap. Mrs. Hinkle left the room, closing the door behind her.

Darlene plopped down in the matching chair next to Trish. "Now that we've got the formalities out of the way, let's get down to business."

"Yes. Why do you need my services, Mrs. Jameson?" David asked as he sat down.

"It's Ms. Truman. I'm getting a divorce. I need an attorney to represent me."

David clasped his pale hands together on the desk and leaned forward. "I'm truly sorry."

"Thank you, but there's no need for sympathy. It's obvious that it wasn't meant to be."

"I see. What is the reason for the separation?"

"He decided to leave me for his mistress."

"Who is fifty-five years old and rich," Darlene added.

"I see. When did you two officially separate?"

"I got legal separation papers from Robert's attorney six months ago," Trish said and pulled a folded contract out of the folder. She handed it to David.

David skimmed the document. "It looks like your typical legal separation document. Nothing tricky. I take it that you're looking for a settlement."

"Yes. I think I deserve compensation. After all, I used the money my parents left me after they died to pay for his pre-med education. I also sold my grandmother's restaurant after she died to pay for him to attend medical school. Throughout our marriage, I worked at various places to keep the household bills paid and food on the table. I wore many hats in L.A. - waitress, secretary, finance assistant, taxi driver, I was even an extra in a couple of movies and two TV shows. For the exception of the past two years, I worked my butt off to support him- financially and mentally."

"She also dropped out of college her sophomore year to be with him in California," Darlene added.

"Yes, that too," Trish said flatly.

David leaned back in his chair. "Now that he's made it big as a doctor in L.A. he has bigger fish to fry."

"Yes," Trish stated.

"How much do you know about the other woman?"

"Not a lot. Her name is Helen Daughtrey, and she's old enough to be Robert's mother. She's been married twice. One husband died - he was a producer who left her a lot of money - and the other she divorced. Rumor has it that she got a pretty hefty settlement from him as well. Big time socialite. She invited Robert and me to one of her garden parties at her estate."

"Is that when you two first met her?"

"She was a patient of Robert's while he was finishing up his internship. But, yes, I first met her at the party she invited us to."

"Do you know what he was treating her for?"

Trish scoffed. "Treatment? Robert is a plastic surgeon. God knows what Helen had tucked or lifted. When I met her the first time, her face was tighter than a pin cushion."

David's eyebrow went up. "I thought he was a general practitioner."

"That's what he was studying at first, but he changed his mind. He said if we stayed in L.A. he could make more money as a plastic surgeon."

"I see," David said.

"Do you?" Trish asked. "I wish I could have seen how he changed. When I first met him, he was a man who wanted to heal people or at least alleviate their suffering. He was a charitable man. Robert would give the shirt off his back if someone needed it. Now, he's a money hungry cheat who would sell his soul to make a buck."

It was silent for a moment.

"Please excuse my... personal and bitter words, Mr.

Shaw," Trish said.

"No excuse needed. You're right. You deserve compensation," David said and grabbed a legal pad and pen. "Can you list the assets that you and Robert acquired during the marriage?"

"Does that mean you are taking her case?" Darlene asked.

David's eyes lingered on Trish's face. "If she'll have me."

"Trish?" Darlene asked.

Trish almost got lost in David's eyes. She quickly composed herself. "Yes," she said in a voice just above a whisper.

"Great. David is going to chew Robert's skinny behind up and spit him out with nothing but the shirt on his back. Aren't you, David?" Darlene asked.

David humbly glanced down. "I'll do what I can - as soon as I get an idea of what to ask for."

"Oh. Here," Trish said and reached into the folder and gave David a piece of paper.

David looked over the list of assets. "You typed this up for me?"

"Can't take credit. It came from his lawyer's office. They said to give it to my attorney- when I found one."

"I have to say, he's done well for himself in a short amount of time."

"Tell me about it. Eighty percent of that stuff I didn't know we had."

"Really?"

"I mean, I knew how much cash we had on hand...as a couple, but apparently he's been stashing cash and buying stocks and bonds for quite some time…in his own account- not to mention the properties."

"Do you have specific requests of what you want as a settlement?" David asked.

"I think two million dollars, one of the rental properties, and the house in the Bahamas is fair to ask for. The house in the Bahamas was an anniversary gift, but it's in his name."

"I think he can afford to give you more than that - especially since he is remarrying a rich woman."

"I'm afraid if I ask for any more, it would hold up the divorce. Robert's attorney has called me every two weeks for the past three months asking me who my attorney is. It got to the point that I don't answer the calls anymore."

"You have his business card?" David asked.

Trish pulled the card out of her black purse and handed it to him.

David took to from her. "I'll call him today. You shouldn't hear from him anymore. We should discuss my retainer."

"How much do you want?" Trish asked.

"Eleven hundred," he said.

Darlene's face went pale. "Dollars?"

"That figure is a bit too ambitious, don't you think?" Trish asked.

"It's not all for me. I need half of it to retain the services of a P.I."

"What do you need a P.I. for? He admitted to cheating on me," Trish said.

"I just have a feeling more is going on than meets the eye. Robert leaves his pretty young supportive wife for a fifty-five-year-old woman. I don't care how much money or how much plastic surgery this woman has had; something is not right, judging from what you've told me. If I'm right, I can use it as leverage. What are you? Twenty-five?"

Darlene's eyebrows shot up at David's statement.

"Twenty-eight," Trish corrected.

"Next month," Darlene added.

"Maybe Robert really does love her. Sometimes age doesn't matter. After all, it's not like I understood all the medical talk. Perhaps they have good conversation," Trish said, and then shrugged.

"I doubt it. From what I can remember, you're intelligent and can hold your own in a conversation. He's definitely looking to raise his social capital and bank account with Ms. Daughtrey."

Darlene's lips parted as she watched the two exchange words.

"I'd like to satisfy your curiosity, but…I have money, it's just I need to buy a car soon, and I need to watch my pennies. I'm afraid a P.I. would be a waste of money. Let's say six hundred up front, shall we?"

"You didn't have a car in California?" David asked.

"Of course, I did. A Bentley, actually. But, without a steady income coming in I didn't want to waste money on car payments and insurance on a luxury vehicle. So, I sold it," Trish answered.

"I have an idea," Mrs. Hinkle said over the phone intercom. "I'm having surgery next week, and David, I mean Mr. Shaw, will need someone to take over for me while I'm out. I'll be out for at least two months. Ms. Truman has office experience. She can pay six hundred now and work off the rest with cash to spare."

"Maybe she can take your place permanently. What do you think you're doing?" David asked.

Trish's mouth dropped open.

"I was just monitoring the conversation to make sure you didn't say anything else dumb to the young lady. We haven't had a new client in here for a month. We can't afford you chasing her away."

"That being said, it's a wonderful idea," Darlene said trying to lighten the mood.

"No. It's not," Trish whispered to Darlene.

"Didn't you work in a law office in California?" Darlene asked.

"I was a temp in one for two weeks - four years ago," Trish stressed.

"If you can read and write, you can do it. Mr. Shaw said you were smart. I bet you catch on quick," Mrs. Hinkle said.

"This is my practice, which means I'm the boss. I have a say who works here," David said.

"It would do you good to get out the house," Darlene said.

"I can go outside to get out of the house," Trish said.

"You need something constructive to do. Keep your mind busy," Darlene continued.

"She's right. Working here would take your mind off your divorce," Mrs. Hinkle said.

"I have not agreed to this ridiculous arrangement," David said.

"Why is it ridiculous? You don't think I can do a good job?" Trish asked.

"I didn't say - I didn't mean it that way," David

stuttered.

"I can do it. I wasn't that spoiled in L.A.," Trish said to him.

"That a girl. David will pay you the same amount as he pays me. Since you have experience," Mrs. Hinkle said.

"What!" David exclaimed.

"Come back tomorrow, sweetheart, so I can show you the ropes," Mrs. Hinkle said. "Deal?"

"You got a deal," Trish said.

"Wait a minute," David said.

"Oh, thank God. We got someone to fill in, and we can pay the electric bill this month. It's been a-."

David jerked the phone jack and cords out of the phone.

Chapter 4

Mrs. Hinkle walked into David's office and closed the door behind her. He continued typing on his computer.

Her grayish brown hair was in a loose bun. "Still mad at me?" she asked.

He continued typing.

"We won't see each other for a while, young man. The least you can do is wish me luck on my surgery," Mrs. Hinkle said as she walked closer to his desk.

David stopped typing and coolly looked up at her. "You're getting a boil removed from your foot. It's not life or death."

"At my age, you never know. Besides, you know helping Trish out is the right thing to do."

"I do?"

"Yes. Another reason why I pushed this is because I don't want you to be alone in this depressing place while I'm gone. If anything, she's something pretty for you to look at."

"Ha!" David spat out.

"You said it yourself during her appointment."

"I did not," David said. He remembered that he had, but he refused to admit it.

Mrs. Hinkle leaned against his desk and stared down at him. "Listen to me very carefully. I'm not speaking to you now as Mrs. Hinkle, your assistant. I'm speaking to you as Mrs. Hinkle who baked you and your brother cookies when you were children. Before you left Clary, you were a bright, caring, and happy young man. That was not the David Shaw that returned. The David that returned is cold and irritable. You're turning into a bitter old man way before your time, and I care about you too much to keep standing by and watching it happen. The only time that you have any life in you is when you're in a courtroom. But, work is not enough to breathe life into a man. Now, I never asked for any details as to why you came back, but I always had a feeling about what it was. It's time to heal and move on."

"Mrs. Hinkle-."

"I'm not finished, young man. I saw and heard something come to life in you when Trish walked in here last week. Yes, it was animosity, but her appearance got a rise out of you outside of a courtroom. That girl is the only one that can handle your....attitude. Maybe she can help you loosen up, and you can stop her from bottling up her feelings. We both know she's more upset about the divorce than she's letting on."

David remained silent.

"You said I could leave around noon today. My last day - for a while, at least. Let's end it on a good note."

David stood up and took Mrs. Hinkle's slim, wrinkled hand. He kissed it. She smiled up at him. "There's my boy," she said and took her other hand to brush the side of his dark wavy hair above his ear.

"Good luck on your surgery, ma'am."

"Thank you. Goodbye, dear," she said and walked to the door and opened it. She took a few steps, and then she looked back at David, and then back out to Trish. "You two try not to kill each other."

After Mrs. Hinkle left, David walked to Trish's desk and looked down at her.

"You follow the rules around here and everything will be fine."

"What do you mean?" she asked.

"Yes, you're my client, but you're also my employee."

"I'm aware of that."

"Good. So, I'll make sure you are aware of other things."

"Like?"

"No smoking in the office. No personal calls unless it's an emergency. If you need a day off or will be late, call to let me know. You get an hour for lunch."

Trish stood up and saluted. "Sir, yes, sir. Anything else, sir?"

His mouth twisted at her sarcasm. "This is going to be a real treat."

"I'll do a good job. I promise I won't embarrass you around your long list of clients. I don't smoke, and for the exception of a distant cousin, I have no family left, so no emergencies should come up. Here," she said and handed him a blue folder.

"What's this?" he asked.

"It's the research into the Manley custody case. There is a list of references that set a precedence of reversing adoptions."

"Oh, thank you," David said.

"If it's all right, Sergeant. I have a lunch date. May I go?"

"Sure," he said and walked back into his office.

Chapter 5

Darlene and Trish ate club sandwiches in a booth at the Bullock Café. The café was located a couple of blocks away from Clary University's main campus and four blocks away from David's office.

"So, how's the job coming along?" Darlene asked.

"Ugh. I can't believe I let myself get goaded into this. He is so infuriating and a total grouch. I don't know how Mrs. Hinkle put up with him for two years. David is so depressing to be around."

"Are you two still fighting?"

"We don't fight. We throw out a couple of zingers and occasionally bicker. Although, it might get worse now that Mrs. Hinkle is gone."

"It will work out. You'll see. Have you seen his brother, yet?"

"Teddy? No. David just said he hired Teddy to be the P.I. for my case. His brother has connections in L.A."

"I knew it. I knew he would get Teddy to be your P.I. Do you think you'll talk to him personally?"

Trish looked up from her sandwich. She stared at

Darlene's glowing face and hope - filled blue eyes. "You stinker," Trish whispered.

"What?"

"You set this whole thing up - how could I be so stupid?" Trish said and dropped her sandwich on the white plate.

"What are you talking about?" Darlene asked in a high-pitched voice.

"I can't believe you still have a crush on Teddy after all these years. I wondered why you were so insistent that I hire David. You were hoping to see Ted. And getting me or goading me into working off the balance of David's retainer. You have an excuse to drop by the office because I'm there- to see if he's there. Unbelievable. You're playing with my future you know."

"I can't believe you would accuse me-." Darlene stopped talking when Trish raised her eyebrows and gave her a penetrating look.

"I...if David really wasn't a good lawyer I would have come up with something else."

"I know what you could have come up with. Go to Ted's office yourself and ask him out to lunch or dinner."

"I can't do that."

"Why?"

"He'll think I like him."

"You do. Hell, I'm thinking you're in love with him."

"I'm hoping he notices me. Asks me out first."

Trish's eyes widened. "You've been pining for the man since you were eighteen years old. Playing hard to get is not the strategy for this situation."

Darlene blew out in frustration.

Trish sighed. "If I happen to notice that Ted's coming in to see David, I'll call you. Okay?"

Darlene blushed. "I'd appreciate that."

"I just don't understand why you can't walk up to the man and start talking to him instead of pining for him from afar. You're an outgoing, friendly person."

"I've always been tongue-tied around him. At my graduation picnic, he approached me. I was a blubbering mess. All he said was congratulations and asked me about my plans for the future. I stuttered so badly; I know he thought I was a complete idiot."

"I'm sure he just thought you were a sweet, shy young lady," Trish eased.

"He's so...so....handsome, smart,...and really successful. He's really successful as a P.I. I heard from the girls at the beauty salon that he's worth a couple of million dollars."

"Hell, you wouldn't know it. Does he still wear that black leather jacket and wrinkled T-shirt?"

"Not all the time," Darlene said sheepishly.

Trish chuckled.

Two African American males approached the booth. Darlene and Trish looked up at them as they approached.

"Good afternoon, ladies. We were wondering if you two would be interested in joining us at our table for dessert?" the one with dreadlocks asked.

Trish and Darlene looked at each other in amazement.

"That's very friendly of you," Trish breathed out as she sized up the muscled specimens before them.

"Thank you, but I can't. I have errands to run," Darlene said.

"I don't," Trish replied.

"Trish, you've got a job to get back to."

"I'll call the sergeant and tell him I got held up in traffic," Trish said as she stared at the more muscular man closer to her left.

"Trish, you just got that job."

"Temp job," Trish said as she smiled at her admirer.

"You said you would do me a favor at that temp job," Darlene said.

Trish gave an 'I'm sorry' look to her potential young suitor. "She's right."

"Maybe you and I could…get together later. How's Saturday night?"

"That would be great," Trish said trying to suppress her excitement.

He reached into his backpack and pulled out a pen and mini post-it note. "You mind jotting your number down, Trish?"

Trish's smile widened as she took the pen and post-it. She wrote her name and cell phone number down. "So, what are we going to do Saturday night?"

"I figured we could meet here around eight for a quick bite, then go to a club," he said.

"That sounds like fun," Trish said.

"Is it a date?"

"Absolutely, uh- uh-" Trish stuttered because she didn't know his name.

"Jamal." He reached into his backpack again and handed her a card. "It's my business card from my part-time job, but it has my cell phone number on it."

Trish took the card and gave him back his post-it and pen. "Telecom Global?"

"Yes, I'm just a part-time sales rep. I have to pay for my books somehow."

"Oh, of course," Darlene said and smirked at Trish.

****

Darlene and Trish walked along the sidewalk in the downtown district of Clary. They were heading to David's office.

"I can't believe you are going out on a date with that child," Darlene said, shaking her head.

"Did you see the muscles coming out of his shirt? Honey, he is no child," Trish said proudly.

"Did you see the fraternity letters on that shirt? He's a college student."

"I saw everything about that chest, thank you very much," Trish said with a mischievous grin.

"Oh, my."

"You know, I admit I was depressed about this divorce, but now I'm realizing how free I truly am. Hot, young flesh, free for me to sample."

"Daddy said no overnight guests," Darlene spat out.

"I didn't say I was going to sleep with him, and if I was, I wouldn't bring him back to your father's house. That would be disrespectful. Nice to know what you think of me."

"Sorry. I have never seen you flirt like that before. I thought you lost your mind for a second."

"Not exactly, but I'm afraid that my libido is in

overdrive."

Darlene rolled her eyes. "We should have stopped for some ice water."

Trish laughed. "It's cold enough out here. I've cooled down now."

"But, seriously, if you're ready to date again, you should keep an eye out for more realistic and long-term options."

"And where am I going to find eligible men that want a serious relationship? Dating is difficult in the nineties. Seems like it's harder to meet people."

"What about Internet dating?"

"No way," Trish said as she turned her nose up.

"There's nothing wrong with it. I've heard plenty of success stories. That's how my cousin in Tulsa met her husband."

"I prefer to meet men the old-fashioned way," Trish said.

"I do, too, but that's not how it's done, now. We are living in the age of the world wide web." Darlene stopped walking.

Trish stopped. "You want me to post an ad looking for love?"

"Just think about it. That's all I'm asking," Darlene said.

"No way."

****

Trish walked into the reception area of the law office just as David was walking out of his office with his briefcase and a black trench coat in hand. His face was like stone and devoid of emotion as usual.

"Good, you're back. I'm meeting a potential client for a late lunch. I'll be back around three. Try not to burn the place down while I'm gone," he said and walked passed her.

"Hell, if the place burns down it won't be because of me. It will be because it's a fire hazard."

"Smart aleck," he mumbled and slammed the front door after himself.

"Ass," she said as she rolled her eyes and whipped off her black coat with fur cuffs and collar. She walked to her desk and plopped down in the chair, slamming her purse down in the drawer as she sat.

Chapter 6

Theodore 'Teddy' Shaw sat down next to his brother at the sports bar. Ted's skin had a yellowish glow, his hair was dark and curly, and his jaw wasn't as chiseled as his younger brother's. Ted wore his signature leather jacket with a black turtleneck and blue jeans. He looked up and down at his brother's gray bagging sweatshirt and pants.

"I take it you've been to the gym," Ted said.

"Yep," David said and sipped his scotch.

"What ya havin'?" the female bartender asked.

"Whatever you have on tap, cuteness," Ted answered with a wink.

She smiled, nodded, and walked away.

"Why'd you call me down here?" Ted asked.

"I thought we could hang out for a while. Have a couple of drinks," David replied without looking at him.

"It's Saturday night - date night - and you call me here to decompose with you? Figures. I thought at the very least you needed me to be your wingman, and you look like you just rolled out of bed."

"If you had plans, why didn't you say so?"

The bartender placed a mug of beer in front of Ted. He smiled and nodded his thanks. She smiled back and walked away. "I didn't have plans. What I'm getting around too is why don't you have plans? When was the last time you went out on a date?"

An ape-like grunt escaped from David's throat. "I don't know, and I don't care."

"You should. You still can't be brooding about what happened in New York with Heather. You didn't need that girl - she was a gold-digger and a slut," Ted said and took two big gulps from his mug.

"I'm not interested in dating."

"Sex. Are you interested in sex, at least?" Ted asked so loudly that the bartender and a guy sitting next to them looked over.

"He's my brother. I'm trying to get him out of the life of celibacy," Ted explained.

The bartender snickered, and the patron just turned his head.

David coldly looked at Ted. "Are you done alerting everyone to the details of my social life?"

"Sorry, man. It's just, for the past two years I've watched you die before my eyes. What happened to that happy-go-lucky guy who was my kid brother?"

"He grew up," David answered and twirled around on his barstool. His mouth dropped open when he saw Trish standing at the door with a guy who looked like a college student. The guy had on a fraternity jacket and black jeans. Trish wore a tight purple angora sweater with leather pants that hugged her in all the right places. "Damn."

"What?" Ted turned to look where David was

staring. "Hey, is that Trish Truman?"

"Unfortunately," David mumbled and reached for his glass.

Ted let out a deep chuckle. "This is going to be fun. Hey, Trish! Over here!"

"What are you doing?" David asked.

"Livening up the evening," Ted answered and grabbed his beer.

David was incredulous. Her outfit was entirely inappropriate for a first date - for any date. She was advertising for attention.

Trish and her date walked to them. "Teddy!"

They embraced.

Ted gave her a kiss on the cheek. "You look good enough to eat. Who's ya friend?"

"This is Jamal Jackson. Jamal this is Teddy Shaw, the best P.I. in the state," she proudly said.

"Well, maybe in town, but not the state. Nice to meet you," Ted said and shook Jamal's hand. "What are you doing here?"

"We were supposed to eat at the Bullock Café, but the place was packed. There was a forty-five-minute wait," Trish answered.

David grunted. "If she's your date for the evening, kid, you have my condolences."

"Jamal, this sorry sap, who is dressed like a sack lunch, is David Shaw, Teddy's brother," she sternly said.

Ted laughed. "Oh boy, I'm sure the office is full of some interesting days with you two in it."

"Try to behave yourself this evening. We wouldn't want your case jeopardized," David said with a deep voice.

The college student's eyebrows shot up, and his eyes widened. He rubbed the back of his fade. "Case?"

A brunette approached them. "Your table is ready."

"I'll tell you about it," she said to Jamal. "We have to go, guys. Enjoy your evening…Teddy," Trish said – making it clear to David she had nothing more to say to him.

"You, too," Ted replied.

The waitress led Trish and Jamal away.

"What was that about?" Ted asked.

"What?"

"It's obvious she's on a date. Why did you bring up her divorce?"

"I didn't - would have been a breach of confidentiality. I brought up a case. I didn't say what it was about," David said and sipped his scotch.

"I can't believe you are still mad at her for beating you up all those years ago."

"She didn't beat me up," David said defensively.

"I was there, remember? You couldn't blame her. Poor thing was what? Twelve when you kicked that snake on her."

"It was an accident, and she was a little older than twelve I believe."

"People have been known to apologize for accidents you know. Have you tried to apologize to her about that?"

"I tried."

Ted's head leaned back slightly "When?"

"Years ago. I came home for the holidays, and she and Robert were still living in Clary. I bumped into them on Main Street. I guess they were shopping. I took the opportunity to explain and apologize. Do you know what that stubborn, cold-hearted fireball said?"

"What?"

"She told me to eat shit and die, then she stalked off into one of the shops leaving Robert and me perplexed on the sidewalk."

Ted's laughter was heard above the bar noise. "Oh, Trish is a fiery little thing when she wants to be. If it doesn't work out with her and this guy maybe I'll ask her out," he teased.

David's shoulders tingled. The last thing he needed was Ted making Trish one of his chicks. "The hell you will," David said more sternly than he meant, too.

"Whoa! Easy tiger. I'm just joking. I know you've laid your claim."

David's eyebrow cocked up. "Laid my claim?"

"I noticed your expression when she walked in with that guy, and how you reacted to her. Insulting her in front of her date? Admit it. You're jealous."

"I am not."

"Are, too."

"Am not."

"Are, too."

David didn't like the thought of his brother and his enemy cozying up to together- that was all. "Am not."

"Are, too."

She was too good for Ted anyway. Trish was too strong of a female for his brother. Her courage and fearlessness would turn him off anyway. "Am not."

"Are, too," Ted said and sipped his beer.

She needed a man who could handle her – why was he thinking about what kind of man his client needed?

David shook his head. "I loathe the woman. The only reason I'm concerned is because I don't want her to jeopardize her case. There's a lot of money on the line. Money I need to keep my practice going."

"I think you protest too much."

David shook his head with defiance. "Her and I are like oil and water. She's driving me crazy at the office."

"Then fire her," Ted said.

David almost shook at the suggestion. "I can't do that. She's working off her retainer and..."

"And?"

"She's a good worker. She's efficient...and," David scrambled for another excuse.

"And sexy," his brother finished for him.

"I- I didn't notice," David said.

"You're celibate, not dead. Then again... you may as well be. Look if it gets too hot for you, she can come work for me. You'll still get the remainder of your retainer."

"I'll keep that in mind."

"Good. And while you're keeping things in mind, think about dating. Have you ever heard the expression 'use it or lose it?'"

David shook his head at his brother's comments and glanced across the room, watching Trish smile at her date.

Chapter 7

Three weeks later, the first day of the Manley trial had finally arrived. This was the biggest case David has had in a year. David rushed to do last-minute preparations for the adoption trial that was scheduled to start in an hour and a half. Trish walked in David's office with two file folders. She knelt down to file them in the two-drawer cabinet across from his desk. His eyes started from her brown stilettos and traveled up her calves to her thighs. They stopped to linger on her bottom, which was covered by a beige mini skirt. She stood up and left the office. His eyes watched the sway in her hips as she walked. David cleared his throat and looked back down at his briefs.

Trish came back in his office carrying four books. She turned around to face the bookcase. His eyes zeroed in on her generous apple bottom. When she reached up to put the books away, her skirt raised an inch - flashing more thigh and a black strap; which was obviously part of a garter belt. He began to fantasize what it would be like to put his hand on her thighs and raise her skirt to see what the garter belt looked like. What she looked like in it. His chest rose and fell like a starving animal ready to lunge.

David realized what he was doing and shook his head and jumped up from the chair. "Will you stop that?" he yelled.

Startled by his abrasiveness, Trish jumped and whirled around. Her big and innocent eyes stared at him like he slapped her. His jaw was clenched, and he was heaving. David's eyes bulged when he noticed her buds were teasing him through her tight brown turtleneck.

"Stop it! Just stop it!" he angrily snapped at her.

Trish jumped again. Her hand flew up to her chest. Trish's upper arms pressed against her side, which incidentally squeezed her borderline D cups together.

His mouth dropped open. She was daring him. He wasn't going to back down. David whirled around the desk and strode to her like a coyote stalking his prey. Trish's back pressed against the bookcase. He grabbed her upper arms and pulled her into a kiss. She let out a squeak. His tongue pried open her lips. As his tongue swirled around her juicy mouth, David pulled the bottom of her turtleneck from the waistband of her skirt. His hands glided up her bare waist to her bra. Trish grabbed the back of his shirt. He growled against her mouth as his large hands squeezed her breasts. David tore his mouth away from hers and shoved her turtleneck over her breasts. He bent his head down to them. Taking his index finger, David rounded the edge of a bra cup to expose her right breast. Her chest rose and fell with each breath. The dark lobe was hard, thick, and ripe. He licked it with the tip of his tongue, then he blew on it. Trish grabbed the edge of the bookshelf with her left hand.

David opened his mouth and took her gift. His lips and tongue teased and kissed her throbbing nipple. His hands squeezed her hips. She let out a long yearning moan that was like an aphrodisiac to him. She wanted more; he wanted more.

The phone rang, interrupting his morning delight. David slowly pulled his mouth away from her breast, letting the tip of her nipple drop last from between his lips. He quickly stood up straight and walked to the phone.

"David Shaw," he answered with annoyance.

"David, it's Bill." Bill was one of the clerks at the courthouse.

"What's up, Bill?"

"The judge wants to start with opening arguments at eight instead of nine," Bill said with urgency.

"That's outrageous. That's thirty minutes from now. What the hell-."

"Sorry, man. The judge wants to start early because of a last-minute appointment he has this afternoon," Bill said.

"Damnit," David said with raw emotion and looked at his watch. "All right. Thanks for calling." David slammed the phone down on its base and started throwing file folders in his briefcase.

"The judge moved the trial up to eight. I need you to call Mr. Manley and tell him to get dressed and get his butt to the courthouse ASAP," David said as he closed his briefcase.

Trish quietly adjusted her bra and pulled her shirt down.

David threw on his black suit jacket. He hurriedly adjusted the collar. "Trish, didn't you hear me? I said I need you to call Mr. Manley to tell him the trial time is now at eight."

"I heard you," she whispered. She looked dazed and confused.

David grabbed his overcoat from the coat rack. "I'll see you at three." He rushed out leaving Trish standing in the middle of his office.

Chapter 8

Trish was at the library wondering if her little surprise for David was a good idea. She couldn't understand what got into him. What was more nerve-racking was what got into her. She couldn't believe she let David maul her like that. Trish reminded herself that it didn't matter because she only had another three to four weeks left working for him. After he finalized her divorce, she never had to see him again. And it couldn't happen too soon.

Trish was heading back to the law office with three books from the library when her cell phone chimed. After fumbling around in her purse, she finally answered it.

"Hello," she answered.

"Where the hell are you? What's going on at the office?" David barked sternly.

"I...I had to run a quick errand."

"I called the office, and the machine didn't pick up. Matter of fact, it didn't ring at all."

"The phone is out of order. I called the phone company- from my cell phone. They'll have it fixed before the end of the day."

David sighed. "Look, I left my notes and some documents in a folder on my desk. I need them before court reconvenes. I need you to bring them to me- at the courthouse."

"When do you need them?"

"ASAP. I need those notes and documents to cross-examine a witness. It's vital that I have them."

"Okay…okay, what's the name on the folder?"

"It's a brown folder that says Manley Adoption Fall 1994b as in boy. You can't miss it. It's right on top of my desk."

"Okay. I'll grab it and be on my way."

"You have twenty minutes," he said and hung up.

Trish started jogging down the street. She could see her breath in the cold. She only had a block to go. Hopefully, she could make it to the courthouse in twenty minutes.

Trish was out of breath by the time she reached the law office. The door was wide open. The painters were putting the finishing touches on the walls in the reception area. Two painters were about to start painting David's office.

"Hey, what are you doing back so soon?" Charles, the contractor, asked.

"David called me. He needs me to bring a file to the courthouse. What did you do with the furniture and the boxes I packed up?" she breathlessly asked.

"We put all that stuff in the alley. Where you guys park behind the building," he answered.

"Okay, are we on schedule here?"

"Ahead of schedule, since we got to start early.

We'll bring in fans to help dry the paint in here, and then we'll start on David's office. The carpet guys will be here in an hour. Once we're finished doing our thing, we'll call you, so you can get the new furniture in."

"Great. I got to run. If I don't get David that file in time he will have my ass, and not in a good way," she said and ran out the back door to the alley.

Chapter 9

David paced in front of the plaintiff table. Ted was leaning his backside against the table. "Pacing to death is not going to get her here any faster," Ted said.

"Where the hell is she?" he mumbled. "This is her fault you know."

"How?"

"She distracted me this morning."

"How did she do that?"

David quickly pushed the memory of the bookcase tango out of his mind. "She just did, okay," David snapped.

"Don't blame her for your screw up, man. You were probably being a jerk to her as usual because-"

Ted stopped talking because David stopped pacing. Trish power-walked to the front of the courtroom.

"It's about time." He violently snatched the folder from her and stalked away.

****

Trish's eyebrows furrowed together and her bottom lip poked out.

Ted grabbed her shoulders and smiled. "Hey, don't worry about it. Let's watch the floor show together, okay?"

"I broke all the laws of nature to get that thing here as fast as I could," she said.

"I know you did. Now come," Ted said as he escorted her to the spectator seating.

Ted put his arm around her when they sat down. "Let's watch the barracuda take his frustrations out on someone else for a change."

"I rather watch him in a fight with Mike Tyson," she said. "Who does he think he is?"

Ted patted her shoulder.

"All rise!" the bailiff bellowed.

Everyone stood as Judge Wakefield walked in. Everyone sat down when she did.

Ted put his arm back around a still pissed Trish.

"Mrs. Langley, please take your place back on the witness stand," the judge instructed.

A red-haired woman who looked like she was in her late thirties walked from the defendant's table to the witness stand. She wore a black designer suit. She sat down at the witness stand.

"You're still under oath," the judge informed Mrs. Langley. "Counselor, are you ready to cross-examine?"

"Yes, your honor," David said and walked to the witness stand holding a piece of paper. "In 1993, did you approach my client with a job offer in Europe?"

"Yes, in our London offices," she answered.

"Did he accept?"

"Yes."

"What was the job offered?"

"Managing director of marketing."

"Why did you offer him the job?"

"He was a nice young man and very bright."

"Mr. Manley has no experience in management. At that time, he had only been working for Langley International for six months. Is that correct?"

"Like I said, he's a bright young man. I knew he could catch onto the managerial position quickly."

"Despite the fact that he just graduated from college two months before he was hired," David stated and folded his arms across his broad chest.

"Yes."

David unfolded his arms and presented a document to the witness. "Mrs. Langley, do you recognize this document?"

She took the paper from David and looked it over. "No."

David took the paper back from her. "Really, because it has your signature on it. This document is a copy of an employment contract between my client and Langley International. At the time of the contract signing, Mrs. Langley was VP over human resource services. I would like to admit this into evidence."

"Objection," the defense lawyer said. "What does Ben Manley's employment status have to do with the adoption of the minor child?"

"Your honor, this employment contract was signed and dated two weeks before the minor child was born. The Langleys have admitted that they planned to adopt the mother's baby a month before the child was born.

However, there was still a danger that the birth father, my client, would find out about the baby and stop the process. This document shows that Mrs. Langley got him out of the country to make sure he didn't find out that his ex-girlfriend was pregnant."

"Overruled. It will be admitted into evidence," the judge said.

David handed the document to the bailiff. "Now, you said you have never seen that document."

"I signed so many things when I was vice president. It's hard to remember them all."

"Is it customary for the VP to sign hiring contracts? Surely, the director of the department can handle that."

"There were times I had to sign them when the director wasn't available."

David smirked. His eyebrow shot up. "Do you know the penalty for perjury, Mrs. Langley?"

"Objection. Threatening the witness. She answered the question and explained the document."

"Sustained."

"I'll re-phrase. Don't you think it's suspicious that you signed this particular employment contract and not your director, who happened to be unavailable that day?"

"No. It's just a coincidence," she answered with a straight face.

"Really," David said and walked to the plaintiff desk. His client, Mr. Ben Manley, looked at David as he pulled out a document from the brown folder.

"Yes, really," she stated.

"It's a little too coincidental," David said and turned back around to face her. "What I have here is a signed affidavit from the director of human resources at

Langley International stating that he knew nothing about Ben Manley's hiring, and that was the only new hire for that month. This affidavit also states that the director of human resources was in the office during the time that the employment contract was drawn up, signed, and processed. There was no reason for Mrs. Langley to assume that responsibility. I would like to admit this into evidence as well."

The bailiff took the document from David.

"Mrs. Langley knew that the birth father was not aware of the boy's existence, and she wanted to keep it that way, so she and her husband could have the baby for themselves."

"Objection," the defense lawyer said as he stood up. "Your honor, is counsel going to ask a question?"

"I'll retract my statement. No further questions," David said.

"Mr. Ross, do you wish to question the witness?"

"Not at this time, your honor, but I reserve the right to put her on the stand at a later date."

"So, noted. You may step down," Judge Wakefield said to Mrs. Langley. "Mr. Shaw. Call your next witness."

****

Court continued for another hour. David Shaw confidently walked around the room like he owned the world. He showed more charisma than Trish ever gave him credit for. She found it sexy, and she hated herself for it. Court broke for a twenty-minute recess. Teddy and Trish remained standing after the judge left.

"So, what do you think of our little barracuda now? Pretty good at his job wouldn't you say?" Ted asked with a smirk.

"The nickname fits," Trish said flatly.

"Let's go get some coffee," Ted said. "We can catch up. Talk about-."

"How about you let my secretary get back to the office and you find the birth mother before the trial ends?" David asked as he approached them in the spectator seating.

"Good grief, you still can't have pent up aggression after all that," Ted said.

"He's right, I have to get back to the office," Trish said as she threw her purse over her shoulder.

"Excuse me," an older gentleman said as he approached them. He had dark hair with gray around his temples and wore a Brooke's Brother's suit. "David, you are doing a great job. When my son told me he hired you, I had my doubts. Please forgive me for doubting your abilities," he said and extended his hand to David.

David took it. "It's fine. I know my reputation hasn't extended far and wide in Pennsylvania."

"But, that's soon to change," Trish said with a small smile.

"I totally agree, Miss?"

"Truman," Trish finished.

"I'm Benjamin Manley. Ben's father. Pleased to meet you," he said. Mr. Manley took Trish's hand and kissed it.

David's jaw clenched. He couldn't stand it when someone was polite to her.

"Charmed," she said with a smile.

"So, what is a lovely flower like you doing in a dusty old courtroom?"

"She's my assistant. She brought me some papers, but she needs to get back to the office," David said.

"Yes, I should be going," Trish shyly added.

"May I walk you to your car?" Mr. Manley asked.

David was about to speak when Trish said, "That's very kind of you. Thank you."

****

Mr. Manley escorted Trish out of the courtroom. David watched them as they left.

"He's just walking her to her car, barracuda. No reason to get your dandruff up," Ted said.

"My dandruff is not up." It was, though, and David knew it and hated it.

"Ha. It's been up since you came into court. I know that the trial time being moved up didn't get you this rattled."

"I can't talk about it now," David said and started walking out of the courtroom.

Chapter 10

Court had broken for lunch, and Ted and David sat in a booth at Charley's Steakhouse. Ted knew something was bothering David. He kept needling him until David confessed about what had happened with Trish that morning.

"Just don't sit there staring at me like I just told you I wanted to join the carnival, Ted. Say something," David said as the waitress put their food down.

Ted didn't speak until the waitress walked away. "See what happens when you let two years of sexual frustration build up," he said as he glared at his brother.

"You're no help," David said with annoyance and started cutting his steak.

"So, after this morning's um...episode, you rushed out of the office and forgot that very important folder. She was nice enough to almost break her neck to get it to you, and you snatched it from her like she was an annoying gnat. Didn't you see her face? I know Trish would die before she would admit this, but it looked like she was about to cry when you took that folder. She probably had the same expression when you callously walked out on her this morning, after you did- what you did." Ted shook his head and un-wrapped his silverware from the napkin. "You pounced on her, literally, and then you treat her like a pest the next time you see her when all she did was give you what you asked for- when she brought the folder, I mean."

David stopped cutting his steak and put his utensils down. "She didn't deserve that."

"No, she didn't," Ted said and took a bite of his mashed potatoes.

David hung his head with shame. "I need to apologize to her."

"Yes, you do," Ted said and sipped his soda.

"I'll do it when I get back to the office," David said and picked up his fork.

"Good. While you're at it, ask her out on a date. That's something a man should do with a respectable lady like her."

"What?"

"It's obvious you're attracted to her."

David scoffed. "Any man would have reacted to what she was showing off."

"It's not like she was doing it on purpose. She was probably cold." Ted shrugged.

"Of course, I realize she wasn't doing it on purpose. It was just a lapse in judgement on my part, and she's very vulnerable right now. It will never happen again. I'll let her know that as well."

Ted let out an exasperated breath.

****

David and Ted walked to the door of David's law office. David stopped before he opened the door. "Do you really have to babysit me?"

"I feel like I do," Ted said.

"Oh, good grief; we're not kids anymore."

"Then, stop acting like a hormonal teenager."

"Look who's talking."

"You're not me. My charm is so natural women just flock to me." Ted grinned.

"Ha, tell that to the waitress you pinched at the restaurant." David threw his head up in the air and swung the door open.

"Surprise!" yelled Mr. Jacobs, Darlene, Trish, Mrs. Hinkle, and a few people, who were former clients, stood in the reception area.

David looked around the office with his mouth open. The walls that used to be dingy white were now Caribbean green. The furniture that had holes in it was gone and replaced with a light plaid couch and matching chairs. The coffee table with drink rings and ten-year-old magazines was gone and replaced with a white table with updated magazines and a vase of fresh flowers.

"Don't just stand there with your mouth open, boy. Say something," Mr. Jacobs said.

"You don't like it," Trish said.

"No. I like it. It's just…," David trailed off.

Trish took a couple of steps towards him. "Just what?"

"I tell you what. You tell me how much this cost, and I'll tell you if I like it or not," he said with a dazed looked.

"That's easy. Nothing," Trish said.

"Huh?" David asked.

"Trish wanted to surprise you. She said you needed an office fit for a real professional like yourself. We decided to help her and you absorb the costs," Darlene said with a smile.

"I never forgot how you helped my son out of trouble a year ago. When Ms. Truman came into the store wanting to order furniture for your office, I insisted on giving her fifty percent off," Mrs. Charmin said happily.

"Trish called my office to have the walls and carpet work done. When she told me it was for your office, I gave her a discount of thirty percent," Charles said. "If you hadn't taken my case eighteen months ago, I wouldn't have a contracting business."

"You two don't owe me anything. You paid your bills in full," David said with humbleness.

"A humble attorney. They do exist," Ted said.

Everyone chuckled.

"The balance?" David asked cautiously.

"That's between me and Mr. Jacobs, young man," Mrs. Hinkle said. She was sitting on the couch with a cane next to her.

"I see," David said.

"Don't you want to see the rest of it?" Trish asked.

"There's more?" David asked.

"Well, you didn't think I'd do the front office and not yours did you?" Trish asked and pointed an open palm towards his office.

David slowly walked to his office door. He turned the knob and walked in. "Holy mackerel," he mumbled.

His eyes focused on his new desk. Trish walked

around David and stood in front of it. She turned to face him and hopped up on it. "It was delivered in three pieces. I know it's large, but I thought you could use the space. I noticed that you spread papers on the floor when you're working on a case or doing research."

Everyone else came into the room.

"That's not a desk, that's a boat," Ted joked. "Trish got you a boat, man, say something."

Everyone laughed.

David's lips turned up, and his perfectly straight teeth glowed. "It's great," he said and walked around the other side of it. "You replaced my chair, too?"

"Yes, it is supposed to be ergonomic friendly. If you don't find it comfortable the old one is-."

"No, I hated that chair." David plopped down in his new office chair.

"King of the world," Ted said.

"What about the wall color? It's called deep blue sea," Trish said as she turned her body towards him.

"It's fine," David said as he kept staring at his new desk.

Trish couldn't help but laugh. "You didn't even look at it."

"It's beautiful. You did a great job, Trish. You too, Charles and Mrs. Charmin," Ted complimented.

Trish turned around to face Ted. "Darlene helped me pick out some things. She has a good eye."

Darlene looked down at her boots. "Oh, I just interjected here and there."

"Well, your recommendations were excellent," Ted said.

Darlene blushed and turned her head.

"That's not all. We're treating you to dinner tonight, David. At our house," Mr. Jacobs said.

"Oh, no. You already-."

"We're not taking no for an answer. Everyone is invited," Mr. Jacobs said.

"If you insist, sir," David said with a small smile.

"I didn't know you were planning a dinner," Trish said.

"Just thought of it," Mr. Jacobs said. "It's December 1st. It's Christmas time. The time of good cheer. A time you spend with family and friends."

"Well, I better get home and get started on dinner then," Darlene said, and everyone chuckled.

"Come by around 6:30. Will that give you enough time, honey?" Mr. Jacobs said.

"Make it seven," Darlene said.

"Seven o'clock, everyone," Mr. Jacobs announced.

"Yes, sir," David said.

"We'll go and let you enjoy your new office," Mrs. Charmin said.

"See you tonight," Mrs. Hinkle added.

"Goodbye, everyone, and thank you for all your help," Trish said as everyone filed out the office and said their goodbyes.

David stood up and walked around to the front of the desk. "I'd like to talk to you."

Trish was still sitting on the desk. She frowned. "You really hate the office, don't you?"

"No, no. It's great." He glanced down and looked back up at her. "I wanted to apologize for what happened today." David leaned against the desk a few inches from her.

Trish looked down at her lap. "Oh."

"I'm deeply sorry for getting so…amorous with you this morning and for treating you so despicably afterwards- at the courthouse. I've had a lot on my mind with this adoption case. That's no excuse, though. I have no excuse. Please accept my heartfelt apology."

Trish swallowed. She continued to look down at her lap. His head leaned in close to hers.

"And you know what? The snake incident really was an accident. I got so freaked out when I saw it crawling on my foot- I was just trying to get it off me. I didn't mean to cause you all that distress," he said in a deep voice.

Trish cleared her throat. Her cheeks warmed by his boyish charm.

"Will you forgive me? For everything."

His warm breath brushed her cheek. She closed her eyes. "It depends," she whispered.

"On what?"

"Will you forgive me for pulling your hair and scratching you all those years ago?"

The side of his mouth turned up in a half smile. "You punched me a few times, too."

"That, too?" she asked and opened her eyes to look into his.

"Yes."

"I forgive you," she shyly said.

David smiled.

"You better be careful. That's the second time you've smiled today. Don't want to make it a habit."

David stood up straight. "Oh, no, we wouldn't want that. Now that's out of the way, please get off my desk,

Ms. Truman, and get me the Anderson file."

Trish kept looking at him. "Yes, sir," she said softly and slid off his desk.

When she started walking out of the office, David added with a smirk, "After that go home for the day. I want to ensure you are making me a good home-cooked meal tonight."

Trish turned and looked at him. "Chauvinist," she said and turned around to walk away.

David kept smirking.

Chapter 11

Darlene was going through her closet as Trish relaxed on Darlene's bed with her back against the backboard. She watched her friend search as she sat eating a bowl of grapes.

"What about this one?" Darlene asked as she held up the yellow dress.

"Looks like something you'd wear for Sunday brunch," Trish said and popped a grape in her mouth.

Darlene put the dress back in her closet and pulled a black cocktail dress out. "What about this?"

"That might be too much for an informal dinner party. Why are you so hyped up about what to wear?

"Because Teddy is coming," she whispered.

"Oh yes, of course. If that's the case, we need to find a color that doesn't make your blushing noticeable."

"I don't-."

"Please. Your cheeks turned so red this afternoon I thought you were going to faint. How about a blouse and a dark skirt?"

"You don't think it will be too plain?"

"Not as long as you wear some jewelry with it,"

Trish said as she ate another grape.

"You're going to spoil your dinner."

"I'm not attending. I'm going to spend the evening in my beautiful basement apartment eating grapes and reading a cozy mystery."

"You can't do that," Darlene said with anxiety.

"Calm down, Darlene. It's a dinner party not the state of the union. I baked a side dish and made dessert. I've done my co-hostess duties."

"I'll need your support tonight. You know I'll get tongue-tied around Teddy. I'll need your wit to bail me out."

"Darlene, I'm exhausted. Do you know what kind of day I have had?"

"Oh please, you didn't have to move the furniture and paint the walls in David's office."

"I…my day was very draining, okay."

"I think it would be good for you and David to socialize in a more relaxed setting."

"Why?"

"I think you two like each other more than you realize," Darlene said as she laid out a black blouse and navy blue skirt.

Trish turned her nose up. "What in the world makes you think that?"

"Remember, when we first went to his office?"

"How could I forget?"

"He paid you some pretty hefty compliments. On the sly," Darlene said and sat down on the bed next to Trish.

"When?"

"Remember he said something was wrong with Robert's situation? He said he didn't care how much plastic surgery or how rich a fifty-five-year-old was, a man Robert's age wouldn't leave a pretty young wife like you."

"I don't think those were his exact words, but I do remember something to that effect."

"Well..." Darlene said in a teasing voice.

"Well, you need to get out more. If the divorce is finalized with everything I asked for, David stands to get a pretty penny. He was just doing a little buttering up to make sure I would let him be my attorney - especially after he insulted me."

"Okay, what about today?"

Trish's mind flashed to what happened this morning. Trish's guard went up. "What about today?"

"I swore I picked up on something. Even, Daddy said something to me on the way home about it."

Trish took a deep breath. "Perhaps you two picked up on some awkwardness."

"What? Tell me."

"Okay, but you can't tell anybody," Trish said already regretting what she was about to tell her friend.

"I won't. You know I keep your secrets. If you had any," Darlene teased.

"Well, I got one now. This morning, before David went to court, I walked in his office to put some books away before the painters got there. They were just going to cover it up with plastic since it was wood and built into the wall."

"Okay, so?"

"So, David...seemed like he snapped. He yelled at me, and then stared at me like...like I don't know what. Then, he came towards me so fast, all I could do was brace myself. I didn't know what he was going to do."

"What did he do?"

"He kissed me. Hard. Next thing I know my turtleneck was pulled up."

"Whoa!"

"Yeah, then…then he..," Trish trailed off as she felt heat in her forehead and cheeks.

"Okay, I got the picture. What happened in the end?"

"The phone rang, and he answered it. Said the case been moved up, told me to call the client, and then he left. He just left me there like…nothing had happened. Then, he called and barked at me to bring a file folder to him at the courthouse. I did what he asked, but he seemed like he was annoyed with me."

"Why that rascal," Mr. Jacobs said from the door that was cracked an inch.

"Daddy! Stop eavesdropping!"

"Mr. Jacobs," Trish scolded.

"I'm old, not deaf," he replied.

"Daddy, go away," Darlene said. "You don't need to hear this kind of girl talk."

"All right, pumpkin," Mr. Jacobs said.

"Geez," Darlene said with wide eyes.

"Anyway, we sprung the surprise on him."

"Which was nice of you to arrange," Darlene said.

"Thank you. After you guys left, he gave me a sincere apology about the whole thing. He apologized for this morning and his unkind behavior at the courthouse. He even apologized for the snake thing."

"Awe, now you see. He's not all that bad."

"Darlene, he practically mauled me this morning."

"Yeah, but it doesn't sound like you were fighting him off," Darlene said with a playful grin.

"You're impossible," Trish said and popped another grape in her mouth. She had to admit Darlene was right. She didn't tell him to stop.

"Did you accept his apology?" Darlene asked with hope.

"He was so...sweet and charming about it. How could I say 'No, David, you're a complete ass' and walk out?"

Darlene squealed. "I think he likes you," she sang in a child's voice.

"I think he does, too," Mr. Jacobs said from the slight crack in the doorway.

"Daddy!"

"Oh, good grief," Trish said with embarrassment.

"Daddy, start frying the chicken and stop eavesdropping. We're not in high school anymore."

Mr. Jacobs chuckled as he walked down the hall to the staircase.

"David said that he's been under a lot of strain, which he has been. It was just a lapse in judgement like he said - on both our parts." At least, she hoped it was a lapse in judgement. David was a complicated man. The last thing she needed was to get involved with someone as volatile as him.

"Either way, please come to dinner. Purdy please...please..," Darlene begged.

"Oh, all right. If I'm doing dinner, I better get downstairs, freshen up, and change my clothes."

"What are you going to wear?"

"A chastity belt."

Chapter 12

Trish sipped white wine as she sat at the breakfast nook watching Darlene and Teddy. Darlene washed dishes as Teddy dried.

"That dessert was great, Trish," Ted said.

"Thanks, but the macaroni and cheese was the best part of the meal. Darlene made that," Trish said.

Teddy turned and looked at his dish partner. "Indeed it was."

Darlene's cheeks turned pink as she shied away from him. "Awe, it was okay."

"It was more than okay. I love my macaroni and cheese as cheesy as possible," Teddy said.

Darlene giggled.

Trish stood up.

"Where are you going?" Darlene asked nervously.

"To the living room with the rest of our guests. You two have everything in hand, and you're almost done."

"Don't rush off," Darlene said with a little begging in her voice.

"Go, Trish, we got it handled. Don't we, Dee?" Ted asked.

Darlene smiled and looked down in the soapy water.

Trish took that as a cue to leave them alone. She quickly walked out of the kitchen, letting out a sigh of relief as she left the awkward situation. She had felt like a third wheel. The whole evening was awkward. Trish could have sworn she caught David looking at her a few times from across the table, but she wasn't sure, and she didn't want to find out. Her plan was to say her goodnights to the guests and head directly to the basement. All she wanted to do was curl up between the sheets and fall asleep as she read a book.

"There she is," Mr. Jacobs said as he raised his glass of brandy towards Trish. Judging by his glossy eyes and cheesy grin, he had had one brandy too many.

"Hey. It's just the two of you?" Trish asked. David and Mr. Jacobs sat in armchairs a few feet away from the fireplace. The fire blazed between four logs.

"Yes, everyone else went home. It started snowing," David answered.

"Really?" Trish said with surprise.

"The wind is blowing really hard, too," Mr. Jacobs said and took a sip of brandy.

"As soon as Ted finishes helping Darlene, we're going home before the weather gets too rough."

"Have a safe trip home. I'm going to bed."

"It's still early," Mr. Jacobs said.

"Not for me. As you know, I woke up at 5 a.m. this morning. I've had a very busy day," Trish said.

Mr. Jacobs chuckled. "Yes, that I remember," he said and chuckled again as he glared at David.

David's eyebrow cocked up.

Trish was about to grab the glass of brandy out of

Mr. Jacobs hand when the room went dark.

"Great," David mumbled.

"Powers out!" Mr. Jacobs yelled into the darkness. The sound of keys jingled, and then a small white light shined around the room. "Good thing I keep this on me," Mr. Jacobs said. "Trish, look in the desk drawer next to the stairs. There's a flashlight in there," he said as he shined the light in that direction.

Trish felt around in the desk drawer. She grabbed the flashlight and turned it on. Another light came from the doorway. Darlene and Ted were carrying candles.

"Let's get out of here, Ted, before the roads get bad," David said and stood up.

"They're probably already bad if the power is out," Darlene said.

"Don't worry. Nothing has been able to take the Shaw brothers out, yet," Teddy said proudly.

"I heard sleet on the roof before Trish came in here," Mr. Jacobs said.

"Slippery streets. The power is out, and that means the street lights are out of order. It's dangerous out there," Darlene said.

"We don't have to drive that far," David said.

"Across town usually isn't that far, but it is in weather like this," Mr. Jacobs said.

"Daddy's right. Why take the risk? Spend the night here," Darlene said.

"Really, we'll be fine," David protested.

"I insist. Most accidents happen just a few miles away from a driver's home," Darlene said.

"How do you know that?" Trish asked.

"I just know," Darlene said.

"You're welcome to stay," Mr. Jacobs stated.

"Um," David stuttered.

"You're staying. No more discussion," Darlene said.

Teddy chuckled. "You're a bit bossy. All right, Ms. Jacobs, we'll stay. Good thing I'm prepared for anything. I keep extra clothes in the four runner. I'll go out and get my bag."

Mr. Jacobs hopped up and walked to the closet next to the front door with his keychain flashlight.

"Daddy, what are you doing?" Darlene asked as she walked over to Trish.

Trish shined the flashlight in the direction Mr. Jacobs was walking in.

Mr. Jacobs opened the closet door and pulled out a shotgun.

"Whoa!" David exclaimed.

"No offense, boys. Like I said, you are welcome to spend the night, but I also have two daughters."

Trish couldn't help but smile at the reference that Mr. Jacobs thought of her as his daughter.

"With that being said, you boys are sleeping in my room. I have a small kerosene heater in there. The girls will sleep in the basement, and I'm sleeping right here," Mr. Jacobs said as he plopped down on the sofa.

"Okay, Daddy. Let me get you a blanket and a pillow," Darlene said sweetly.

"Why don't you boys bring in some more wood from outside, since Ted wants to get his bag. Trish, there should be a kerosene heater in your bedroom closet, but you do have the fireplace in the living room," Mr. Jacobs said.

"Oh, what a great idea," Darlene cheerfully said.

"What is?" Trish asked.

"We'll sleep in front of the fireplace. It will be like camping and a sleepover all in one," Darlene answered.

"Absolutely not. Why are we going to sleep on the floor when I have a bed big enough for two?" Trish asked with annoyance.

"I'll get the sleeping bags out of the garage," Darlene said and walked away.

"Darlene," Trish called.

She disappeared into the darkness of the kitchen.

"I don't think she heard you," Teddy said, and then chuckled.

Trish blew out an exasperated breath.

"Can't say I blame you, I prefer a comfortable bed myself," David stated.

An image of David stretched out in a king sized bed with satin sheets sprung in her mind. Shirtless with his hands behind his head. She shook her head, trying to clear away the image. She was immediately grateful that the room was dim; she shuddered to think what her faced looked like at the moment.

Chapter 13

David's arms were full of wood, so he lifted his booted foot to bang on the door. Since the woodpile was in the backyard, he thought it would be best to go through Trish's entrance. Trish opened the door, and David quickly rushed in with blown snowflakes following behind him.

"Whew," she said and quickly closed the door to keep more snow from coming in. "I forgot how these Pennsylvania winters can be."

"Where do you want this?" he asked.

Trish pointed towards the fireplace. "Put them on the left side of that wood stack, please."

David did as she asked. She followed behind him. "You didn't have to bring in any more wood. I already had some."

"I know. That's what you said upstairs. We don't know how long the power will be out. I wanted to make sure you stayed warm," he said and knelt to sit the wood down.

Trish smiled.

There was a green candle lit on the coffee table, and

another one was on the kitchen counter. David stood up and pulled off his gloves, stuffing them in his coat pocket. He ran his hands through his thick dark hair to shake the snowflakes out.

"Let me help you," she said and reached for his coat.

His body tensed as Trish unzipped his coat.

"Turn around," she said sweetly.

He quietly turned so she could pull his coat from his shoulders.

"I'll put this on the banister so it can dry," she said and walked away.

"Thanks," he mumbled. David noticed that she had changed into tight black thermal pajamas that hugged her body like a second skin. He knew he should go back upstairs, but he couldn't bring himself to do it. "I see you got a fire started."

Trish turned around to face him. "Yes, it's small, but it works."

"I'll stoke it up for you." Feeling odd about the words, he quickly grabbed a log and poker. David kneeled down in front of the fireplace. Trish walked over to him and kneeled beside him.

"Expert at handling fires?"

"I have to be in my profession. Usually, I try to put them out, not start them," he said as he blew and poked at the fire.

"I'm sorry you got trapped with us. I assure you that wasn't what Mr. Jacobs had in mind."

David smiled. "No big deal. At least I have good company."

Trish brought a hand up to her chest. "Why, Mr. Shaw, was that a compliment?" she joked.

"I was speaking of Mr. Jacobs and Darlene." He smirked.

Trish laughed. "Of course. How ignorant of me."

David's heart warmed at the sound of her laugh. "You know I think that's the first time I've heard you laugh." He put the poker down and sat on the floor.

She did the same. "I guess I haven't had much to laugh about lately."

For some reason, David wanted to change that. "Well, it's not like I tell jokes at the office."

Trish looked down at her lap.

He turned to look at her. "Did I remember to thank you for today?"

"Yes, you did."

"It was a sweet gesture."

Trish looked up at him. "That was a compliment…for you." She cleared her throat. "I never thought you would use the word sweet to describe me." Her eyes were wide with surprise.

He kept looking at her. "I hate to admit it, but you are starting to grow on me. I guess you can't say the same for a drill sergeant like me."

Trish rotated her shoulder. "Oh, I don't know. Drill sergeant might be a bit harsh. You're just serious. I mean you are a lawyer. I understand that."

"Careful. That almost sounded like a compliment," he teased.

Trish laughed and he did, too.

She looked at the fire. "Wow, you really got the fire going now."

"I can't have my secretary catching a cold."

"How considerate of you."

"I think so."

She looked at him again with a smile. He smiled back at her.

"I appreciate it. Luckily, you only have to put up with me for a short time," she said.

"What are your plans? I mean, after the divorce is final."

Trish tilted her head. "I don't know. I'm not worried about it. I mean, once it's finalized the skies the limit, right?"

"For dating?" He wanted to take the question back, but it was too late. He knew it was none of his business, but he wanted to know.

"I guess," she said and began fingering the end of her dark hair while averting her gaze.

"I'm sorry. It's none of my business."

"It's okay," she stammered.

"No, it's not. I didn't mean-." He placed his hand on her shoulder. "I didn't mean to make you feel uncomfortable."

"You didn't. I was just…surprised by the question."

His hand moved to her cheek. David's thumb lightly stroked the lower half of her cheek.

"It's fine. I guess I should get used to the question," she whispered.

David leaned his head closer to hers. His thumb gently rubbed her full lips, and her eyelids fluttered closed. He cursed his lack of self-control. He closed the distance between them with a kiss. Gathering her into his arms, he planted her across his lap. The tip of David's tongue slid across her bottom lip as she wrapped her arms around his neck. David leaned her down an inch, and his tongue dipped into her warm, welcoming mouth. He breathed her in. God, he wanted her- more than he had this morning. There was no use in denying it. It was more than raging hormones, it was her- something about her made him feel alive.

"David!" Ted yelled. "You down there?"

A deep groan escaped from his throat, and he broke the kiss. He turned his head towards the stairs. "Yeah," he answered with as little frustration in his voice as possible.

"Good. You're back inside. What are you doing down there?" Ted asked.

Trish tried wiggling out of his embrace. He tightened his arms around her to keep her from escaping.

David turned his head back to Trish and smiled. "I'm starting a fire for Trish."

Her dark brown eyes widened.

"Oh, okay," Ted replied. "See you when you come up."

"Okay," David said. He was about to kiss her again when she placed two fingertips over his lips.

"We shouldn't be doing this," she said.

David opened his mouth. The tip of his tongue grazed her fingertips.

Her breath caught, and she moved her fingers away. "We really shouldn't be doing this."

"Why? Is it because I'm white?"

Trish's eyebrows shot up. "What? No," she said shaking her head.

"Then, what is it?" he asked and brought her hand back to his mouth, kissing the back of it.

"We hate each other," she answered.

He pulled her hand over his shoulder, and her arm rested next to his neck. "Do we, really?" He gave her a quick kiss.

She took in a sharp breath. "I work for you."

He pulled her closer and nuzzled his face against her neck. His lips lightly pressed against her neck. "I don't think we hate each other as much as we thought. Also, if you want to get technical about it, I work for you as well. So, we work for each other...in more ways than one," he said in a deep voice. He continued kissing her neck.

She let out a moan. "Oh, you do have a way with words, Mr. Shaw."

"I have to be in my profession, Ms. Truman," he mumbled between kisses.

"We should set boundaries," she breathed.

He raised his head and looked into her eyes. "What do you propose?"

"Okay, we are attracted to each other- physically, but mentally we have nothing in common. Our personalities don't match."

"Have you ever heard of opposites attract?"

"Nevertheless, we should...I propose that we keep an arm's length distance between us at all time. Maybe even two arms."

A wicked smile crossed his lips. "I'll try. That's all I can promise."

Trish's mouth dropped open.

"Hey, I hope you guys got it toasty down there!" Darlene yelled.

The sound of Darlene coming down the stairs made Trish wiggle her way out of David's hold. She pushed her hands against David's chest and scrambled to her feet. She was walking away from him as Darlene opened the door. David chuckled.

"What's so funny?" Darlene asked as she came down the apartment stairs.

"Ah, you know, Trish's wit," he replied.

"You're actually laughing at something she said?" Darlene commented with confusion.

Trish kept her back turned to David.

Darlene walked to Trish. "Are you okay? You look like you got a fever."

David coughed to cover up the laugh he wanted to let out as he stood up.

"I'm fine," Trish said and looked down at the plastic bag and sleeping bags Darlene was carrying. "What's that crap? I told you I wasn't playing camping Ms. Daisy."

"Oh, come on. Where's your sense of fun?" Darlene asked.

"Yeah, Trish," David said with a smile.

Trish whipped her head around and glared at him.

"Hey, boy! Get yourself upstairs so the girls can get settled!" Mr. Jacobs yelled with a slur.

"You ladies stay warm. Sweet dreams," David said and started whistling as he headed for the stairs. He grabbed his coat off the banister without missing a beat in his melody.

****

Darlene stared at David leaving. After the door closed, she looked back at Trish "Did I interrupt some-"

"You just interrupted him being a jerk as usual," Trish said and folded her arms.

"I see. Are you sure-."

"Just lay down the sleeping bags."

"Yes," Darlene said. She celebrated her victory by dancing towards the fireplace.

"I'm not eating any s'mores. It's too late for that." Trish grabbed the bag of food Darlene brought.

"Oh, all right. We'll do it tomorrow."

Trish blew out a breath and placed the bag on the kitchen counter and walked back to the living room.

Once the girls laid out the sleeping bags, they lay down. After a couple of minutes, Darlene spoke.

"Trish?"

"Darlene, I am not telling you a bedtime story," Trish said with her eyes closed.

Darlene chuckled. "No, I'm going to tell you one."

"Oh," Trish said drowsily.

"In the kitchen, after you left….before the power went out, Ted was about to kiss me."

Trish smiled and opened one eye. "That's nice, honey."

"Yes, but it would have been nicer if we actually got to do it."

"Maybe we can arrange for you two to be alone again, without interruptions," Trish murmured and closed her eye.

"Trish?"

"What?"

"What were you and David doing down here? He

seemed awfully cheerful when he left."

"I told you. He was being a jerk as usual. He likes getting a rise out of me."

"Oh."

"Goodnight, Darlene," Trish said and drifted off to sleep as she fantasized about David.

Chapter 14

Ted and David wore sweat suits under the covers to stay warm. Since they were in Ted's size, David's were a little tight. The sleeves didn't come to his wrists and skin showed around his ankles. David didn't complain; it was good to have a brother who was always prepared for anything.

David felt a nudge in his side. He opened his eyes and turned on his back to look at his brother.

"Were you sleep?" Ted asked.

David's temper flared. "You know I was," he said through gritted teeth.

"All right, man, sorry. Look, let's go downstairs to see what the girls are doing."

David would love to see Trish, but he wanted to on his terms. "I'm not getting shot by Devil Anse Hatfield."

"That old man got so drunk he probably won't wake up until noon."

"Forget it," David said and rolled back over to go back to sleep.

"What were you doing in Trish's apartment?"

"I told you. Getting a fire started."

"Yeah, but your tone when you said it. Sounded like you were doing something else."

It was a good thing David's back was turned to hide the smile on his face. "I wasn't," he said and closed his eyes.

"I almost kissed Darlene tonight," Ted confessed.

David opened his eyes. "What?"

"I said-."

"I heard you, but why? She's not your type."

"And what is my type?"

"Cheap and easy."

"Ha."

"Seriously, Ted. Darlene is a nice girl."

"I know that."

"You're a playboy. Nice girls want to settle down, get married, and have children. You're not that type."

"Yeah, but I find her shyness cute…and refreshing."

"Just don't break her heart."

"Flirting isn't hurting. With that being said, let's see what the girls are doing."

"They're probably asleep, like we should be…like I was."

"How often do we get to hang out with beautiful ladies- together?"

David groaned. "You're not going to let me go back to sleep are you?"

"Nope."

"All right, but if Mr. Jacobs wakes up, I'm pushing you towards the barrel," David said as he slung the covers off.

"If they are sleeping, we will wake them up with our charm." Ted cheerfully hopped up and grabbed a silver flashlight from the nightstand.

Ted slowly opened the bedroom door and gingerly walked into the hall. David followed him. "It's a good thing we're wearing socks."

"Shh," Ted said.

They made their way to the stairs. Ted held his hand up to David, motioning him to stop. Ted took two more steps down and peeked out under the overlook. David could hear Mr. Jacobs snoring. Ted waved David to follow as they made their way down the rest of the stairs. On the last step, David stepped on a squeaky floorboard under the carpet. It was loud enough to make Mr. Jacobs stir, and the Shaw brothers stopped dead in their tracks. David itched to go back upstairs, but he was afraid he would make more noise going up than they did coming down. David's heart started to race. Mr. Jacobs was covered with what looked like three blankets. The fire in the fireplace was going strong, and the light from it illuminated the room. They waited until Mr. Jacobs was in a deep sleep again. Ted cut his flashlight off.

Ted took a couple of steps into the living room, and David followed a few steps behind. They passed the back of the couch and reached the basement door. Ted opened it - slowly. The hinges hummed a long, loud creak. The brothers looked at each other and slowly turned their heads towards the couch. David could see the shotgun on the floor in front of the sofa- close enough for Mr. Jacobs to reach it if roused. Mr. Jacobs let out a few loud hog snorts, but he continued to slumber.

Ted squeezed through the crack, and David followed suit. He was about to close the door behind him, but Ted turned around and shook his head. Ted turned his flashlight back on. They slowly went down the stairs. Ted opened the door to Trish's apartment a little faster than the previous one. It didn't make a sound. David was relieved that they got this far without hassle. Ted opened it wider to let David walk through first. Ted walked behind him and closed the door. David made his way down the stairs - a little less carefully.

They walked around the sofa. The girls were sound asleep as the firelight glowed across their bodies. The candle on the coffee table was still lit. Trish lay on her stomach and Darlene laid on her side. David could tell the fire needed another log.

"They look like angels," Ted whispered. "It's almost a shame to wake them."

"Maybe we shouldn't," David whispered as he watched Trish breathing deeply.

"Psst...psst," Ted hissed out.

Darlene stirred.

"Wake up, sunshine," Ted said.

Darlene's eyes fluttered open. She turned her head and gasped.

"Ah, look at those natural baby blues. We're looking at the deep blue sea, David," Ted said with a grin.

Darlene giggled.

The side of David's mouth cocked up with amusement.

Trish's head popped up and quickly turned to look at the Shaw brothers. "And I'm looking at a natural ass-whoopin'. What are you two doing down here?"

"We couldn't sleep," Ted said cheerfully.

"Correction. He couldn't sleep," David said.

"Let's get the party started," Ted announced.

Trish was incredulous. "Party- my- ass. What if Mr. Jacobs catch you down here?"

Ted looked at David. "Ooo, she's grumpy when she wakes up," he teased.

"That happens when I only get two hours of sleep," Trish snapped.

"Actually, three. Maybe some beer will improve your mood," Ted said and headed for the kitchen.

"I don't have any beer," Trish said.

"Yeah, but I bet you got wine," Darlene said and hopped up from her sleeping bag.

"What about Mr. Jacobs?" Trish argued.

"He's sound asleep," David said and walked towards the fire.

"Yeah, he was calling the hogs," Ted said and opened the refrigerator, flashing his light inside.

Darlene grabbed wine glasses out of the cabinet, and Trish blew out an exasperated breath and plopped her head down on the pillow. David threw another log on the fire.

"You might as well give it up. I tried all ready," David said and sat down on the floor across from her.

Ted and Darlene walked to them with full wine glasses and a bowl of chips.

"Brother, give one of these to Trish," Ted said.

David took two glasses from Ted.

Darlene sat down next to Trish holding a wine glass and sat the bowl of chips on the floor. Ted sat next to David.

"You guys weren't comfortable in Daddy's room?" Darlene asked.

"I was," David said. "But, this isn't so bad either."

"I was comfortable. I just wasn't sleepy. I only go on about three-four hours sleep anyway," Ted answered. "Get up, Trish. It's not like you have to go to work tomorrow."

"Who says?" David asked.

"With the power out? You know this could last for days," Ted said.

"Let's play a game," Darlene suggested and popped a potato chip in her mouth.

Trish admitted defeat by sitting up in her sleeping bag. "Like, what?" She rubbed her eyes.

David noticed her long hair was fluffy and tousled. She even looked sexy half asleep. David handed her a wine glass. She quietly accepted it from him and took a sip.

Ted took a gulp from his glass. "Let's play truth or dare."

"Ugh, what are we in high school? No way," Trish said.

"I have to agree. It's not a good idea," David stated.

"I don't know. It might be a giggle," Darlene said with a smile.

"That's the spirit, sunshine. Are you two chicken or what?" Ted teased.

"Fine. Since you're so gung ho for this, Darlene, you go first," Trish said.

"Okay, David, truth or dare?"

"Truth."

"Why did you leave New York?"

His body tensed. With years of practice in a courtroom, he was able to quickly recover and transition in a nonrevealing answer. "There were many reasons, but the main one was I got homesick. The firm I worked for became too…impersonal for me."

"My turn," Ted announced. "Trish, truth or dare?"

Trish rolled her eyes. "Dare."

"I dare you to kiss, Darlene."

"Oh, my God," David said and rubbed his forehead.

Darlene's mouth dropped open.

"Eww. I never realized how juvenile you are. It would be like kissing my own sister."

"But, you're not sisters, technically," Ted said.

"Oh, all right," Trish said and grabbed Darlene's head and kissed her on the cheek.

"Hey, I wanted some tongue action," Ted said with a frown.

"You did not state any stipulations. Therefore, take what you got," David said and sipped his wine.

"Can you take your lawyer hat off for one night?" Ted asked with annoyance.

"No. Ted, truth or dare?"

"Dare me. Sock it to me."

"I dare you to take your shirt off. Since you're such a rough and tough type of guy; a little chill shouldn't phase you."

"Hell, that's not a big deal," Ted bragged and quickly pulled his sweatshirt off. He had some muscle definition, but it wouldn't hurt for big brother to join David in the gym a few days a week.

Ted tossed his shirt to the side and proudly flexed his arms for the ladies.

Darlene looked down in her lap and giggled. Her cheeks turned pink.

Trish placed her hand on the side of her face and shook her head. "Are you okay?"

"Of course," Darlene said in a high-pitched voice.

"Yeah. David, truth or dare?" Trish asked.

"Truth."

"What was her name?"

"What?" he asked with confusion.

"The woman you tried to forget in New York. What was her name?"

Everyone fell silent.

Damn, how did she pick up on that? "Heather," he answered and took another sip from his drink.

"Let's keep the ball going," Darlene said. "David, truth or dare."

David shook his head. "I'm going to get hounded now I see. Truth."

"Here - in the apartment earlier tonight - did you kiss Trish?"

Ted's face perked up. He slowly sipped his wine to hide an amused look.

Trish's mouth dropped open. "What the hell is the matter with you?" she asked as she turned to look at Darlene.

David smirked. He looked at Darlene and smiled.

"That's a ridiculous question, Darlene. Of course, he didn't-" Trish started.

"Yes," he proudly and happily admitted.

Ted spat wine out of his mouth at the revelation. The liquid sloshed back into his glass.

Darlene laughed. "I knew it. David and Trish sittin' in a tree, k-i-s-s-i-n-g."

Ted coughed and laughed at the same time.

Trish furiously got out of her sleeping bag with her wine glass and stomped away.

"Where are you going?" Darlene asked with a smile.

"To my bedroom to get some sleep," Trish said and left the room.

"Party pooper," Ted teased. "Don't just sit there, David. Go after her."

"All jokes aside, I don't think that's a good idea," Darlene said as her smile disappeared.

"Part of the game, sunshine. David, truth or dare?" he asked his brother with a mischievously smile.

David contemplated what Ted wanted to say. He returned his brother's grin and said, "Dare."

"I dare you to go after her," Ted said.

"I accept that challenge," David said. He grabbed his wine glass and stood up.

"That a boy," Ted said with pride.

"Oh, dear," Darlene groaned.

Chapter 15

Trish finished lighting the kerosene heater. A white pillar candle was lit on the nightstand. She grabbed her wine glass from the nightstand and sat down on the edge of the bed. Before she could take a sip, the door opened. David lazily walked in holding a wine glass.

She couldn't believe he had the nerve to follow her. "What are you doing in my bedroom?"

David closed the door. "I think Ted wants to be alone with Darlene."

"Then why didn't you go back upstairs?"

David shrugged and took a couple of steps into the room. "I guess I wanted to be alone with you."

Trish turned around. "You could have lied when Darlene asked you that. You're a lawyer; you know how to lie."

He took a drink from his glass. "I didn't want to lie," he said and sat down on the other side of the bed. "Why did you want me to?"

"Because, it was none of their business, and nothing is going on anyway," she said and took a sip of her wine.

"I have to disagree on the statement about nothing

going on," he said.

She sat her wine glass on the nightstand. "Of course, you disagree. We always disagree. Will you please go so I can go to sleep?" Trish stood up and pulled the covers back on her bed.

A smirk played across his lips. "You're going to kick me out into the cold?"

"Yes."

David smiled and placed his wine glass on the other nightstand. He stood up and pulled down the covers on the other side of the bed.

Her eyes bulged. "What do you think you're doing?"

"I'm sleepy."

He was insufferable. Her body tingled with anticipation, but her mind was reeling. They didn't have anything in common. How could this be happening? Why was it happening? "Then go back upstairs."

"I'll sleep better down here. The view is better."

She sucked in her lips to keep from smiling. Trish walked around the bed. She was heading for the door to open it for him to leave. David grabbed her by her arm. She whirled around to face him. He scooped her up like she weighed two pounds.

"David!" she shouted.

"Shh. You don't want to wake the whole world do you?" he asked.

Flustered, all she could do was pout like a child. It was the only way she could cover up the fact that her heart was pounding, and her body warmed at his touch. He leaned over and laid her down on her side of the bed. Then he crawled on the bed next to her. He pulled the covers over them and put his arms around her.

"David, please," she protested.

"Relax, I'm too tired to do… anything." He nuzzled his head underneath her neck. "Now, go to sleep. I don't want you to have bags under your eyes in the morning."

Trish wanted him out. Away from her while she still had her wits about her. She started to squirm.

"Be honest. You really don't want me to leave, do you? This is nice, don't you think- just relaxing? Warming each other on a cold winter night," he mumbled.

She exhaled. Yes, it was nice to have a hard body-confident man who found her irresistible next to her. For it to be David, that was a surprise but not totally unwelcomed considering how skilled he was in seduction. However, she wasn't going to admit it- not tonight. Not any night. "You're incorrigible," she whispered and closed her eyes.

******

Trish woke up a couple of hours later. The candle still burned brightly on the nightstand, and David was lightly snoring on her chest. A part of her didn't want to wake him. She wanted to rub her hand through his luscious hair, but he had to go before Mr. Jacobs woke up.

She shook his shoulders. David stirred and tightened his hold around her. He groaned.

"David, wake up."

"Uh huh," he mumbled.

"The sun is about to come up."

He pressed his groin against her outer thigh. She felt something long and hard. Her nipples started to get aroused, and her eyes widened. "What is that?"

David opened his eyes as he let out a deep chuckle. "You know what it is."

Her mouth dropped open "Put it away. What has gotten into you?"

"You. I think it's your stellar wit and luscious lips. They can drive a man insane."

"Yeah, right. Please go back upstairs before Mr. Jacobs wakes up," she begged.

David quickly lifted his head and kissed her on her lower half of her cheek.

Her breasts started to ache. "David, please."

"I make you a deal. You let me kiss you goodbye, and I'll go upstairs."

"Pretend that you did and go anyway."

David cupped one breast and gently massaged it. He started kissing her neck.

"David," she pleaded.

He pressed his erection against her again.

She let out a sigh.

He moved on top of her, using his knee to spread her legs. David propped himself up on his knees. Trish cursed the clothes they wore. He pressed his pelvis against her wanting vagina.

Both of David's hands squeezed and massaged her breasts. Her eyes fluttered closed, and she exhaled.

"Can I kiss you now, sweetheart?"

"Don't...don't call me that," she breathed. Her womanhood moistened with want.

He took in a breath. "Why not? You are sweet.

Cooking for me and decorating my office."

She sucked in. "It was a dinner party. Everyone pitched in. Please…go back upstairs."

"Kiss me goodbye, and I'll stop and go upstairs."

She let out a moan. "Okay."

He brought his weight back on top of her. He kissed her parted lips - lapping at them. Trish moved her hips to press against him as David continued to kiss her and massage her breasts.

"You taste sweet, too," he mumbled against her mouth.

All reason left her head. She wanted him – now – all day- all night. His tongue explored her mouth. Trish moved her head to the side to break the kiss when she heard a tapping on the bedroom door.

"Trish? Can I come in?" Darlene shyly asked.

A snarl of frustration escaped through David's gritted teeth. David let Trish scramble to her feet. He swung his legs over to the side of the bed as Trish went to the door and opened it.

Darlene stood at the door twiddling her fingers. "Hey, Daddy is still asleep on the couch. This could be a good time for David and Ted to go back upstairs."

"I agree. David, you better hurry," Trish breathed.

Chapter 16

For a week and a half, David's flirting and seduction attempts were becoming more difficult for Trish to resist. He always found a reason for he and Trish to be closer than an arm's length apart. She did everything she could to schedule meetings with old clients and new. She even went out of her way to drum up new clients just to keep him busy with other things.

Two days ago, David said he needed help with his computer. When Trish leaned over to see what was on the monitor, he pulled her onto his lap. He stole a long, searing kiss. She didn't know how long they made out, but she was grateful when she heard a delivery man come through the door.

Today, David was dictating a list of tasks to Trish. "I also need you to call Mr. Cockly and set up an appointment. It can be here in the office or a business lunch."

Trish was too busy writing on her notepad to notice David taking off his tie and unbuttoning the top three buttons and cuffs on his dark-blue dress shirt.

"Also, make a note for me to call my brother about

updates on pending investigations," David said and stood up.

Trish kept writing and said, "I think we should start placing ads in the newspaper and possibly online. I think part of the reason you don't get that many clients is because people don't know-" Trish looked up from her notepad to see David walking around the desk towards her. "What are you doing? Where is your tie?"

"I got hot," he said with a smile.

"I'll turn the heat down," she said quickly and stood up to go to the thermostat.

David lightly caught her arm. "You look a little overheated yourself." He pulled her into his arms and kissed her. David reached for the bottom of her purple turtleneck sweater, and Trish let her pen and pad drop to the floor. He broke their kiss to raise the sweater over her head, tossing it on the floor.

Admiring the lacey white bra, David grazed his fingers over the curve of her breasts. "I can't believe you're not protesting."

She couldn't resist anymore. She wasn't made out of stone. Trish looked down. "Don't take it as encouragement; that sweater was getting hot."

He lifted her chin to look at him. After giving her a quick kiss on the mouth, he kneeled down in front of her. His hands slid up her black stockings- under her purple suede skirt. He grazed her white garter belt before he reached her panties. She shifted her hips when his hands grabbed the edge of her panties. He pulled them down her legs to her ankles. Trish lifted her feet, so David could pull them away from her black high heels.

David stuffed her panties in his pants pocket. He

hiked her skirt up around her hips as he stood up, and they came together for a long kiss. Their tongues caressed each other's as David unhooked her bra. Without breaking their kiss, he maneuvered her to the edge of his desk and lifted her up on it. He blindly brushed off a couple of items, so she could get comfortable. David broke the kiss, pulled her bra off and tossed it behind the desk. Trish braced herself with her arms and leaned back. David bent his head to suckle and play with her breasts. He kept it up until she begun to whimper with want.

David stood up straight as he let his hand glide down her body. Her legs opened to allow his hand between her thighs. David's eyes darkened with lust as he admired her sex, and his finger begun to rub her button. Trish's mouth dropped open and her eyes closed. Deep breaths echoed from David's direction. Trish knew she should stop him. She knew she should get off the desk, grab her sweater and run back to the reception area. Yet, when she placed her hand on top of the one that was pleasing her- she caressed it. She let out a deep moan. He massaged her for another minute.

"You know what it does to me to see you like this? Do you want to know what I'm thinking now?" he asked in a deep voice.

Scared of the answer because she knew it was what she wanted, she shook her head, no.

"Yes, you do. Perhaps it will be better if I show you," he said and fingered between her folds.

She let out a gasp.

His middle finger slowly entered her wetness. Trish's head swung back as she let out a little cry.

"Lay down flat. Relax," he said as he moved his finger in and out. "Sometimes I think you're more tense than I am."

She slowly lay down on the desk.

"That's it," he soothed as she got comfortable. "Relax and just… enjoy, and I'll enjoy watching you." His thumb started to massage her nub again as his finger continued to go in and out of her.

Trish stretched out her left leg and lifted it. David grabbed her calf and placed her leg against him- her ankle rested on his shoulder. Her black heel stayed on because of the belt strap around her ankle. He used his free hand to slowly stroke the leg she had on him.

Her breasts felt full and tight. She placed her hands on the side of them. "Oh," she breathed out.

"How do you feel?" he asked with a lazy smile.

"Mmmm, wonderful," she seductively answered.

"You'll feel better than that if you played with them, I think," he said and nodded towards her chest.

Her eyes opened at the suggestion. "I….I… you want," she breathlessly stuttered.

"I want to watch you please yourself. Show me what you like," he admitted without shame.

Her cheeks warmed, but she did what he wanted. She pressed them together, then moved her hands to nipples. Her eyes glanced down at what she was doing. She squeezed the front of her breasts lightly. The buds became slightly peaked. Her manicured fingers rubbed and flicked them. She sighed and moaned. Between David's leg caress, his finger massaging down below, and her playing with her mounds, Trish couldn't keep a sane thought. She could only feel the pleasure and the expertise of David's hands.

"Do you want me as much as I want you? I want you so much, sweetheart. It's everything I can do to keep from devouring you right now. But, I wanted to please you. I wanted you happy," he said in a husky voice.

She squeezed her breasts then let go and squeezed them again. She kept repeating the motion. "Oh, yes," she moaned.

"Yes? Yes, what, sweetheart?" he pushed.

"Yes, I want you. I want this. I want….I want," she faded into a haze.

David began to move his finger in and out of her a little faster. His thumb kept the pace as well. "What? You want something else?"

She whimpered.

"Tell me. What do you want?"

"I want….I want it all," she admitted.

David smiled. "I do, too. You're so beautiful. So sexy, so-," he stopped because he felt Trish's body tense. He slowed down and started pushing his finger deeper into her.

"Oh, yes. I like that. Just like that," she breathed.

He growled. "Yes, talk to me. Let me know what you like."

Her hips met his rhythm. She continued to pump her breasts. "Oh, yes… oh, David."

Trish closed her eyes, a smile curved her lips. Her walls tightened around his finger.

"That's it, sweetheart. Let go," he said as he watched her under lowered eyelids.

Trish gave her breasts a good hard squeeze, and she cried out his name as her back arched up from the desk.

OLIVIA SAXTON

David waited until she came back to Earth before he gently lowered her leg from his shoulder. He pulled his fingers away. Trish's eyes fluttered open to see him licking his fingers. She hugged herself and turned her head to face the clock on the wall. David was gently rubbing his fingers around her folds again. He placed them back in his mouth - tasting her.

Panic rose in her mind when she realized what she had let David do to her. The things she said- what he was doing now. Embarrassment entered her heart as she bit her lower lip. She cleared her throat. "David," she whispered.

"Yes, sweetheart," he said quietly.

"It's almost 10:15."

A lazy smile crossed his lips as he continued to play in her wet center. "So."

"So, you have an eleven o'clock lunch with a potential client. Mrs. Layne's attorney had to be excused from her case because of a family emergency. She owns three restaurants. If she likes you, maybe she will put you on retainer," Trish said and sat up.

She pushed David's hand away and hopped off the desk. She quickly pulled her skirt back down and walked a few feet to fetch her sweater.

"Trish. It's okay," he said as he walked behind her.

She pressed her sweater against her to cover her chest. "No-"

"Yes," he said and bent down to kiss her neck.

She turned around to face him-clasping her sweater in front of her. "No, it's not. You need clients, and if you do a good job for Mrs. Layne you could get future business," she said nervously.

His eyebrows rose. "That's not what I'm talking about, and you know it."

Trish walked away from him. She headed towards the other side of the desk searching the floor for her bra.

"Trish, talk to me," he said as walked to the front of the desk.

She found her bra next to his tie. Picking them both up, she threw his tie to him. He caught it. She turned her back to him and lowered her sweater to put her bra back on. She quickly pulled her sweater on.

When she turned around, David was staring at her with his hands lazily his pockets. His collar on his shirt was pulled up around his neck. His tie loosely hung from around it. "It's okay."

"There's no time to- just make yourself presentable before you leave," she said and started looking around again.

"Now, what are you looking for?" he asked as he rolled his sleeves down.

"Um…where are my panties?"

The side of his mouth cocked up. "I don't know."

She gave him a stern look. "You have them don't you."

"Not sure. Maybe you should search me."

"Ha, forget it. Keep them. Besides, it wouldn't be the first time I walked around without underwear," she stated as she walked to the office door.

His eyes grew wide. "What does that mean?"

She opened the door and turned to face him. She had a smirk on her face. "You're the clever one. Figure it out." She winked at him and closed the door behind her.

Chapter 17

It took Trish fifteen minutes to get David out of the office before he was late for his lunch appointment. He couldn't let go of her comment about walking around without underwear. He demanded details. She laughed at him and told him after his lunch with Mrs. Layne, he had to interview a new witness for the Manley custody trial. Then, he had to go to the law library to do research on a criminal case that was starting next week. He also had to go to court to represent a client who was arrested for a DUI at two-thirty. With any luck, he would be out of the office until four or four-thirty, and she was planning to leave the office around three to do some Christmas shopping.

The door opened. It was Teddy. As usual, he was wearing his leather jacket and blue jeans. "Hey, beautiful," he happily greeted.

She smiled. "What's up, Teddy? What are you doing here?"

"I came to see if that knucklehead brother of mine was free for lunch."

"No can do. He's having lunch with a potential

client. He also has other things scheduled, and he probably won't be back until four."

"Sounds like business is picking up."

"I think so. During the time I've been here he's gotten seven new clients," she said proudly.

"That's great, but I'm sure you had something to do with that."

"Why do you say that?"

"My brother may be the best attorney in Clary, but no one knows it because he is not a social butterfly. I mean he does the minimum to keep himself relevant, but he's not a big networker. But, you. You're very sociable and approachable; you know how to flatter people and make other people look good."

"I'm flattered by the compliment, but I haven't lived here in years. My sociability, as you put it, isn't that strong in Clary like it was years ago."

"Bull. I just bumped into Mr. Wine. He's been having problems with one of his business partners. He said he saw you at the grocery store last week and you suggested that he make an appointment with David to see if he could help him," Teddy said with a smile.

"Well, maybe I've put a bug in people's ears here and there," she shyly admitted.

"Did Mr. Wine make an appointment?"

"I can't tell you that. Lawyer-client-"

"Privilege," he finished for her.

The phone interrupted their conversation.

"Oh, will you wait? I just love our little chats," she asked sincerely.

"Of course."

She picked up the receiver. "Shaw Law Office."

"Trish? It's Mrs. Hinkle. How are you, dear?"

"Mrs. Hinkle. Hey, Teddy-"

"I heard," he said with amusement.

"Is Teddy there with you?"

"Yes."

"Well, put me on speaker phone, so I can talk to both of you."

Trish pressed the blue button and hung up the receiver. "Mrs. Hinkle?"

"I'm here, Trish. Teddy, you handsome devil, how are you?"

"Missing you," he flirted.

Trish smiled as Mrs. Hinkle laughed. "Oh, Teddy, how's the P.I. business? Still making the big money?"

"You know it, and it appears my baby brother is going to catch up with me as long as he's smart enough to keep Trish by his side."

"Really? That's wonderful. I knew Trish and David would make a good team."

"I wouldn't go that far. Let's just say we get the job done. So, how are you healing?" Trish asked, desperate to change the subject.

"I'm fantastic. I've been walking around without my cane for four days. The doctor said I've healed quicker than expected, and I can go back to work at any time."

"That's great. You wouldn't be interested in coming back early would you?"

Teddy's eyebrow shot up the same way David's would, which unnerved Trish a little bit.

"Well, I have been bored. I got an early start on my Christmas shopping and my daughter-in-law decorated my house for Christmas as soon as I got out of the hospital. There really isn't anything for me to do around here. I won't see my family again until Christmas Eve. I would love to come back on Monday, but what about you?"

Considering what happened this morning, Trish had to get away from David before it was too late. She wasn't ready for another relationship or even a fling. She couldn't bear for her heart to be broken again. "That's perfect. Don't worry about me. I've paid David the retainer I owe him with money to spare - just like you planned."

"Yes, but what about you? Don't you need a job until your divorce is final?"

"Don't worry, Mrs. Hinkle. I'm sure I can get Trish some work- if she wants it. I could use some help around my office," Teddy said.

Trish didn't know if he really meant that or if he was saying it to keep Mrs. Hinkle from worrying about her. Either way, she was grateful. "Yes, don't worry about me. After all, I only had another two weeks to go anyway. You coming back to work early would be a nice surprise for David."

"Definitely a surprise," Teddy said with a little sarcasm, and he looked at Trish like she was pulling the biggest con job known to man.

Trish rolled her eyes and said, "You know, Mrs. Hinkle, you should come in tomorrow, so I can catch you up on everything. That way you'll be able to hit the ground running on Monday."

"I'd love to, dear, but answer me this. Why are you so willing to leave early? Are you and David still bickering?"

Teddy chuckled.

Trish gave him a stern look.

"Not really, ma'am. I mean we squashed a lot of things during my time here, but there is still some…uneasiness. I really think this is for the best."

"Oh, that's too bad. You know, I was hoping…well I probably shouldn't say," Mrs. Hinkle said.

"Oh come on, Mrs. Hinkle. Don't leave us on the hook. What were you going to say?" Teddy asked.

"Where's David?"

"He'll be out of the office until four. What was it you were going to say?" Teddy asked again.

"I was going to say that I hoped that you two would spend enough time together where nature would take its course. Oh, Trish, I know David can be strict, tense, has no sense of humor, and is downright… Oh my, I'm not doing him justice. Nevertheless, he wasn't always like that. Ask Ted."

"It's true," he interjected.

"There was a time he was a fun loving, charismatic, even charming young man. But, something happened in New York. I don't know what. I never could get him to open up to me, but whatever it was, it robbed him of his joy. I thought an attractive girl like you could bring it back. Yes, I figured you two would fight like cats and dogs for the first week or two, but like I said, I thought nature would eventually take its course," she admitted with disappointment.

"Mrs. Hinkle, I'm not David's type, and he's not my type. It's sweet that you tried to do something for him, but I am not the one for him."

"I disagree," Teddy said.

"What?" Trish said.

"I said I disagree. All my brother needs is a nice woman who is supportive, yet smart enough to run her own life. That's you, Trish," Teddy said.

"Exactly. It's a shame you two didn't get together years ago, but then again you were so in love with Robert Jameson," Mrs. Hinkle said.

"Yes, and now that you are divorcing that weasel, I can come out and say that he's a weasel and wasn't good enough for you," Teddy spat out.

"I agree. There was something always weaseling about him. Your father said he was the type of young man that was always looking for the best deal, and at that time you were it. One of the prettiest girls in town, both parents had good jobs, your grandmother owned a restaurant..." Mrs. Hinkle trailed off.

"What a minute, my father spoke to you about Robert before he died?"

"Oh yes. Your mother had passed on by then. He would come by the house once or twice a month to have lunch with me. He hated Robert, but at the same time, your father didn't want to destroy your happiness. So, he kept quiet. He was also worried about you being alone after he was gone. I told him that he didn't have to worry because James Jacobs was his best friend, and he'd make sure you would be okay no matter what lay ahead of you."

Trish was stunned. Her father did such a good job acting like he liked Robert. Matter of fact, everyone did a good job acting like they adored Robert. "Were you guys the only three that disliked Robert?"

"Hell no. Oh excuse me, Mrs. Hinkle," Teddy said

with embarrassment.

She laughed. "Oh, honey. I've heard worse in my day."

"Half the town couldn't stand him or his parents. Walking around like their you-know-what didn't stink. Loads of people couldn't understand why you were with him; people that really liked and respected you and your parents. That's why no one said anything bad about him while you were in hearing distance," Teddy confessed.

Trish felt like someone struck her. "I don't believe it." How could she not notice that people were pretending to like Robert for her sake? "Wow."

"You know who else didn't like him?" Teddy asked.

"Who?"

"David."

"Oh, please. Why would David care who I was seeing? We hated each other anyway."

"Yes, but he saw what most people saw. A smart, yet sneaky young man," Mrs. Hinkle said.

"That's right, cutie. You made the right decision getting rid of him," Teddy stated.

"Yes. Anyway. I better go. I don't want to tie up the line. I'll see you tomorrow, Trish. Goodbye, Teddy," Mrs. Hinkle said.

"Goodbye, gorgeous," Teddy said.

"Goodbye, Mrs. Hinkle, and thank you," Trish said and pressed the blue button again to end the call.

"Talking about Robert, did you find out anything… irregular?" Trish asked.

"Not yet," he answered as he played with the pens in the pen holder on her desk.

"I figured there wouldn't be any surprises." David

wanted to hire Teddy to make sure Robert didn't have any hidden assets or another girl on the side, but Trish couldn't see how Robert could have another woman. When would he have the time?

"I didn't say I didn't find anything. I just said not yet. David's instincts are right on with this one. I just have to connect the dots."

Trish shrugged her shoulders. "Okay."

David perched himself on Trish's desk. "So, tomorrow is your last day?"

Trish just looked at him.

"What are you doing? David is going to smash something over you leaving early. Why did you lie to Mrs. Hinkle? You two are getting along the way she hoped."

"Teddy, I don't want to talk about your brother with you."

"But, he likes you - a lot. And you like him. Don't try and deny it."

Her heart jumped. "He told you that he liked me?"

"He didn't have to. The sparks were flying during that dinner at Mr. Jacobs's house, and I'm not just talking about when we spent the night in your apartment. During dinner, David could barely take his eyes off you. You two made eye contact a few times, but you kept looking away. I also know what happened that morning in the office, too."

"Oh, my God, he told you about that," Trish said putting her hand on her forehead in embarrassment.

"He felt bad about it because it seemed like he mauled you. I guess he needed to talk to someone. I don't think he realized how much he liked you until that night."

Trish shook her head. "Well, whatever. It's not going to happen."

"Why? You two are perfect for each other."

"We are not. We have nothing in common."

"You're wrong."

"Can we change the subject please?"

"Sure. So, you're in the job market again. How do you feel about working for me?"

"Doing what?"

"Being my secretary. I love my job, but I hate typing reports. I may ask you to do some personal errands for me like pick up my dry cleaning."

"Dry cleaning. You have other clothes other than a leather jacket, blue jeans, and two T-shirts?" Trish asked with sarcasm.

Teddy chuckled. "Of course, I do. I even own a couple of suits."

"Suits! My God, I think I'm getting light-headed," Trish said mockingly fanning herself.

Teddy laughed. "Do you want the job or not?"

"How long do you need me for?"

"For as long as you want to work for me. What do you say?"

Trish pretended to think. "Hmmm. We'll give it a try."

"Great. Come by Monday afternoon to get a feel for the office because the first thing I want you to do is redecorate. The place needs a woman's touch."

"All right."

Teddy stood up and reached for his wallet. "Also, I need you to do some shopping for me. Christmas shopping."

"Okay, for who?"

"My parents, David, and other various family members. I'll give you a list. Oh and I want you to get lingerie for Mary, Tina, Charlene, Debbie…hmm, who am I missing?"

"I'll shop for your family, but I'm not shopping for your bimbos," Trish said sternly.

Teddy laughed. "I'm just kidding. I'm not seeing anyone that would warrant buying a gift for."

Trish relaxed, if Darlene thought Teddy was interested in another woman right now it would kill her. "Oh, sorry."

"Not a problem. Here is my credit card," he said and handed it to her.

Trish slowly took it. "You're giving me your credit card," she said with amazement.

"I trust you. No ties. I get my dad and David ties every year. Get them something different. I don't care what it is, just something different."

"All right. I'm actually leaving to do some Christmas shopping today. Do you want me to use this credit card to redecorate your office?"

"Yes."

"Budget?"

"For what?"

"For Christmas gifts and redecorating."

"Oh, don't spend more than fifteen hundred on gifts, and redecorating… well, I'll let you look at the office first then we'll discuss it."

"All right. You got a deal."

"Terrific," Teddy said happily.

****

Trish and Darlene sat at the island in Trish's kitchen as they drank white wine and ate cheese.

"I thought you would be happy that I will be working for Teddy," Trish said as she looked at Darlene's perplexed expression.

"Why?"

"So, you'll have an excuse to come by his office. You know, meet me for lunch- see Teddy, drop off my sweater- see Teddy. Get what I mean?"

"Yes. I guess it's a good idea."

"What's wrong? I thought you'd be jumping for joy."

"I would if I thought he was attracted to me," Darlene said with a pout.

"He is. You told me he was about to kiss you before the power went out the other week."

"Yes, or I thought, but he must have changed his mind because after you and David went into the bedroom, he just wanted to talk."

"Maybe, he wanted to get to know you better. He knows you're not like those bimbos he usually dates," Trish said and sipped her wine.

"Perhaps. Talking about the night of the snowstorm- ," Darlene started with a mischievous look.

"Why rehash that again? I already admitted that David and I kissed in my bedroom," Trish said and took another sip of her wine.

"Yes, but that wasn't the end of it. What's been going on at the office?" Darlene said and popped a cheese cube in her mouth.

"I told you. He's been... incorrigible. I spend most of my time fighting him off."

"Does that count for today as well?"

"Why do you ask?"

"You seemed distracted when you came home. You gave in, didn't you?"

Trish exhaled. "I let him take certain... liberties, but I shouldn't have. I don't think I can resist him much longer. Thank God Mrs. Hinkle called in today. I got the perfect out."

"What I can't understand is why you want to resist him. It's not like he's a bum. He's a smart version of a Baldwin, an attorney; he's in good shape-."

"We have nothing in common and we hate each other."

"That's not true, you do like each other. And have you ever heard of opposites attract?"

"Yes, and it always ends badly. What's your point?"

"My point is that you could be running away from the perfect guy...for you, and opposite personalities sometimes balance a couple out. Wait a minute, was David right to ask?" she trailed off.

"Right to ask what?"

"You don't want to be with him because he's white."

"Of course not. You know better than that."

"Well, there's only one thing left. You're afraid."

Trish looked at the shimmering liquid in her wine glass. She exhaled. "I...well. My divorce isn't final, yet. I was married for so long, and then I got traded in for a bag of dried bones. That's a real blow to a woman's confidence. And today, I find out that half the town - including my best friend, her dad, and my father - thought Robert was a no-good weasel, and nobody bothered to say anything to me about it all those years ago."

"Now, honey, no one wanted to destroy your happiness. You hadn't smiled since your mother died, and when Robert came into the picture-."

"I know. You've explained. I'm not mad at anyone. I understand. It's just, I have nothing to offer David. I don't have a college degree, I don't have a career, and I hardly have any money."

"The money thing is temporary."

"The point is, I think he just wants to sleep with me. As far as the race thing goes, let's face it – interracial couples still have a hard time. It won't bother me, but it could affect him and possibly his business."

"You shouldn't let other people's ignorance affect your future or happiness. And I don't think David cares what people think. As far as him just wanting you for your body-he's not that kind of man. I believe he is drawn to you in every way."

"Hopeless romantic," Trish said and shook her head.

"Just give him a chance. Talk to him. Have a serious conversation with him about how you're feeling and what you want."

"What if it isn't what he wants? I'll make a fool of myself."

"Tomorrow is your last day, so what do you have to lose?"

"I don't even know what I want. I haven't thought about love or dating again. My plan was to make the divorce final, then think about my future."

Darlene laughed. "Plans change. Looks like your future is now."

Chapter 18

The next day, Trish was preparing checks for David to sign when a tall blonde woman walked in. She wore a long white fur coat, and her thick curls cascaded around her shoulders.

"Good morning. How may I help you?" Trish greeted with a smile.

The woman glided to Trish like she was walking on air. "Good morning, dear," she said with a deep southern drawl. "I have to say you are very pretty. What's your name, hon?"

"Thank you. My name is Trish."

The woman smiled. "How cute, but surely that's not your real name."

"My full name is Patricia, but everyone calls me Trish."

"I think Patricia suits a pretty thing like you a lot better. I realize I just walked in off the street, but I was hoping Mr. Shaw was available."

"I'm sorry he is in court, but he will be back this afternoon. Would you like to make an appointment?"

"Normally, I would, hon, but I don't want to leave

my name. I want to surprise him."

Trish's curiosity was peaked. "Oh, I see. Did you two go to school together?"

"No, but David and I go way back. I tell you what," she said and reached into her Luis Vuitton purse. "This is the hotel I am staying at and...," she trailed off and picked up a pen from Trish's desk and wrote on the card. "This is the room number. Ask him to come by when it's convenient for him."

Trish's skin tingled with rage, hurt, and the feeling of inadequacy. She slowly took the card from the Southerner. "I can tell him, but I can't guarantee he'll come since I can't give him a name."

"Hmmm. You may be right. Tell him I'm a desperate wife who is frightened and will only speak with him... in person."

Trish had the sudden urge to tell her to get the hell out and stay away from David. Then, she realized that this was a sign. A sign for her not to get involved with David. She straightened in her chair. "I don't like to lie to Mr. Shaw."

"If he gets mad it won't be with you, darlin'. It will be directed at me. So, don't worry."

"What will you do if he gets mad at you?" She regretted asking as soon as it came out of her mouth, but she couldn't help it.

The woman laughed. "I have my ways to calm a man down. I'm sure you have that talent as well."

Trish couldn't believe she said that. "What makes you say that about me?"

The woman continued to smile. "Pretty women like us can get out of any jam when we put our minds to it."

Trish forced a smile on her face. "Right."

"Can I ask you one more favor, Patricia?"

Trish wanted to tell her to go directly to hell. She swallowed. "Sure."

"Would you stand up and walk around the desk. I must have a good look at you," she asked sweetly.

Trish was taken aback. "Why?"

"I realize it's a strange request, but I am a slave to fashion. Would you indulge me, please?"

Trish had an eye for clothes too, but she never asked complete strangers to model for her. Trish decided to play along to see what this woman was up, too. She stood up and walked around the desk. Trish stood in front of the woman. She looked up to meet her stare.

The woman took in Trish's form. Trish realized that this woman was sizing her up. The woman circled around Trish- examining her black business suit with the white cuffs and collar. "You have a sharp sense of style. Nothing cheap. The shoes - Chanel?"

Trish turned around to face her. "Yes. Good eye. I noticed your ring. It looks to be about two carats."

The woman's blue eyes brightened with amused surprise. "Very good. It appears that I'm not the only one with a good eye." The woman lifted her hand for Trish to get a better view of her ring. The two carat round diamond was surrounded with smaller diamonds. You could barely see the wedding band behind it, but Trish did see it.

Trish smiled. "It's lovely. Your husband is a generous man."

"Yes and it seems like yours is as well. It's obvious he wants you to be well dressed."

"Yes, it seems like we're both lucky."

The woman smiled. "It has been a pleasure, Patricia, but I should go. Don't forget to give David my message now."

"Oh, I won't," Trish said – thinking she'd give it to him all right.

"Thank you. I hope to see you again, dear. Au revoir," the woman said and glided out of the office.

****

Around noon, Trish was catching Mrs. Hinkle up on current cases and appointments - since she was starting back full time on Monday.

Teddy and David walked in.

"It warms my heart to see two beauties as soon as I walk through the door," Teddy said as they approached the reception desk.

Trish smiled and rolled her eyes.

Mrs. Hinkle laughed. "You're a devil."

David sat down a white plastic bag in front of Trish. It smelled like hot oriental food. "I brought you Chinese food from Wong's."

Trish's eyes grew wide. She opened the bag. It was true; it was from Wong's because they were the only Chinese place in Clary that put takeout food in round cartons that looked like wood and tied it up with string. "That is all the way across town."

"It's not far from the courthouse. Ted and I had lunch there. I got you pork fried rice and chicken with that red sauce you like."

"How did you know that was my favorite dish from Wong's?" Trish asked.

"I pay attention when you order takeout from the office," David said with a smile.

Trish returned his smile. "Thank you."

"You look great, Mrs. Hinkle." David said happily.

"Thank you, dear. I feel great especially since I'll be coming back to work Monday," Mrs. Hinkle replied.

David's eyebrow shot up. "Come again?" he said.

"Yes, I didn't get a chance to tell you this morning. Mrs. Hinkle recovered quicker than expected and she was bored sitting at home. I was just catching her up on what's been going on.

"I...I see, but won't you get bored sitting at home?" David asked.

"She won't be sitting at home. Trish is going to work for me- starting Monday afternoon," Teddy chimed in.

David's head snapped towards his brother. "Like hell she is."

Everyone's eyes grew wide.

"What do you need with a secretary?" David asked in a stern tone.

"I've got paperwork that needs to be done, too. I hate paperwork. Worse thing about my job. Besides, I'm tired of my clients having to talk to my answering service when I'm not in during the day," Teddy explained with a cool look.

David glared at his brother.

Teddy's lips curved up. "She's going to redecorate, too."

"Trish, I'd like to see you in private," David said and

walked into his office. He stood in the doorway waiting for her.

Mrs. Hinkle and Teddy slowly turned their heads in Trish's direction. Trish picked up a blue folder and quietly entered David's office. He closed the door behind her and turned around to face her. "So, today is your last day, and you didn't see fit to tell me."

"I was going to tell you," she stated coolly.

"When? At five o'clock today?" he asked with cold sarcasm.

"No," she said in a defensive tone. "This morning, but you rushed out the door so fast when I was coming in that I didn't have a chance."

David took a deep breath and walked away from the door. "You're not working for my brother."

"I beg your pardon? I work for who I like. You have no say in my work life or my life period." Her tone was indignant.

"My brother is too....personal as an employer," David said as he stared down in her dark brown eyes.

"Personal? Is that your way of saying he's a flirt?"

"Well, yes," David said and folded his arms across his chest.

"He may be a flirt, but it doesn't make him dangerous."

"Not dangerous like me," he stated.

"What?"

"You've been denying our attraction for almost two weeks. I got too close yesterday, didn't I? Too close to breaking down your walls. I got back to the office, and you were gone. I come in this afternoon, and you've plotted a quick escape."

"No. Mrs. Hinkle is ready to come back. This was not a permanent arrangement, David," she said coolly.

"Just an excuse. What are you afraid of?"

"Nothing," Trish said and turned her back on him. She placed her hands on her hips willing her body not to tremble.

"Yes, you are," he walked up behind her. "Are you afraid I will hurt you?"

She remained silent.

"I know my interest in you is sudden. It surprised me, too. But please know that I have grown to care for you a lot. Actually, I've always found you attractive, but we seemed to be like oil and water. But now..." He placed his hands on her shoulders. "I would rather cut off my hands than hurt you, sweetheart."

She swallowed, but remained silent and still like an ice sculpture. It took all her strength to not respond to his touch.

"I want to start seeing you- socially. I don't care where you work. But, I can't go without seeing you, talking to you every day." He leaned his head down into her hair. "Let me take you to dinner tonight. Where do you want to go?"

She cleared her throat. He started to massage her shoulders. "Please, answer me, sweetheart," he said into her hair.

The memory of the blonde beauty flashed in her mind, and Trish's temper simmered. She slowly pulled away and turned around to face him. "You won't be able to take me out tonight. You need to meet a client." Trish took a few steps back.

"No, I don't."

"Yes, you do." She opened the blue folder she was holding and pulled out the hotel business card. "A blonde came by asking for you. She's staying at The Wingate, suite 720. She said come by anytime."

David took the card and stared at it like he had never seen a business card before.

"The folder has checks you need to sign and letters you need to proof before they go out. Oh, and there are three messages from clients you need to call back," she finished. Trish walked over to David's desk and dropped the folder on top of the desk calendar.

"Is this why you won't accept my dinner invitation? Because of this?" David asked as he held the business card up.

"No. I just don't want to have dinner with you," she answered with no emotion.

David dropped his arms to his side. "Right. What was her name?"

"She wouldn't tell me. She said she wanted to surprise you. That you two went way back," she said, putting an infuses on the word, way. Trish folded her arms across her chest.

"I don't know who this could be. What did she look like?"

"Like I said, she was blonde. She's only a few inches shorter than you- taller than me obviously. Pouty lips, she had a bit of a southern accent, and she wore a white fur coat," she answered with annoyance.

David furrowed his eyebrows. "Did she use endearments at the end of her sentences, like, hon, sugar, darling, or dear?"

"As a matter of fact, she did," Trish answered and

watched him intently.

David's face went pale and looked down at the business card again. "It can't be," he mumbled.

"So, you do know her. She wouldn't tell me what she wanted. She wanted me to tell you a crock of bull story about being a desperate wife in need of your-." Trish cleared her throat. "Services. She would only talk to you alone."

David shoved the business card in his black trench coat pocket and walked over to Trish. He pulled her arms away from her. David picked her up and sat her on the desk.

"David!" she exclaimed.

He met her eye to eye. "Listen, to me very carefully. I want to be with you. But, I have to find out what this is about. I'll explain everything to you when I get back. Do you understand?"

"David, I don't care who-."

"Yes, you do. Your body language is screaming of jealousy, but you have no reason to be. Please, believe me," he urged.

Trish glanced down to his lips.

"Kiss me goodbye," he said.

"No," she pouted stubbornly.

"Kiss me goodbye, please. Let me borrow some of that famous strength of yours."

Her eyes closed for a moment. When she opened them again her steel stare was replaced with soft moist emotion. Trish wrapped her arms around his neck, pulling his head closer to hers. He claimed her mouth, kissing her like a starving man.

Her mouth opened, and the tip of her tongue pressed

against his lips. The heat from her tongue sent him into overdrive. He wrapped his arms around her waist and pulled her up and away from the desk. She tightened her arms around him. Her feet were a few inches off the floor. Their breathing grew deep and wanting.

Trish tore her mouth away and leaned her cheek against his. David kissed around her ear. He started sucking her earlobe.

"Go," she whispered. "Go."

"No," he said in a husky tone. "I don't care about anything outside of this office. I'm not leaving you."

"You must. Deal with whatever this is. Then, you can move on," she reasoned between heavy breaths. She patted him on his upper back as a signal to put her down and leave.

He understood and reluctantly placed her feet on the floor. David cupped her left cheek. She placed her hand over the one he had on her face. "Go," she repeated

"I'll be back. We'll talk. Okay?"

"Okay," she said. *If you come back, and even if you do, I won't be around. The kiss goodbye really is goodbye*, she thought.

He turned away from her and walked to the door. He swung the office door open. Teddy and Mrs. Hinkle were rushing away from the doorway. David stopped for a moment to look at them, and then walked through the reception area.

Chapter 19

David paced like a lion in a cage in The Wingate Hotel elevator. *No, way. No, way, it is her.* She was married, and attending high society parties in New York. He willed it not to be her.

The elevator door opened, and David stepped off it with purpose in his stride. The desk clerk refused to give David the name of the guest in suite 720, but was proud to say that it was a deluxe room and that there were only three rooms on that luxury floor. The desk clerk also called the room to let the guest know that company was coming.

David reached the suite's double doors. He knocked, hoping it was someone other than who he thought it was. The door slowly opened to reveal the blonde bombshell he met several years ago. The color went out of his face at the sight of her.

"My God, darlin', you look like someone died. Please come in," she said and stepped aside.

He felt like he had died from shock. He walked passed her, yet kept looking at her.

She closed the door. "Come in. Sit." She gestured

towards the lavish living room.

David just stared at her.

The woman walked passed him. He followed.

"Sit down, sugar, before you pass out. You act as if you've seen a ghost."

David finally plopped down on the ivory couch.

She walked to a credenza bar and picked up a bottle of Johnnie Walker scotch. She held it up to show him the label. "I remembered," she said with a smile and opened it. She poured a generous amount of the brown liquid into two tumblers.

"What are you doing here?" he finally asked.

She walked over to him with the scotch and handed him one glass. He quietly took it from her. His favorite brand when he lived in New York. After he left the law firm, he couldn't afford it anymore. He settled for a cheaper brand for two years.

"Nice room, isn't it? It's a lot nicer than I thought it would be considering Clary is such a small city.

"What are you doing here?

"What do you think?" she teased and sat down next to him. She sipped the scotch she poured for herself.

"This is not the time for games, Heather," he said solemnly and took a big swallow of his drink.

She smiled. "I've missed you, sugar."

David's jaw clenched. "Your husband doesn't keep you company?"

Heather looked down in her drink. "He died - six months ago."

David's mouth dropped open. "Died? Are you serious?"

"Of course. I wouldn't joke about something like

that," she said and kept staring in her drink.

David shook his head. "Of course not. How stupid of me. I'm sorry for your loss." He sat up straight and looked at her. "How did it happen?"

"Heart attack."

David furrowed his brow. "George was only fifty."

"Fifty-three actually. I tried to tell him about eating all that fatty and greasy food," she moaned.

"You came here to tell me that your husband died?"

"Partly, but it wasn't working anyway. I mean we got along, and he was really sweet to me, but he wasn't you."

"Heather-."

"Please, let me finish. It took me months to build up the courage to come here. To face you. To say what I need to say. You never gave me a chance two years ago. You left New York so fast-."

"All right, what is it that you have to say to me."

She looked into his eyes. "Oh, sugar, I'm so sorry for what happened two years ago. I never meant for you to find out about George like that."

"So, you were going to leave me for him anyway."

"Yes. I was going to break off our engagement to marry him. He proposed to me two days before you came back from your trip."

"Came back early, you mean," David bit out.

"Yes. I accepted George's proposal and told him that I would break it off with you."

David exhaled and slumped back on the couch. "If you didn't love me- you led me on," he said with incredulousness in his voice.

"No, I loved you. I still love you."

David couldn't believe what he heard. "If you loved me, how could you leave me for him? Cheat on me with him!"

Heather jumped up from the sofa. "You know how poor I was growing up in Georgia. I worked like a dog to put myself through community college. I worked even harder to save money to move to New York. I didn't want to be poor white trash for another twenty-two years."

"You wouldn't have been if you married me. You weren't in the first place. I had a career at Lakedale. I was one of their best lawyers. And you- you were the executive assistant to a partner."

"I was an over-glorified secretary. And yes, you were the best at the firm. Everyone respected you. I was proud to be your fiancé. But, it would have taken you years to make partner. Look at the time you had already put in."

"You make it sound like I was destitute. I damn near made a six-figure salary at Lakedale. I had a great apartment. One that you liked, as I remember."

"Yes, you had money, but not the type of money that George had. Not the large condo and the house in the Hamptons. You didn't have that. It would have taken years for you to get it. When George took an interest in me I went for it."

"No, you made a calculated decision to choose money over me," David spat out and took another gulp of scotch.

"Yes. And I've regretted that decision for two years. Like I said, George was good to me, but he wasn't you," she said and sat her drink on the coffee table. "He...he couldn't make love to me the way you could," Heather said as she sat down next to him again, but this time closer. Her leg grazed against his.

She leaned in close. "I've never been with a man who was so giving and attentive as you- in bed and out. Of course, I love you, but you were so angry with me. My plan was to tell you everything and work out a compromise."

David's eyebrow shot up. "You mean your plan was to marry George and make me your lover on the side?'"

She shook her head.

"You know me. You knew I wouldn't share you with another man. Much less be your lover on the side," he said with disgust.

"I convinced myself that I could make you see the bigger picture. We both would have benefited from the marriage. I was going to explain that to you after you caught George and me together, but…you quit your job and moved away so fast. I called and called you until one day the phone was disconnected. I could have gotten you a bigger salary, a bigger office-."

"All I wanted was you. As long as I had you…," he trailed off and shook his head. It didn't matter now. It was too late for them.

They were face to face – eye to eye.

"I'm so sorry, sugar. Please forgive me. We can start over. I received a lot of money from George's estate. We can go back to New York, and you can start a law firm there. We'll buy a home or a condo. Get married like we planned to before," she said with a hint of desperation. Heather started rubbing the center of his chest.

David recoiled. He jumped up and walked to the

middle of the floor. "Two years is a long time, Heather. Things change. Feelings change."

"Mine haven't. As angry as you were at me, I believe you thought of me while we were apart."

David looked down at his feet and back up at her. Heather's eyes were watery. "I admit, I have thought of you during the past few years. You know what I felt?"

"What?"

"Hurt, anger, disappointment, and foolish," he said.

"Love, what about love? Admit that you still care for me, at least," she urged.

David glared at her. At one time, he didn't think it was possible to stop loving her. That's why he stayed away from other women for two years. He didn't want anyone, but her- until now. "I have realized that I've been living the last two years in mourning over losing you. Not from love, but from anger and hurt. What you did changed me, but not for the better. I lived my life like a caveman because of you. But, I digress, you want an answer to your question."

She sat in silence.

"No, I don't love you anymore. Go back to New York, Heather. Move on with your life because that is what I intend to do." He sat his drink down on the coffee table and turned to leave.

"It's her, isn't it?"

He turned back around to look at her. "Her?"

Heather leaned back on the sofa. "Don't play coy, sugar. The one you decided to move on with your life for. Your secretary. The woman I met this morning."

"She's not my secretary. She's a temp."

"Pretty temp, Patricia is. You talk of not being

someone's lover on the side, but you're willing to be hers."

What was Heather going on about? There wasn't another man in Trish's life- as far as he knew. Is that why Trish was resisting him? "What are you talking about?"

"She's married. I mentioned how well her husband takes care of her. She didn't deny it."

David's muscles relaxed. "She's getting a divorce."

"Is that what she told you?"

"She is. I'm her attorney."

Heather was astonished. "Let me get this straight. She works in your office, but you're her attorney for her divorce. Why does she work for you? It's obvious she doesn't need the money judging from the clothes and shoes she had on."

"It's complicated."

"I see. So, her future ex-husband is rich. I'm sure you'll get her a good settlement."

David's senses went up. He didn't want to give Heather any personal information about Trish. "I'm doing my best."

"No matter how good of a settlement she receives, Patricia won't be as rich as I am now. Bigger picture, sugar."

"I don't want her because of money."

"So, she has captured your eye."

Damnit, he didn't mean to reveal that to her.

"I don't blame you. She has a very sexy shape and the face of an angel." Heather's eyes narrowed. "Have you had her, yet?"

"That," he said loudly and then concentrated on

lowering his voice, "is none of your business."

Heather examined him for a moment. "I take that as a no. You would be a little more confident in speaking about her if you had. Hmm, I thought the girl was smart, but she can't be if she turns down your...well-endowed talents."

"That's enough."

"Are you sure she isn't still in love with her husband?"

"None of this is your business, Heather."

"Oh, but it is," Heather said and stood up. She took a few steps towards him. "I love you. Can you say the same of your Patricia? Do you love her, and does she love you?"

David shook his head. "I'm not getting into this with you. No matter what happens between me and Trish it is too late for us. Go back to New York, Heather. I wish you luck," David said and strode to the door. He didn't hesitate to open the door and walk out of the hotel room.

Chapter 20

It was seven o'clock by the time Trish walked through the front door of the Jacobs home. She took her coat off and dropped it on the sofa. Then she pulled her shoes off and leaned back on the sofa.

Darlene came from the kitchen. "There you are. We were starting to get worried."

Trish turned her head towards Darlene who stood a few feet from the doorway holding a dish towel. "Worried? Why?"

"David has called here four times looking for you. He said when he got back to the office this afternoon you were gone. Mrs. Hinkle said you wanted to leave, so she finished out the day. What happened? Where have you been? Why didn't you finish your last day?"

"Geez, so many questions at one time," Trish complained and turned back around. "I see you two finally got the tree decorated. Looks good."

Darlene walked around the sofa and sat down a few inches away from Trish. "Where have you been? Mrs. Hinkle said you left the office hours ago."

"I treated myself to a manicure and pedicure. I

bumped into some old friends I haven't seen since high school- had an after dinner drink with them. Okay, two drinks. Then I drove around for twenty minutes and came home."

"Uh huh. What happened with David today? Did you two talk?"

Trish groaned. "I actually had a better evening than I did morning and afternoon, so let's not talk about it."

Darlene pressed her lips together. "You know I'm not going to let this go."

"Oh, all right. This morning a blonde bombshell pranced into the office claiming to know David from way back and left the name of her hotel and room number for me to give him when he got back from court"

"What!" Darlene exclaimed. "Who was she?"

"I don't know. She wouldn't give me her name, but she was wearing a wedding ring. She had the nerve to size me up like competition, so it was obvious she didn't want to discuss legal matters with David."

"I don't believe it. You think David is messing around with a married woman? No way. You must have misunderstood."

Trish looked at Darlene and shook her head. "You should have seen his face when I gave him the message. He turned white as a ghost. Whoever she is, David is very familiar with her. But, I think she's separated from her husband and decided to look up an old flame."

"Yeah, that's it. She's some old floozy he probably dated in college and she needs an attorney. That's it. Give him a chance to explain. He's called here four times asking us to tell you to call him when you got in."

"What is there to explain? He held me in his arms and told me he had to go to another woman's hotel room. He made his choice."

"There's got to be more to it. Whoever she is she can't hold a candle to you."

"Thanks for the boost, but you didn't see her. She had long blonde hair, tall, full lips, and sparkling blue eyes. And she wore a white fur coat. And her skirt....if you guys think my skirts are short, you should have seen the one she had on."

"Mmmm. She sounds like a tall glass of water," Mr. Jacobs said as he tried to hide around the doorway.

"Daddy! What have I told you about eavesdropping? And you shouldn't be commenting on a woman like that."

"I'm old, not dead," Mr. Jacobs said as he entered the room.

"Daddy, you go back in the kitchen and finish the dishes so Trish and I can finish talking."

"They're finished," he said and walked around the sofa to face them. He stood a few inches away from them.

Darlene let out an aggravated breath.

"Oh, let him stay. I'm sure he got the gist of what's going on now- with the eavesdropping and all."

"Eavesdropping? This is my house," Mr. Jacobs said.

"Yes, sir," Trish said.

"Now," Mr. Jacobs said and folded his arms in front of him. "This is how I am interpreting this situation. David is attracted to you, and you are attracted to him. But, you are desperately trying to keep your distance because you're not sure if you're ready for a relationship. Am I right so far?"

"Yes, sir," Trish mumbled.

"My daughter, in her wisdom, advises you to talk to him about your futures until this what did you call her? Blonde bombshell? Walked into the office before you two had a chance to talk."

"Yes, sir," Trish mumbled.

"So, he comes back into the office. You give him the message. David acts like he's about to have a stroke. He tells you that he wants to talk to the woman and catch up with you later. Right?"

"Right," Trish said.

"Trish, you don't know what this is about. Maybe he had some unfinished business with this woman and wanted it finished before he moved on with you," Mr. Jacobs stated.

Trish grunted.

"You won't know if you don't talk to the boy," Mr. Jacobs said.

"Talk to him for what? For him to tell me that he made a mistake, or he changed his mind. He wants to be with this other woman. He really wants to be with her, but couldn't have her before. No thank you. That's a conversation I don't need to have. And it's not like we were dating or anything. What're a few kisses here and there? It's not like he was proposing marriage."

Darlene just sat in silence.

"All right. It's your life. We'll support whatever you decide. Right, Darlene?"

Darlene was silent.

"Darlene?" Trish inquired.

"Of course, I support you, Trish. I just think you are doing the wrong thing."

"Ugh," Trish groaned.

The phone rang and Mr. Jacobs walked to the desk to answer it. "Hello, Jacobs residence."

He was silent for a moment then he said. "Hey, David."

Darlene and Trish whirled around on the sofa. Trish started waving her arms in a negative motion - putting her finger to her mouth.

"No, David, she hasn't come home."

Trish gave him a thumbs up.

"Yeah, David, I'm sure she didn't use her private entrance because I just got off the phone with her."

Trish shook her head up and down and mouthed the words, she'll be gone until tomorrow.

"Yeah, she called and said she'd be gone until tomorrow. Where did she go?" Mr. Jacobs looked at Trish for an answer.

Darlene shook her head with disapproval.

Trish mouthed the words, with friends.

"She's with friends. She met up with some friends from high school this afternoon and they invited her for an overnight trip. Where?"

Darlene threw her hands up and fell back on the sofa.

Trish was lost on ideas. Where would she go at a moment's notice? Then, Mr. Jacobs spoke.

"Philadelphia," he answered. Mr. Jacobs was quiet for a minute.

"It's only a four-hour drive, son. Yes, she drove." Mr. Jacobs went quiet for a second. "She didn't tell me what hotel she was staying at, she was calling from her cell phone." Mr. Jacobs was quiet again. "No, son, she didn't give us the name of the friends she was with."

Trish was getting antsy. Why was David torturing poor Mr. Jacobs?

"David, she's a big girl who lived in California for years. I'm sure she's safe and will continue to be so." Mr. Jacobs was quiet again. "If I hear from her before she gets back I'll tell her to call you, son. Stop worrying so much. Have a stiff drink and get some rest, okay?"

Darlene ran her hand through her short blonde hair.

"You're welcome, son. Get some rest. Bye." Mr. Jacobs finally hung up the phone. "You need to put your car in the garage, Trish. I wouldn't put it past that boy to drive by the house at this point."

"It sounded like he believed you," Trish said.

"He might start thinking about it. David could have picked up on something. I'm not used to lying."

Guilt formed in her mind. "I'm sorry, Mr. Jacobs. I'm sorry for the inconvenience. I just need some time for myself right now. To think. To figure out what I want. I know I can't avoid him forever, especially since he is handling my divorce."

"It's all right. I'd do it again for you. Take all the time you need. How about something to eat? We saved you a steak."

"Yeah, Daddy let the moths out of his wallet and bought Black Angus steaks for us," Darlene said when she sat back up.

Trish gave off a weak smile. "Thanks, but I'm not hungry."

"How about some cocoa for both my girls? I'll put

marshmallows and a wafer in it like Darlene's mother used, too."

"Awe, Mom used to make hot cocoa for us all the time when you stayed over. Remember, Trish?"

"Of course, I do. I would love to have some hot cocoa," Trish said.

Chapter 21

Ted Shaw was watching an episode of Law and Order while drinking a beer when the doorbell rang.

"Damnit," he mumbled. Then, he decided to be quiet. Whoever it was would soon go away.

The doorbell chimed again followed by loud banging.

"What the hell?" Ted said and got off the leather couch. He walked slowly to the door.

"Ted! I know you're home," the invader said and banged on the door again.

"David?" Ted yelled and started unlocking the door. He swung it open.

David stood there. His clothes were wrinkled, and his black trench coat halfway hung off his shoulders. He stalked past Ted like a wild man.

"What the hell is going on? This better be good, I'm missing Law and Order. Even though it's a rerun, I haven't seen it," Ted said with anger and shock.

"I need you to go to Philadelphia and find Trish."

"What? Wait a minute. What is Trish doing in Philadelphia?"

"She went on an overnight trip with some friends, but I don't know who they are. I need you to find out who they are and what hotel they are staying at," David said and stuck his hands in his pockets.

"Why?"

"Because I don't know who she's with. I just need to know that she's okay. When I got back to the office she was gone. No one has seen her since this afternoon."

"But, you know she's in Philly."

"I called the Jacobs house. Mr. Jacobs told me she went to Philadelphia with some friends from high school, but he didn't know where they are staying or why they went."

"Why do you think she's in trouble?"

David sat down in the leather arm chair. "I'm not saying she's in trouble. I just need to talk to her. She ran off."

Ted leaned his head back in slight amusement. "Ah. I see now. You have something to explain, and she doesn't want to hear it," Ted said and took a swig from his beer.

"I need to talk to her, but I can't do that if I can't find her and she refuses to return my calls. I called her cell phone and her house….," he trailed off as he leaned back with exhaustion.

"I'm missing something," Ted said. "The last time I saw you two, you were at the office. You left her there – in a hurry. Who was the mystery woman?"

David huffed. "Yes, you and Mrs. Hinkle were trying to eavesdrop. How much did you hear?"

"Enough to know that you asked Trish to dinner, she said no, and then she said something about a blonde and a hotel room. Tell me what happened. Start from the beginning," Ted said and sat down on the sofa.

David explained what happened with Trish and Heather. "When I got back, Trish was gone, and Mrs. Hinkle finished out the day. I called Trish's cell phone three times – she didn't pick up. I called the Jacobses, they haven't heard from her until an hour ago. On the last call, Mr. Jacobs said she went to Philadelphia with friends. She's supposed to come back tomorrow."

"Then why not wait until she comes back?"

"I can't. God knows what she's doing in retaliation or out of hurt or anger," David said desperately.

"Trish isn't the type to do something reckless unless it is extenuating circumstances."

"That's easy for you to say. Nevertheless, I would feel better if you went."

"I'm not driving to Philly at 8:30 at night without any leads."

"I think Mr. Jacobs knows more than what he was telling me," David said.

Ted finished his beer and sat the bottle on the table. "Maybe he was lying. I don't think she's left town at all."

"I can't see him lying. Hiding something? Yes. I think he knows exactly who Trish is with and what hotel they are staying at."

"I can if it concerns Trish's wellbeing. He's been known to do out of character things for Darlene."

"So."

"So, he thinks of Trish as a daughter. I believe he would do the same for her. Let's face it, you are in a very emotional state. You probably didn't pick up on any telltale signs of a lie when you talked to Jacobs."

"Maybe," David mumbled.

"And what the hell is wrong with you? Sometimes I wonder if we really are brothers."

"What do you mean?"

"Sometimes you know how to treat a woman, and sometimes you are just dense. You left the woman you claim to want, who by the way, you had eating out of your hand, to go see what your ex-fiancé wanted. No wonder Trish won't speak to you. You should have thrown that stupid card away, scooped Trish up and taken her back to your apartment. Why did you go see Heather, David?"

"I had to see what Heather wanted. I wanted it finished- done and that's what happened when I went there. I left my baggage from the past in her hotel room, so I could move forward," David said defensively. He leaned forward and buried his face in his hands.

"Are you sure you're not still in love with Heather?"

He raised his head and looked at Ted. "Positive," David said with conviction and placed his head back in his hands.

"You know Heather is the type of woman that gets what she wants. She's not the type to pack her bags and go home. That's how she's gotten to where she is today."

David looked up again and ran his hands through his thick dark hair. "She can do what she wants. I'm not interested." He leaned back in the chair.

"Okay, so Trish is the woman you want?"

"Yes. I've grown to care for her very much, and I enjoy her company."

Ted's eyebrows rose. "Well, I have to say I never thought you'd admit it this easily. Then again, you've never been one to play games. I tell you what. Stay here, spend the night."

"I don't need a babysitter. I need-."

"I know- you need to talk to her. But, that's not happening at the moment, and I would feel better if you stayed here tonight. You've still got clothes in the guest room. Wash your face, get a drink, and some food. I'll be out doing some footwork for you."

"You're going to Philly?"

"No, I'm not driving three or four hours on a wild goose chase. But, like I said, I don't think she's in Philly," Ted said and stood up. He went to the closet and grabbed a pair of boots.

"Then, where are you going?" David said and started pulling his arms out of his coat.

"Don't worry about it, right now. Just relax. My legwork should take no more than two hours."

****

Ted parked his SUV across the street from the Jacobs house. He had only been watching the house for fifteen minutes. The Christmas lights lined the front of the roof, the windows, and the doorway. The nativity scene was a few inches away from the walkway. Light came from the windows on the front of the house. He didn't see Trish's car in the driveway, but Mr. Jacobs' and Darlene's were there.

Ted figured that Trish parked her car in the garage.

Judging from the silhouettes from the windows there were three people inside. Ted opened the car door and got out. He jogged across the street and up to the front door. After he carefully opened the storm door, he leaned his head against the front door. He heard Christmas music and muffled voices. There were definitely two women talking. Ted knocked on the door. The voices got quiet. He waited for a moment.

"Who is it?" Darlene asked.

"Your favorite neighborhood P.I.," he replied.

"Oh… um just a minute," Darlene said.

She definitely sounded surprised and nervous.

"Come on, Darlene, it's freezing out here," he said.

"Okay, coming," Darlene said in a high-pitched voice. After another twenty seconds, she opened the door.

"Hi," she greeted with a nervous smile.

"Hey, sunshine," he said and squeezed past her to walk into the house.

"It's past nine o'clock," she said.

"I know it's getting late, but I had to come over. Where's your father?"

"He's upstairs. Why?" she asked as she clenched her pink bathrobe around her chest.

Teddy unzipped his leather coat. He ignored the question. "Where's Trish?"

Darlene looked down. "She's out of town. She'll be back tomorrow."

"When tomorrow?"

"I don't know," she said defensively.

Ted softened his tone. "I just want to help. I just want to make sure she's okay," he said and took a few steps closer to Darlene. He looked into her blue eyes. There was only an inch between them.

"I…she's fine. You better go before Daddy comes downstairs," she stuttered.

"Too late," Mr. Jacobs said in a deep voice. He stood in the middle of the staircase staring daggers at Ted.

Ted took two steps back. "Mr. Jacobs, just the man I was looking for."

Mr. Jacobs came down the rest of the stairs. "Oh, it's a little late for a financial consultation, Ted."

Darlene walked to the other side of the room.

Ted smiled. "I'm not here for your financial advice, sir. I wanted to ask you a few questions about Trish's whereabouts. I heard she went to Philly with some friends."

"She did. She'll be back tomorrow," Mr. Jacobs said.

The old cogger was going to hold his ground. Ted tried another tactic. "Was she already in Philly when she called you?"

"No, she called from her cell phone."

"Who was she with?"

"She didn't say."

"Did she say how many friends she was with?"

"No."

"You didn't ask?"

"It was none of my business. She's a big girl."

Ted turned to look at Darlene. "Why didn't you go with her? If they were friends from high school, surely you knew them."

"I did…I mean didn't, I just didn't want to go on an

overnight trip," Darlene stuttered.

"Why? Your best friend is going through a divorce - she wants to go on a trip. Why didn't you go with her for moral support? You've been by her side so far."

Darlene's mouth opened, but nothing came out.

Ted walked to the couch. "Yeah, she's not in Philly. She's here, isn't she?"

"It's time for you to leave, son. I'll tell Trish to call you when she gets back," Mr. Jacobs said.

He was close. "Trish, you may as well come out. I know you're here."

No one said anything.

"Trish, if you don't come out I'm not going to help you and David with your divorce case anymore. And believe me, you need what my contacts are pursuing on the west coast. And are you really going to keep making Darlene and Mr. Jacobs lie for you? It isn't in their nature."

Trish slowly emerged from the hallway that led to the kitchen. She wore a black silk robe and slippers with black fuss on the top. Her hair was down- the ends grazed the top of her shoulders. Ted could tell she wasn't wearing a bra. If David was here, he'd go nuts.

"What do you want, Shaw?" she asked with annoyance.

"My brother is beside himself with worry. All he wants is to talk to you. I'll take you to him. Get dressed- I'll wait," Ted said and sat down on the couch.

Trish walked around the sofa and sat down next to him. "I'm not going anywhere, and if you are my friend, you would leave and not tell David where I am."

"I am your friend, but David is my brother- my kid

brother. He's in agony," Ted said and crossed his arms.

"Oh, he can't be that bad off. All because he can't find me," Trish huffed.

"Listen to him, Trish," Darlene implored and sat down on the other side of Ted.

"Did he ask you to look for me?" Trish asked.

"Yes. David is a wreck. Why won't you return his calls? Is it because of that woman?"

Trish blew out. "Partly."

Mr. Jacobs quietly watched and listened.

"She means nothing to him, and he went to The Wingate to tell her that. Now, what's the other part?" Ted asked.

"I need some time to myself. I need time to find me again. I lost so much of myself these last seven months. I need some time to think. I know that's hard for a man to understand, but sometimes a woman needs to do that," she answered with desperation in her voice.

"I do understand, but David-."

"Just tell him you spoke to me, and I'm fine. Just to leave me alone for a while," Trish said.

"I'm not lying to him," Ted said.

"I'm not asking you to lie. You did speak to me. Just don't tell him how or where you spoke to me."

"He's going to ask," Ted said.

"Just ask him to give me a few days, better yet, a week. Please, Teddy," Trish begged.

Ted looked into Trish's dark brown eyes. He had never heard Trish so desperate. She was always so confident and strong. Ted's mind churned possible ideas that could make both parties happy.

"Please, Teddy," Darlene begged with a pout and

lightly placed her hand on his arm. Her watery blue eyes could melt a glacier.

They were ganging up on him, and it was working. "Oooh, I'll tell David I spoke with you, and you're fine. I'll try to stall until tomorrow afternoon about your whereabouts, but that's all I can promise you."

"Thanks, Teddy. You're the best," Trish said with a smile.

"Yeah," Darlene said with a smile and squeezed his arm.

******

Ted told himself this was the last stop for the night, and then he was going back home. He knocked on the door of suite 720. David had told him Heather's room number earlier.

Heather opened the door. Her opened white silk robe revealed a low cut, lace-lined nightgown. Her cleavage didn't leave much to the imagination.

"Teddy!" she exclaimed happily. "How good of you to come to see me. Come on in, sugar."

Ted stepped into the suite. The room screamed money. Heather had got all the money she wanted and needed.

"Come..come...sit. I'll make us some drinks. I'm afraid I don't have any beer. Then, again I could call room service and have a couple of bottles sent up."

"Don't bother. I'm not staying long," he said dryly.

Heather turned off her southern hospitality. "This sounds serious. Has something happened to David?"

"Yes. He's finally forgotten about you and wants to move on- with a vivacious exciting woman that can breathe life into him again. I don't want you messing that up for him with your mind games."

"I didn't come here to play games. I love, David. I want him back."

"I love, David. More than you will ever know or probably understand. I'm not going to sit by and watch you break his spirit or mind in half again."

She smirked. "Don't you think David is a little too old for you to be fighting his battles for him?"

"I'm not fighting his battles. I'm watching his back. That's what family does, Heather. You're a beautiful woman. Go back to New York - find a man there. David has finally moved on."

"Actually, I am going back to New York in the morning. I have some business to attend, too."

"Good. Moving on is your best bet, now. You had a good man, and you blew it. Not trying to rub it in your face, people make mistakes, but sometimes you can't make up for the mistakes you make. And believe it or not, I wish you luck."

"Thank you," she said and let her eyes linger across Ted's face. "But, I always wondered…"

He looked at her face and let his eyes linger on her cleavage. "Always wondered?"

They let the question hang out there. Heather broke the silence. "Are all you Shaw men terrific in bed?"

The little vixen, he thought. There was no way he was bedding her – not even if her nightgown dropped to the floor. Ted couldn't help but smile. "Yes, we are, but unfortunately I can't prove it to you."

Heather's bright teeth slowly appeared between her red painted lips. "That's all right, sugar. I'll take your word for it."

"Goodbye, Heather," Ted said. He turned and left the suite, closing the door behind him.

Chapter 22

David groggily woke up on his brother's sofa. He remembered taking his shirt off and loosening his pants, but not covering himself with a blanket. He quickly realized Ted must have done it when he came back last night. There was a slight throbbing in his head. David rubbed his forehead with his first two fingers. The last thing he remembered was drinking a glass of scotch. It had been eleven and Ted still hadn't come back.

David sat up and looked at the table. His glass of scotch was gone- including the bottle he had sitting next to it. Sunlight was trying to come in through the white mini blinds. David grabbed his watch from the coffee table. It was nine forty-five. He put his watch back on the coffee table and slowly stood up. He couldn't believe he had slept past nine. The smell of bacon and coffee slowly led him to the kitchen.

"Hey, sleepy head. I got bacon and sausage on the burner. Going to whip up some eggs and toast," Ted said cheerfully as he poured a cup of coffee.

"I'm not hungry," David mumbled and sat down on a brown stool next to the kitchen island.

Ted handed his brother a cup of coffee.

"Thanks," David mumbled and took the cup from him.

Ted started whipping the eggs he had sitting in a bowl. "You should eat. You must have a headache. That was a full bottle of scotch. Only half of it was left."

"Sorry, Mom," David said sarcastically and sipped the coffee.

"I'm not riding your ass. Just stating the concern of an older brother," Ted said and checked on the bacon and sausage in the frying pan.

"Did you find, Trish?"

Ted grabbed a plate that had a paper towel on it and started placing the bacon and sausage on it.

"Ted, will you stop messing with the food and tell me what you found out last night," David said and sipped his coffee again.

Ted sat the plate down on the island in front of David. He grabbed the bowl of eggs. "I talked to her. She's fine. She just needs some space right now." Ted turned around and poured the eggs into a fresh warm pan.

"Did you talk to her on the phone or did you see her? Where is she?"

"I'm not going to tell you anything else until after breakfast. Both of us are running on empty. Meaning, you're eating"

"Damnit, Ted."

"After breakfast," Ted said.

David quietly conceded.

****

Ted's food was better than his coffee. They finished eating, and David wiped his hands with a paper towel. His head felt a lot better.

"We're finished eating. Now tell me what happened last night," David demanded.

Ted looked at the clock on the wall. It was after ten thirty. "Why don't we take a shower and get dressed. We'll have another cup of co-."

"Ted!"

"Damn, all right. I tracked Trish down, and I got to speak with her. She's fine, she's beautiful, and she needs time to herself."

"She said that?"

"Yes. Sometimes women need time alone, like men do sometimes. It happens," Ted explained.

"Where did you find her?"

Ted was quiet for a moment then answered. "She never left town, David. Like I suspected."

"And?" David asked.

"She's at home. That ole cogger lied and said Trish was out of town," Ted finally said.

David jumped up from the stool. "She's been in Clary the whole time, and you're just telling me now." David strode to the living room.

David grabbed his dress shirt from the leather armchair. Ted rushed into the room.

"What are you doing?" Ted asked.

"I'm going over there," David said as he put his shirt on.

"The least you can do is shit, shower, and shave first. How will she hear a word your saying with you smelling like day old scotch?"

David stood at attention. "I don't stink."

"The hell you don't! Your hair is lopsided, too. If you never heard a word I have said to you in your life, hear me now - take a damn shower, brush your teeth - cause your breath is rank, comb your big hair, and put on some fresh clothes," Ted said a little more loudly than he intended.

David whipped his shirt back off and balled it up. He threw it down on the carpet. "You don't have to be such an asshole about it. But, afterwards, I'm going over there," David said and left the room.

****

Ted waited until he heard the shower running before he made the call. Someone picked up on the third ring.

"Hello, Jacobs residence," Mr. Jacobs said.

"Hey, Mr. Jacobs it's Ted. Is Trish there?"

"Hold on a minute," he said, and the line went quiet.

Ted waited impatiently.

"Hello," Trish answered.

"Hey. Listen I did what I could, but I couldn't hold out until noon. I bought you another thirty – forty minutes at the most, but that's it. He is coming to see you."

"It's okay. Darlene and I are about to leave anyway. I'm driving her around to deliver Christmas cookies to half of Clary. That should take hours," Trish said with little enthusiasm.

"I didn't call to give you a heads up, so you could run. I called so you wouldn't be blindsided when he showed up on your doorstep. Surely, you figured out what you want by now," Ted said with impatience.

"Ted, please. I need more time. No one can figure out what they want for their future in less than twenty-four hours," she reasoned.

Ted blinked a couple of times. "I suppose not. It's just hard to watch David agitated like this."

"Oh, Teddy, I don't mean David any harm. I'm not doing this to hurt his feelings. I'm just trying to look out for myself. To make the right decisions, and to do what's best for me."

"I know, kid."

"Who are you talking to do?" David asked. He walked a few steps into the living room. His hair was wet, and a white towel was wrapped around his waist.

"Um…" Ted stuttered.

David walked over to him.

"Ted? Are you still there?" Ted heard Trish ask.

"It's her, isn't it?" David asked, but he didn't wait for an answer. He snatched the phone out of Ted's hand.

****

"Trish? Is that you?" David asked in desperation.

"David," she said.

"Sweetheart, I need to talk to you. I tried to reach you yesterday."

"I know."

"Then why didn't you return my calls?"

"I wasn't ready to talk to you. I'm still not. David, I need time to myself without you around to confuse me," she explained.

"All right, but before you take this time, I think you should listen to what I have to say. It could affect whatever conclusions you come to. It could affect both our futures," David said in a desperate tone.

"I can't. I can't even if I wanted, too. I'm busy today."

"Busy with what?"

"I'm sorry, David. I have to help Darlene load the car."

"Load the car? Where are you going?"

"I'll talk to you later. Goodbye," she whispered.

David didn't get a chance to say goodbye because the line went dead. He slammed the phone down on the base.

"Easy," Ted said.

"She can be the most stubborn, infuriating woman," David said through gritted teeth. He stalked into the guest room.

Ted followed him. "What are you going to do now?"

"I'm going to get dressed and catch her before she leaves. What did she say to you?" David asked and tore off his towel.

"Jesus!" Ted exclaimed and turned his back. "It's no use. By the time you get dressed and drive over there, the girls will be gone."

"Where are they going?" David asked as he pulled on a pair of black boxers.

"She's helping Darlene deliver Christmas cookies

today. She said they had to make a lot of stops. It will take them hours."

"That's fine. I think I might know some of the places they would go," David said and pulled on a pair of black slacks.

"You got your drawls on, yet?" Ted asked.

"Yes."

Ted turned around and walked over to his brother. He placed his hands on his shoulders. "David, you need to get a grip. She's going out to spread some Christmas cheer. That's all. The last thing you need to be doing is crawling the streets hunting her down. Take a deep breath- relax. Try to talk to her tomorrow."

David looked at the concern in his brother's eyes. "I guess I am becoming a bit unglued, huh?"

"A bit. But, it's understandable. You're a man in love, and the woman you love won't talk to you- won't see you. You're afraid you're going to lose her. You can have her, David, as long as you play it cool. Don't go hunting her down like she's a doe on the run," Ted said and took his hands off David's shoulders.

David looked at Ted. "Love? I didn't say I loved her."

"You didn't have to. Look at how you're acting. Calling her twenty times in a span of five hours, banging on my door like a wild man that lost everything he owned, and drinking yourself to sleep - which is definitely not like you - and dropping your towel in front me like I wasn't even in here, again not like you. You're in love with her."

Could it be? David plopped down on the bed. He took a quick inventory of his emotions during the past month. Flashes of her smile, her laugh, and her body invaded his mind. David's mouth dropped open. He was falling in love with Trish the whole time, and he didn't know it. Now that he did, would he tell her now or later?

"Are we having an epiphany, dear Watson?"

"Yes," David said slowly. "I do love her."

Ted let out a high-pitched opera note. "And there it is."

"Now that I know this, what am I going to do?"

"Relax. Take this time to think while she's thinking. Give her a few days and then call her."

"Yes, I'll do that."

Chapter 23

When David told Ted he would give Trish some space he meant it. Though he only lasted until nine o'clock that evening.

He knocked on the door at Mr. Jacobs's home. The old man opened it, and surprise registered on his face. "David."

"Good evening, sir. I know this is not the usual time for a social call-."

Before David could finish Mr. Jacobs interrupted him. "Oh, get in here, son." Mr. Jacobs stepped aside to let David pass.

David stepped into the living room, and Mr. Jacobs closed the door. "Have a seat, son."

David sat down on the couch, and Mr. Jacobs walked to the credenza where he kept alcoholic drinks. He poured himself a brandy. "Name your poison, son."

David was going to refuse, but he thought better of it. Maybe having a friendly drink with Mr. Jacobs might give him an edge in winning Trish's affection. "Scotch, on the rocks," he answered.

Mr. Jacobs shook his head and grabbed a fresh glass.

He opened the ice bucket and dropped two cubes in the glass before pouring the scotch. "You've cause a bit of a commotion these past two days."

"Yes, sir. I didn't mean to," David said, feeling like a ten-year-old boy again.

Chuckling, Mr. Jacobs walked over to him and handed David his glass. Mr. Jacobs then sat down in the same chair that he had sat in during the night of the dinner party.

"It's all right. Sometimes a woman can do that to a man. I take it that you're here to see Trish."

"Yes, sir."

"She's not here. Trish and Darlene went out for the evening. I dropped them off myself. I'm not lying to you this time, son."

"Yes, sir. I know."

"I'm sorry about that, by the way. I was doing what I thought was best at the time."

"I understand."

"But, since we got some time alone, this gives us a chance to talk. Eye to eye – man to man."

David didn't blink, even though the words made him a bit nervous. Years of presenting cases in courtrooms trained him to not reveal his emotions through his body language or voice when it was necessary.

"Did you know I was Trish's godfather?"

"No, I did not."

Mr. Jacobs smiled. "Yeah. A lot of people don't know that. Just me, her parents, Trish, Darlene, and my beloved wife - may she rest in peace. See, Trish's father and I were close friends. Did you know that?"

"Yes, sir, that I did know."

"You know how we became friends?"

"No."

"I was a young man - meaning this happened many years ago - and I worked at Welts Bank as a teller. One day, two masked men came in and stuck the place up. There was me, two other tellers, and one manager on duty. There were three customers in the bank that day. They made us come around the counters and kneel on the floor along with the customers. One guy had a gun on us and the other cleaned out the teller drawers." He stopped and took a sip of brandy before continuing. "The robber with the money said, 'Let's go, I got it all'. But, the other - he wasn't satisfied with that. He started taunting us. Pointing the gun at each of our heads. Russian roulette, you see. This guy had a six-shooter. When he got to me, he had already gone through five clicks. So, my chances of survival was zilch. You know that bastard had the nerve to goad me to beg for my life. 'Come on, kid. You're too young to die. You beg me the right way, I let you live.' But, my father," Mr. Jacobs leaned forward and looked David in his eyes. "My father raised me to be a man. So, I looked that SOB in the eye and told him to go to hell. He laughed and said, it was a shame he was going to have to kill me because I had real balls. Before he could pull the trigger, a big bear of a black man was all over him. He ripped that gun out of that guy's hand and knocked his front teeth out with the butt."

"Wow," David said like a wide-eyed child.

"You want to guess who that man was, David?"

"Mr. Truman," David said with a smile.

"If it wasn't for him, Darlene wouldn't have been

born. I don't think the girls know that story. Since that day, I had a friend for life. As time went on, our wives became friends just like our daughters did. I helped him get a loan for his construction business, which was successful, but I don't think it ever began to repay what that man did for me. Ole Bear was a tender-hearted soul, but if you messed with innocent people, and he knew about it, that's when things got ugly. He defended and protected his family, too. Trish and her momma were that man's heart and soul. At my age, I know I forget a lot, but that day at the bank I'll never forget – not as long as I live."

"Yes, sir. I understand."

"Do you, boy? You see Ole Bear he could do just about anything he put his mind to. I wouldn't be surprised if he rose out of the grave to give hell to anyone that caused Trish pain or harm. Like Robert, I wouldn't be surprised if he can't sleep at night these days. I wouldn't be surprised to learn that Trish's daddy was working through you to make Robert pay for breaking her heart. With that being said, what are your intentions with my goddaughter?"

David was lost for words. He wasn't expecting this. He said the first words that came to his mind. "I'm in love with her, Mr. Jacobs. Please know it is not my intention to upset her or hurt her."

Mr. Jacobs's eyebrows rose. He leaned back in the chair. "I have to say I didn't expect you to say it so bluntly, but I do respect that. If you love her, son, what is this I hear about a blonde at a hotel?"

David definitely didn't want to get into this with him, but it was obvious that he wasn't going to get Mr.

Jacobs to help without divulging the information that he asked for. "Her name is Heather. I was engaged to her when I lived in New York, but it didn't work out. She chose to be with someone else. Fast forward to the present, she came here to see if we could get back together."

"What did you do?" he asked.

"I told her no. I don't love her anymore and she needs to go back home."

Mr. Jacobs nodded his head with approval. "All right, I won't bring her up again. So, now you are here to win Trish's heart."

"Yes, sir, if I can find her," David said with a small smile before sipping his drink.

Mr. Jacobs thought for a moment. "You know, son, sometimes it's best to give women some room. Give them time to think."

"Yes, sir, but-."

"You can't wait. That's why you're in my house at nine o'clock at night."

"Well, yes, sir."

Mr. Jacobs chuckled. "Oh, you do look and act like a man in love; I know you're a good young man. I dropped Trish and Darlene off at The Clover Club over an hour ago. The place is hosting some sort of Christmas Blowout Bash."

"I'm surprised that you would drop them off at a nightclub."

"They're both grown. Besides, the guy that owns the place is a client of mine. He won't let anything happen to them. Plus, the owner is one of the old high school friends Trish bumped into yesterday. He invited her to the club. Trish talked Darlene into going with her. They'll call a cab when they're ready to come home. That is if they don't find a ride home," he said with a smile.

"Yes, sir." David finished his drink and put it on the coffee table. He stood up.

"You know where the club is?"

"Yes. I never been there, but I know where it is."

Mr. Jacobs also stood.

David extended his hand to Mr. Jacobs, and they shook hands. "Thank you for your help, sir."

"You're welcome and good luck."

****

There were two lines formed outside of the club. It was a thirty-minute wait, but David finally got to the front of the line at The Clover Club. He reached for his wallet to pay the doorman.

"David? David Shaw?" the African American man said. He was dressed in a green dress shirt and black jeans.

"Yeah," David said.

"You don't remember me, but maybe you remember my mom, Ruth Davis? You were her lawyer when she sued her employer two years ago."

Recognition registered in David's eyes. "Oh, yes. Mrs. Davis and you must be Chuck."

"Yeah...yeah. You were able to prove that my mom's new supervisor fired her because she was black. You got her a settlement out of court and got the supervisor fired."

"How is she?"

"Oh, she's great. She started a catering business a year ago. It's really working out for her," Chuck said.

"That's great. Listen, do you know Trish Truman?"

"Yeah, man. My mom used to work at Trish's grandmom's restaurant years ago."

"Have you seen her tonight?"

"Yeah, she came bee-bopping through here with the blonde she hangs out with all the time...Dolly?"

"You mean, Darlene?" David asked.

"Yeah, that's her name. Anyway, they're inside. I didn't see them leave."

"Thanks, Chuck. How much do I owe for the cover charge?"

"It's on me," Chuck said. He turned to the skinny kid behind him. "Hey, Bobby, hook my man, David, up with a green wristband."

The two men shook hands. "Thanks, Chuck. I appreciate it."

"And I appreciate what you did for my mom. Have fun in there."

After David got his wristband and checked his coat, he started walking behind a group of six. Two bouncers opened the double doors for them to enter the main area of the club. The rap music and flashing lights blasted David in the face.

"How can anyone hear themselves think in here?" He meant it as a rhetorical question to himself, but a girl with pink streaks in her hair looked up at him.

"What? What did you say?" she yelled over the music.

"Nothing!" he yelled. "I was talking to myself."

She smiled and shook her head. "Oh. You want to dance?"

David smiled back at her. "No thanks. I'm looking for someone. Maybe later, okay."

She continued to smile. "Okay, handsome." She started squeezing through the crowd.

David had no idea where to look first. It was like a million people were crowded into one place. He decided to start on the dance floor. After a half a dozen 'excuse mes', he got to the dance floor. His eyes widened at a familiar face.

Ted was holding a mixed drink and grinding against a brunette with short hair who was wearing too much makeup. Her legs were shoulder length apart- giving Ted better access. David made his way over to them.

"Ted. Ted!" David yelled. The music grew louder the closer he got to the dance floor. Eventually, David got close enough to pat Ted on the shoulder. "Ted!" he yelled.

Ted turned his head around to look at him. His eyes grew wide. Then, he started laughing. The girl he was bumping his pelvis against kept wiggling against him. She didn't seem to notice or care that Ted had stopped dancing. Ted kept holding her by her waist. She had her hands around his neck.

"What the hell are you doing at The Clover? Not necessarily your type of hang out!" Ted yelled.

"What do you think?"

Ted looked at him. "Beats the hell out of me."

"Trish is here."

"How do you know?"

"Mr. Jacobs told me. He dropped Darlene and her off earlier."

A sudden look of panic appeared on Ted's face. "Darlene's here?" Ted asked.

David smiled. "Yep."

Ted tightened his grip on his dance partner, which made her stop wiggling. "Hey, Barb, let's get another Christmas Volcano."

"Okay!" she yelled.

"Let's go to the bar, man!" Ted yelled.

It took them ten minutes to make it to the bar, but the music wasn't as loud there.

The bartender approached them.

"Get us three Christmas Volcanoes, my man," Ted said.

"No. Nothing for me," David said.

"Make that two Christmas Volcanoes," Ted said with a sour look at his brother.

The bartender nodded his head and went to make the drinks.

"Why don't you live a little? The Christmas Volcano is The Clover's signature drink of the season. Try something new," Ted said.

"Try something new? Look where the hell I am. And the only volcano I'm interested in is about yah high," David said and put his hand out next to him estimating Trish's height. "With beautiful brown eyes and luscious lips," he said and sat down on a free bar stool.

"Aw," he heard Ted's companion swoon. "She sounds pretty…and feisty."

Ted laughed. "Only when provoked. David, you remember Barb?"

"No. I never met Barb."

"Oh. Well, let me make the introductions. Barb, this bleeding heart sap is my brother, David. David, this wild bodacious beauty is Barb. She's a hairdresser."

"Oh, the lawyer brother. Nice to meet you," she said sweetly.

"Nice to meet you too, Barb," David said.

The bartender returned with two drinks in tall hurricane glasses. The liquid at the bottom was green, and at the top was red. White smoke rolled out of the drinks like they were on fire. David cocked his eyebrow up.

"Twenty dollars, Shaw," the bartender said.

"What?" David said in amazement at the price.

"Here's twenty-five. Keep up the good work."

"Thanks," the bartender said and walked away.

"You two are going to drink a drink that's smoking?" David asked with astonishment.

"Sure am," Barb said and grabbed one. She quickly started to suck it through the green straw.

Ted laughed and took a quick sip of his drink. "Take a sip of mine. See if you like it."

"No thanks. I don't know what your mouth has been doing tonight," David said.

"Ha… ha… ha," Ted feigned sarcastically.

A black man with short dreadlocks approached them and stood in the same place as the bartender did. "Hey, Ted. David, I haven't seen you in years."

David's mouth dropped open. "Barry Bartman? The last time I saw you, you were playing for the Broncos."

Barry smiled. "Yeah, I blew my knee out three years ago. Luckily, I finished college and didn't live a lavish lifestyle while I was in the NFL. As you can see, I'm a business owner now."

"You're the owner of this place," David said with shock.

"I've been the proud owner of The Clover Club for two years now. Glad you decided to come to our Christmas party tonight," Barry said and he leaned closer to the brothers. "We got some fine looking honeys in here tonight. You are single, right? I didn't notice a ring."

"Yeah," David said, and before he could say anything else, Ted interjected.

"Barry, you know my brother is a lawyer. Maybe you can put him on retainer."

"Ted."

Barry laughed. "I think Ted is trying to help both of us out. See he knows I don't have a lawyer anymore."

"What happened?" David asked.

"He got disbarred."

"Ooh, someone was a bad boy," Barb said.

"You got that right, baby. The idiot got busted in a whore house in New York – that had underage girls working there. He was so hiked up on cocaine he didn't realize he got arrested until the next morning - in jail. Can you imagine that?"

David shook his head. "No. What do you need a lawyer on retainer for?"

"Oh you know, I get the occasional lawsuit from patrons. Like, a fight broke out, someone feigns injury. Of course, my bouncers take care of any disturbances as quickly as possible. Then there's the occasional 'My eyes were strained from the flashing lights in your club' routine. I also have a couple of rental properties, too. My lawyer drew up the rental agreements."

"I see," David said.

"David, give the man your business card," Ted encouraged.

David was about to say that he didn't have any, but he remembered that Trish pestered him to carry some in his wallet. He reached for his wallet and pulled out a business card and gave it to Barry. "If you're interested, call my secretary and make an appointment for next week."

Barry smiled and took the card. "Maybe we can do some business."

With that out of the way, David got to the business he wanted to attend to. "You invited Trish Truman to your club tonight, right?"

Barry looked surprised. "Oh. You're looking for the number one honey. Can't say I blame you. That hair, those eyes, and that body. Damn, she really filled out nice-," Barry stopped talking when he noticed how David was looking at him.

Ted had one hand on David's shoulder. Ted was also making cutthroat motions across his neck trying to signal, Barry.

Barb watched with wide eyes.

"Hey, David. I didn't mean no disrespect. I didn't know you and she had something going on. Look, let me get you a drink - on me. What do you drink?"

"He likes scotch on the rocks," Ted answered for him.

Barry reached underneath the bar.

"David, Trish is a pretty woman. Men are going to

look at her. It's just something that we do. You know that," Ted said.

"Yeah, Barry's a sweetie. He didn't mean any harm," Barb said.

Barry poured a generous amount of scotch in a glass over ice. "There you go. I apologize, David. I didn't know she was your lady. Are we cool?"

"David?" Ted asked.

David took a deep breath. "It depends. How good is this scotch?" he asked as his face softened.

Barry laughed. "The best in the house."

David took a sip. It tasted like his old brand in New York. "We're cool," he said with a smile.

Barry, Ted and Barb smiled.

"I'll sweeten the pot. I'll tell you were Trish is hanging out in here. I gave Trish and her gal pal the hook up."

"The hook-up?" David repeated trying to figure out what he meant.

"Yessiree. They're in the VIP section of the club. You got to have a green wristband to get in."

David looked down at his green wristband and was even more grateful to Chuck than he was at first. Ted looked down at his green wristband.

All three men looked at Barb, who was looking down at her black wristband. Her lower lip poked out. "That's fucked up," she said.

"Sorry, baby. Rules are rules," Barry said.

"Sorry, Barb. I have to go play wingman for my brother," Ted said.

"It's all right, Teddy. Thanks for the drinks and the dances. I had a fab time with you as always," she said with a smile.

Ted knelt down to give her a hug. Barb grabbed both sides of Ted's face and gave him a kiss. It lasted longer than a 'just friends' kiss. Ted didn't try to fight her off.

"Mmm. Still the best kisser at The Clover Club. Come by the salon sometime. Maybe we'll get to close the shop together again."

"Yeah, I hope so," Ted said with a mischievous grin.

"Bye, fellas," Barb said and walked away with her drink.

"Bye," Barry and David mumbled.

"Come on, guys, I'll take you to the girls," Barry said.

"I know how to get to the VIP, Barry," Ted said.

"It will take you fifteen minutes to make it to the elevator or the stairs in this crowd. I can get you up there a lot quicker."

"Yeah, how?" Ted asked.

"Grab your drinks and meet me at the end of the bar," Barry said and pointed to his left.

They did as Barry said. They stood next to the wall and waited for him. They didn't have to wait long because Barry opened the bar walk through and let them behind the bar before leading them to the back where there were loads of liquor bottles and boxes. He made a sharp right and opened a door that was painted black. There was a staircase in front of them.

"Keep following me, guys. Ted, do me a favor and close that door behind you," Barry said.

Ted closed the door. The stairwell was dimly lit, but you could see where you were going. Barry got to the top of the stairs and opened another door. David could hear music again, but it wasn't as loud as it had been downstairs. Barry held the door open for them, and Ted and David walked through. They were behind another bar.

"This is it, fellas. The VIP section. It has all of the same things, but less people, more lighting, and some luxury booths."

"Where's Trish?" David asked.

"There, David. Looks like her and Darlene are getting down on the dance floor," Ted said and pointed.

They watched the girls for a moment. David examined Trish's red dress with the halter neckline. Her cleavage was pronounced and the hem was midway up her thigh. She wore matching red heels. Her hair was parted on the side and full of curls at the ends. He wanted to walk over and carry her out of the club right then and there.

A tall, skinny white man approached them. He had brown floppy hair, and the girls looked happy to see him - too happy. They embraced him at the same time, and Trish gave the guy a kiss on his left cheek as Darlene kissed him on his right.

"Who the hell is that?" Ted and David asked in unison.

Barry slowly looked at the brothers. "If I didn't know you two were a couple of years apart, I'd say you were twins. The young man in question is Phillip."

"Phillip what?" Ted asked with a frown.

"Dunn. Phillip Dunn. He's from England. Seems to be another childhood friend of Trish's and apparently Darlene's, too."

"Know anything else about him?" Ted asked.

"He's some sort of international banker or investor or something like that. Dunn goes back and forth between the states and Europe. He has an aunt that lives in Clary."

The brothers kept watching the girls make a fuss over Phillip.

Chapter 24

Trish and Darlene danced to What's My Name, by Snoop Dogg, when an old friend approached them.

"Hey, double trouble!" he yelled over the music in a British accent.

They both turned around. "Phillip!" they exclaimed in unison. Trish hugged the left side of Philip, while Darlene hugged his right side.

"I haven't seen you in ages," Darlene said with excitement.

Trish kissed Phillip on his left cheek as Darlene kissed the other side.

"Mmmm, that's because I have to work for a living," he joked.

"Hey, we work for ours. Darlene is getting her masters," Trish said with a smile.

"And Trish works hard at being fabulous," Darlene slurred.

They all laughed.

"Who are you here with?" Trish asked.

"No one. I've been coasting back and forth between VIP and steerage most of the night."

"Well, in that case, join us at our private booth," Trish invited and bragged at the same time.

"I'd be honored, love."

The girls hooked their arms around Phillip's. On their way to the booth, Trish asked the waiter to bring them three Christmas Volcanoes. When they reached the half oval shaped booth, Trish slid in on the left side, and Darlene and Philip slid in on the other.

****

Ted and David stared across the room as David sipped his drink slowly. Ted gave his back to the bartender, he didn't want it anymore. The waiter that Trish spoke to approached the bar.

"Hey, Drew, what did Trish order?" Barry asked.

"Three volcanoes," Drew answered.

"From the dance floor they don't look like they are feeling any pain," Barry said.

"Trish is pretty relaxed, but the blonde is straight up drunk. Not sure if she needs anymore to drink."

"Have they eaten? Had water?" Barry asked.

"Very little water and they've only been eating the free bowls of chips."

"Okay, let them have the volcanoes, but take them some water and food. Order some nachos and wings."

"What kind of wings?"

"Get them a large order of plain, mild, and BBQ. Try to make it quick," Barry said.

"You got it, boss," Drew said and left to follow instructions.

Barry turned around to face the Shaw brothers. "Okay, guys, I got an idea."

Ted and David listened as they stewed.

****

Phillip was pleased that he was in between two ladies. "Ah, what a delicious sandwich we make."

The girls laughed again as they got cozy next to Phillip. He put his arms around both lady's shoulders. He read the sign out loud in the middle of the table, "Reserved, Truman. Where's Robert?"

"Oh, that's over. We split. He left me for an old lady with money. Lots of money," Trish slurred.

"Yeah, men are pigs. Except you, Phillip," Darlene slurred.

"Thanks, Darlene. Trish, darling, I'm so sorry," Phillip said with sincerity.

"It's okay, I've started a new life," Trish said proudly.

"Yeah, me too," Darlene said.

"Sound like you two beauties are nursing broken hearts," he said and gave them both a quick squeeze.

Darlene laid her head on Phillip's shoulder. Trish did the same thing, yet she said, "We didn't come here to mope. We came to party...have a good time."

"Have you been having a good time?" Phillip asked.

"Mostly," Darlene said and placed the palm of her hand on Phillip's chest. She started fingering his shirt. "Is this silk?"

"Yes, it is," Phillip answered.

"It feels….nice," Darlene said.

Phillip smiled at her. "Well, it feels even better, now. It's been a long time since I've had the company of such gorgeous ladies."

"Oh, Phillip." Trish smirked and raised her head from his shoulder.

Darlene giggled.

"Darlene, has anyone ever told you that your smile would light up a stormy night?"

"No," she answered slowly.

"Well, it can," he said and winked at her.

Darlene lightly rubbed his chest for a moment. "Oh, Phillip; thank you."

"Should I leave you two alone?" Trish asked jokingly.

Phillip gave Trish a light squeeze where he had his arm around her. "Absolutely not, I'm sure I can give both you ladies the attention you need."

"Oh my," Darlene gushed.

Trish smirked. "I have to say I like a man who doesn't back down from a challenge."

They all chuckled.

Two waiters approached the booth. One sat down three Christmas Volcanoes, three glasses of water, and a fresh bowl of chips. He picked up the empty bowl. The other waiter had a tray of food.

"Wow, I am hungry, but we didn't order that," Trish said.

"I took the liberty. It's on me," Barry said with a smile as he approached the booth.

"Barry!" the girls chimed.

He chuckled. "Ladies….Phillip," he greeted.

179

"What did you hook us up with this time?" Trish asked.

The waiter started sitting down the food.

"Nachos!" Darlene screeched.

"And wings," Trish added.

"Smells delicious," Phillip said.

"Yes, you really know how to take care of your customers," Trish said.

"Of course, you're VIPs, baby," Barry said.

Darlene giggled. "You got that right," she said.

The waiter placed silverware, three small plates, and some extra napkins on the table.

"Thanks, Drew," Barry said.

"No problem, Barry," Drew said and left.

Trish happily took in the sight. "Smoking drinks and smoking food, it doesn't get any better than this."

Everyone was all smiles and laughs until the Shaw brothers approached them.

"May we join the party?" Ted asked with a serious look on his face.

Trish looked at David like he was a Martian. "What are you doing in a nightclub?" she asked in a high-pitched voice.

"Um, looking for you," David answered with a little attitude. He crossed his arms in front of him.

"I thought you boys were going to hang back until I assessed the situation," Barry mumbled.

"We got tired of waiting," Ted said. He looked at Darlene, who still had her head on Phillip's shoulder and her hand on his chest. "Who's your friend?"

She slowly raised her head, but kept her hand where it was. "Who were the whores?" she asked back.

Phillip let out a slow whistle.

Barry and David's eyes widened.

Trish stifled a chuckle.

Teddy's eyebrows furrowed. "Whores?"

"Yes, one was a brunette you were dancing with, or should I say damn near screwing in front of the world."

Ted's mouth dropped open.

Trish picked up her drink. "Now you've done it. You got Darlene cussing," she slurred and sipped her drink through the straw.

"We haven't spent the whole evening up here you know and there are monitors in VIP that shows the, ehm, party on the main floor. Nice shade of lipstick, Ted. Who's it by? Rover or perhaps Dogiliene."

Phillip started to chuckle.

Trish stopped sipping her drink. "Teddy, you got some explaining to do," she said in a Ricky Ricardo voice, then she laughed. Phillip laughed as well.

Darlene smiled. "Not at all. We're all single here. Isn't that right, Phillip?" she asked and looked at him.

"Whatever you say, love," he smiled and winked at her again.

Darlene smiled and batted her eyes.

Ted roughly rubbed his hand over his mouth.

"Trish, come on. Let's go, honey," David said.

"Go?"

"Yes, I want to talk to you - in private."

"David, I'm hanging out with my friends, and we're about to eat," she said.

"I'll take you to get something to eat. Somewhere a little quieter."

"Eh, I don't know," Trish slurred.

Phillip gave Trish a little squeeze. He started caressing her bare shoulder with his thumb and index finger. "No offense, mate, but I don't think the lady wants to go with you."

"Take your hands off her," David sternly said.

"Or what, mate?"

"Oh, shit," Ted groaned.

"Or I'll break your arm, wrist, and fingers," David said stonily.

"David," Trish said with shock.

Phillip just smirked at him.

"David, the DJ just started playing a slow jam. Why don't you take Trish for a spin on the dance floor?" Barry asked in a deep commanding voice.

Trish pouted. "I don't want to dance. I want to eat."

"Oh, go on, Trish, At least David hasn't bumped and grinded against two brunettes, a redhead, and a blonde all in one evening," Darlene spat out.

Trish burst out in laughter.

Ted jerked his head up to the ceiling and groaned loudly as he grit his teeth.

David cocked his eyebrow and looked at Ted.

"Well, that's true," Trish said with a big grin directed at David.

He smiled at her.

"Okay, I'll dance, but I'm doing it for Darlene and Barry."

"Oh, of course," David said and offered his hand.

She slid out around to the edge of the booth and took David's hand. While they were walking away, Darlene said, "Have fun!"

They got to the dance floor. Trish tilted to the side

and quickly straightened herself as David grabbed her by the waist. "Are you all right?" he asked.

"Yes," she said.

David gave her a quizzical look. "You're drunk, aren't you?"

"No, I'm tipsy. Darlene is drunk. There's a difference," she explained with an innocent look.

He smiled. "Come here, Ms. Tipsy." He gently pulled her against his body and wrapped his arms around her waist.

Trish placed her hands on the front of his shoulders. They started swaying to I'll Make Love to You by Boyz II Men. Trish listened to the lyrics for a moment. Her eye's traveled down his shirt. "Have I ever told you how handsome you look in black?"

He chuckled. "No."

She looked at him. "You do. You look very handsome in black."

"Thank you and you look-" He stopped and let his gaze travel down her dress. "You look good enough eat." David tightened his hold on her.

The nerves in her body started to tingle, and her stomach growled. She got an idea to detract from the intimate situation they were in. "Speaking of eating, maybe we should go back to the table before they eat all the food. I'm famished," she slurred the last word.

He looked into her eyes. "If you leave with me now, I promise I'll feed you," he said in a husky voice.

Trish lightly gripped his shoulder. "This time of night? Or were you not speaking of food."

"It's up to you," David said. "I know a restaurant that's open twenty-four hours. It's only two miles up the road; or we can go to my apartment, if you're comfortable."

Trish's mouth opened. "I'm not sure if we should go to your apartment."

David smiled. "The restaurant it is."

"I didn't agree to anything," Trish said quickly.

David went in for a kiss. It was light and sensual and too short for Trish's liking. He looked at her from under heavy eyelids.

"What about Darlene?" she asked.

"I think she'll be fine. Barry is a client of Mr. Jacobs. He'll make sure she gets home safely."

"Oh, I don't know," Trish said.

David kissed her again. This time it was deeper. His tongue dipped into her mouth, then retreated. He gently broke the kiss. They were nose to nose.

Trish's breathing was heavy. "Oh, all right. Let's go."

He smiled and escorted her off the dance floor. It was good timing because the song had ended. They approached the booth and found Darlene sitting between Phillip and Teddy. She and Phillip were eating nachos. Teddy was eating BBQ wings. Barry was sitting on the edge of the booth.

Trish took a napkin from the table and grabbed two wings. "Darlene, I'm going to leave with David. Are you going to be okay?"

"Sure," she said with her mouth full.

"I'll make sure she gets home," Barry said.

"Yeah, me too," Phillip chimed in. He grabbed a small black purse with a gold chain. "Is this yours?" he asked Trish.

Teddy just stared at Phillip.

"Yeah," Trish said and took it from him. "Thanks, Phillip."

"Anytime, love," Phillip said.

"Barry, thanks for the best Christmas bash I've ever been to," Trish said.

"You're welcome, and please come back soon," Barry said as he nodded his head. "Why don't you let me walk you guys back downstairs? The fast way."

"That would be great," David said.

Barry stood up.

"Bye, guys," Trish said.

Darlene, Phillip, and Teddy mumbled their goodbyes.

Trish ate her two chicken wings as they made their way downstairs. Barry walked them to the double doors of the main floor. "David, I'll be calling you!" he yelled over the music. He took the chicken bones that were wrapped in a napkin from Trish. "You two have a great night."

"Thanks, Barry!" David yelled.

The lobby still had a few patrons entering the club, but not like it was earlier when David arrived. David and Trish walked to the coat check. He gave the attendant his coat ticket. While they waited, David realized Trish didn't give the guy a ticket. "Where's your coat?"

"I didn't bring one. I didn't want to keep up with a coat all night."

David looked at her in amazement. "It's freezing outside."

"I didn't know they had a coat check, and it's not bad if you get here early and go in and out of a warm car."

The attendant returned and gave David his coat.

"Thanks," he said to the attendant and held the coat out for Trish.

"David, I'll be fine."

"Put it on," he said slowly.

She rolled her eyes and turned around to slip her arms into his coat that was two sizes too big for her. "You are so bossy," she said as she adjusted to the size of the coat. She slung her purse strap over her shoulder. The trench coat sleeves hung from her wrists like bathrobe sleeves.

He smirked at the sight of her in his coat. "Yeah, and you love it."

She couldn't help but smile. He put his arm around her waist, and they started walking side by side through the lobby.

Chuck spotted them. "All right, David. I see you got what you came for. Woooo," he said loudly.

A bouncer whistled and another bouncer did a coyote call.

"I ain't mad at ya, bro," the skinny kid who gave out the wristbands said.

Trish giggled and shyly looked down as David opened the exit for her to walk through. "Goodnight, fellas," he said with a smirk.

They all happily returned the goodbye.

Chapter 25

Trish and David entered the diner. The booth and stool seats were red, and the floors were black and white checkered. The table and countertops were white. No customers were in the diner. A middle age man was wiping the counter with a white cloth. A waitress sat at the far end of the counter reading a newspaper. They both looked up when Trish and David walked in.

"Well, look what the cat dragged in. Hey, Dave," the man said.

"Hey. Gus, Dee Dee; this is Trish."

"Hi, honey," Dee Dee said from the end of the counter as she popped her gum.

"Hi," Gus added.

"Hi," Trish said back with a small smile.

David walked Trish to the middle of the diner and stopped at a booth. Trish untied the trench coat.

"Hey, Gus, how about some coffee?" David asked as he stepped behind Trish.

"Yo, Dave, you know where it is," Gus replied.

Trish's mouth dropped open with amusement.

"You see how he treats me. Gus, I got a date I'm

trying to impress." David pulled his coat off Trish's shoulders.

Gus laughed. "Well, you shouldn't have brought her here," he joked, then he got a good look at Trish when David took her coat off.

Gus's mouth dropped. "I'll get the coffee."

"Thank you," David said.

Trish shyly sat down in the booth. David sat down on the other side, placing his coat next to him.

"I want decaf," Trish said.

"Hey, Gus. Make that two unleaded coffee."

"Got it," he said with his back turned.

Dee Dee walked up to them with two waters. "This is the first time Davey has brought a girl in. You sure are pretty, sweetheart."

"Thank you," Trish shyly replied.

"The menus are behind the napkin holder. Just holler when you're ready to order," she said sweetly and walked away.

David grabbed one menu and handed it to Trish.

"You're not eating?"

"Oh yeah, but I know the menu by heart," David said.

"Oh," Trish said and opened her menu. She rubbed one side of her temple.

"Are you okay?"

"Yes. I think the cold air sobered me up a little bit."

"You got a headache?"

"Just a little pounding. Some food will help," Trish said.

"You know what you want?" David asked.

"You seem to be a regular here. What do you

recommend?"

"Everything is good," David said.

"Everything is great," Gus said as he brought them their coffee. "Cream and sugar are on the table."

"I know that, Gus," David said.

"See how he treats me?" Gus said to Trish.

Trish laughed.

"Whatcha in the mood for, young lady?"

"I don't know, but I'm starving. I usually don't get hungry or eat this late at night."

"Did you two just come from that Christmas Blowout at The Clover Club?" Gus asked.

"Yep," David said.

The dishes Dee Dee was carrying rattled in her hand as she walked by. "You went to the nightclub, Davey?"

David laughed. "Yes, there was…something in there I wanted," he admitted as he looked at Trish.

"Uh huh," Dee Dee said and kept walking.

"You two got the place to yourselves for two hours before the drunks from the club come in demanding food and coffee. I suggest you take advantage of it. What about a club sandwich and some hash browns," Gus suggested.

"That sounds good. I'll take that," Trish said and closed her menu.

"I'll have the same, Gus," David said.

"Coming right up," Gus said and left them alone.

"Well, you got what you wanted," Trish said.

"What do you mean?"

"I'm having dinner with you," she said, reminding David that he asked her out to dinner the other day.

He smiled. "Yeah, I guess you are. Trish, I want to

tell you about what happened after I left the office the other day. Before you make any decisions. Will you let me do that?"

Twenty-four hours ago she didn't want to hear a word he had to say about the mysterious blonde. But, David's actions made her change her mind. She had to admit, a man had never chased her all over town before. The least she could do was hear him out. "Yes," she said and put some creamer in her coffee.

"The woman that came into the office, who I met at The Wingate, is Heather Young. But, when I first met her, she was Heather Richards. She was my fiancé."

Trish let go of the end of the spoon. It clinked on the side of her coffee cup. Her eyes were wide. "I see. She was the woman you mentioned the night of the snowstorm."

"Yes, I met Heather at Lakedale Associates. That's the law firm I worked at in New York. Actually, I got a job with them as soon as I graduated from law school. I worked at the firm for a couple of years. I casually dated. I never got serious about anyone until I met Heather. She'd been at the firm almost as long as I had by then. She was a receptionist on the lower floor and worked her way up to executive assistant to one of the partners, George Young. That's when I met her...personally. She was smart and charming. After a couple of months of dating, I introduced her to my parents. Ted had already met her earlier on. When I lived in New York, Ted would visit me pretty often. Heather and I dated for a year before I proposed to her. I thought she was happy, it seemed that way. She accepted my proposal." David stopped and sipped his coffee.

Trish took a sip also and continued to listen.

"Thinking back, I think Ted saw something that I didn't. After I told him I was engaged, he said don't be so quick to walk down the aisle. I laughed him off-thought he was joking as usual. Now, I wish I had listened more carefully. Anyway, six months into our engagement, I had to go out of town for business. I finished my business three days early, and I wanted to hurry back - for her, because I missed her. I had a key to her apartment. When I first walked in I didn't see her. She wasn't in the living room. I thought she was taking a nap." David took a deep breath.

"I opened the bedroom door to find her naked and bent over the bed with George Young behind her." He stopped and leaned back in the booth.

"Oh my God, David. That had to be…I don't know what to say," Trish stuttered.

"Yeah, I didn't know what to say at the time. But, I felt it. I'm standing in the doorway with a bouquet of flowers in my hand like a fool, and she's screwing one of the partners- with my ring on her finger. I must have dropped them at some point, but I don't know when because I had never been so angry in my life. I don't know how long I stood there watching them, but Young saw me first. I believe he said, 'Oh, shit.' He had the decency to stop what he was doing. She looked in my direction. The shock on their faces would have been comical if I wasn't so enraged. Young pulled his pants up and started buckling them. Heather grabbed a pillow and covered herself. A pillow," David scoffed. "Well, it was probably the only thing that was close enough to her at the time. She said something when I entered the room, but for the life of me I don't know what it was. My ears were ringing. My face....felt so hot. Then, all of a sudden, Young approached me. His mouth was moving, but I didn't hear a word. But, I felt. I felt it. I hit Young so hard that he stumbled back and hit the floor. I did hear Heather scream and shout my name. I walked over and grabbed him by the throat. I wanted to kill him. Blood dripped from his mouth. I started to come back to my senses, and I let him go. I turned my back and left the apartment as Heather screamed my name."

Trish fought back tears. She wasn't crying for herself. She was crying for him. She could tell how he told the story that he was devastated by this woman. No wonder he was an infernal grouch when she first started working for him. A woman like Heather made all women look bad. She wanted to kill these two people for what they did to David.

"I knew I was fired. There was no point in trying to keep my job. Even if there was a chance of me keeping my position, I'd be damned if I was going to work under Young and see Heather every other week. I went back to the firm that day and packed up my personal things. I walked out and never looked back. Within a day, I decided to move back to Clary. I wasted no time. I only found out months later that I broke Young's jaw with that hit. My old secretary tracked me down. She told me. She said no one blamed me for my actions and urged me to move back to New York. She was convinced that I could rebuild my life there. I didn't want to. I didn't want to try. I stayed in Clary and slipped into my own little world for two years." David looked up to see a tear stream down Trish's face.

She grabbed a napkin from the dispenser and dabbed the tear away.

"I- I didn't mean to upset you," David said.

"No, it's okay," she croaked. "I completely understand. I don't blame you for wanting to kill that guy. You know, I threw a glass full of orange juice against a door when Robert walked out on me. Actually, I broke a lot of glass in my kitchen that day. Granted, I didn't catch him in the act, but it's upsetting when someone you love and trust betrays you like you were nothing to them," she said and cleared her throat.

"Here you go, kids," Dee Dee said and sat their food down. "If you two need anything else just-" She stopped when she noticed the somber mood. "Is everything okay?"

"Yes, ma'am. We're just talking about a heavy topic," Trish said.

"Oh, okay. I'll let you finish your talk. If you two need anything else, give me a shout," she said and quickly walked away.

"So, now the vixen of NYC is in Clary, Pennsylvania," Trish said.

"Not anymore. Yes, I knew it was her when you gave me the card and described her. I went to The Wingate to see what she wanted. I couldn't fathom what she wanted - especially since she married Young six months after we broke up."

"What did she want?"

"She wanted to start over. She asked me to return to New York with her. I couldn't possibly, not after what happened. Not after what I saw."

"What about her husband?"

"Died of a heart attack six months ago."

"Hmm. She didn't wait long," Trish said and took a bite of her sandwich.

"She claimed she never stopped loving me and that what she did was a maneuver for money and power. Her original plan was to take me along with her. She'd marry Young, and I would be the lover who came along for the ride."

Trish swallowed. This woman didn't know David at all. There was no way a man like David would allow himself to be treated like a gigolo. "You're kidding. She actually had the gall to admit that to you."

"Yes. She was always blunt when it came to me," he said and sipped his coffee.

"Why didn't she tell you about her master plan before you walked in on them?"

"She claimed she never got a chance, but whether it's true or not, I'm finished with her."

"Are you sure?"

David looked into her eyes. "Absolutely. I don't want to be with a woman who manipulates and uses her body to gain wealth and social status. I was long finished with her before I went to see her. After humiliating me like that." David shook his head. "Another thing, she hoped to talk me into being second in her life. Expecting me to go along for the ride like a little lap dog waiting for treats."

"That was an insult to you."

"I told her flat out that it was over between us, and we had no chance."

Trish took a sip of water.

"You believe me, don't you?"

"I do. Especially, after the way she betrayed you. You have too much pride and self-respect to go back to her. What I'm concerned about is how you feel about her. It seems like you loved her a lot. You were going to marry her."

David looked down at his food, exhaled, and then looked back up. "Yes, I was, but I don't love her anymore. I stopped loving her over a year ago. I continued to carry that pain around like a stone, though. But, I let that go when I was in her hotel room. I want my life to be different now. I want to....I actually want to be able to laugh and smile again. Enjoy the pleasures of life again. I didn't realize that until you came along. Trish, you being in my life helped me see how depressing my life has been for the past two years. You've awoken something in me that actually wants to live, not just go through the motions."

"Oh, David, I think you're giving me far too much credit."

"No, I'm not."

"So, the first few weeks of our bickery and zingers, made you want to come out of your shell."

He laughed. "Yes."

She couldn't help but smile. "Strange therapy."

"Yes, but it worked. I...can't have you disappear out of my life without a fight. Anyone that puts up with me in the office is patient, kind, caring, and spunky. That's you. You're beautiful, which I always thought you were, even when you hated my guts," he said and took a hold of her hand.

"What makes you think I still don't hate your guts?" she asked playfully.

"You really want me to prove that to you, here? I don't think Gus would appreciate me propping you up on the table," he flirted.

She giggled. "I was just kidding."

"I was too…sort of," he said and rubbed the back of her hand with his thumb. "I meant what I said. I've really grown to care for you, and I want to start seeing you. I'm willing to give you the time you need to think about it. I just wanted the chance to explain the blonde in the office and make it clear to you that I want you and no other woman."

Trish's cheeks warmed. She always liked it when a man was direct about his intentions. "Okay, you've given me a lot to think about. I would like some time to do so. I promise I won't take long."

He smiled at her. "Thank you."

"Now, let's eat our food, it's getting cold."

"Yes, dear."

Trish smiled and shook her head.

****

It was one-thirty in the morning when David pulled his beamer into the Jacobs driveway. It was an older model from his lawyer days at Lakedale. He would have loved to get the newer model, but he couldn't afford it.

"Your home, Ms. Truman," he announced and cut the headlights off.

"Thank you for a surprising, yet lovely evening," she said.

"Don't thank me, yet," he said and slowly put his

hand on the side of her face. "I haven't walked you to your door."

"You don't have to do that. The porch light is on."

"Actually, I do. You have my coat," he said as he caressed her face.

She smiled and leaned against his hand. Trish closed her eyes.

He moved his hand to her hair - shoving his hand into her thick soft strands, and she responded with a moan. He couldn't help himself; he grabbed her by the waist and positioned her in his lap. Her legs hung over to the passenger's side.

She kissed him. Her soft lips were warm and wanting. David took control, moving his tongue into her mouth as he slid his hand down to the lever next to the seat. He lowered them about two inches to give them room away from the steering wheel. Then, he wrapped one arm around her and shoved the other one through her hair. He pulled his tongue back, and hers followed after it. He groaned and slid his hand down the back of her dress to her bottom – and squeezed. She moaned against his mouth and wiggled against his growing manhood in response.

He tore his mouth away and started kissing her cheek. "Mmmm, I knew I should have taken you back to my place," he said against her cheek.

She smiled. "I thought it was too soon. Besides, this is nice, isn't it?"

"It's more than nice," he said and started to kiss her cheek again. He kissed his way down to her neck as he lifted her up against him. His head was at her chest. Her chest rose and fell with each breath as he kissed and nuzzled her cleavage.

******

Trish cupped the side of David's face. Her other hand ran through his hair. She was about to close her eyes as David kissed her chest and squeezed her breast when she noticed headlights coming down the street through the back window.

It looked like a sports car. It parked across the street from the house. Thanks to the street lights, Trish was able to see that it was Phillip. He got out of the sports car and closed the door. Then he walked around to the passenger side, opened the door, and helped Darlene out of the car. They linked arms and walked to the front of the car.

Then, an SUV came barreling down the street. It came to an abrupt halt, just an inch from hitting the sports car's bumper. The driver cut the engine and the headlights off. Teddy leaped from the driver's side and slammed the door. He started marching towards Darlene and Phillip.

****

David lightly bit the curve of her breast. He was fully erect, and he pushed himself against her bottom.

"Oh uh," she said.

He groaned and kept up his seduction.

"David," she whimpered.

"Mmmm, yes, sweetheart," he said with his lips against her cleavage.

"Shouldn't you get out there and keep Teddy from

beating Phillip to a pulp?" she breathed.

David's body tensed, and he looked up at her. She was looking out the back window. "What did you say?

"Across the street," she said and squirmed backwards.

David quickly moved his head to the right and looked in the rearview mirror. Ted had Phillip by the collar as Darlene looked on helplessly with her hands on her cheeks. "Argh, damnit," he scowled.

Trish squirmed towards the passenger side as David reached around her for the door. He got out as fast as he could. Leaving the car door open, he ran across the street. "Ted!"

When he reached them, David tried to push his body in between them. He grabbed Ted's hands. "Damnit, Ted, let him go."

Ted let go of Phillip's collar with a shove. Phillip stumbled a couple of steps back yet stayed on his feet.

David wasn't sure when Trish crossed the street, but she was there with her arm around Darlene's shoulders.

"What is this about?" Trish asked.

"It's about Teddy being a crazed neanderthal," Darlene cried out. "You stay away from me, you jerk," Darlene said and jogged across the street. She was staggering. Trish jogged behind her.

Phillip gave Ted a crooked smirk.

Ted raised his finger at Phillip. "You better get that smug look of your face, fish and chips, before I punch it off."

David stayed his hands against Ted's chest.

"Don't be mad at me because you made a muck of it. American men, always resorting to brute force. Don't you know a lady likes it when you can handle it like a man?"

Ted tried to lunge towards Phillip, but David held him back. "Get out here, before I decide to let him go," David said angrily.

"Later, boys." Phillip hopped in his sports car and sped off.

"Can you believe that bastard?" Ted yelled and pointed down the street.

"Keep your voice down. Do you want to wake the whole neighborhood?" David sneered.

"I think it's too late for that."

Before David could say another word, they heard a muffled hurl. They looked across the street and saw Darlene on the porch, on her knees, throwing up in the bushes. Trish quickly walked away from Darlene with her hands in the air. He wasn't sure if Trish was giving Darlene some space or if she was disgusted.

Chapter 26

It was ten o'clock Sunday morning when Trish made her way up the walkway of the Jacobs house. She had woken around eight and had gone to the grocery store and bakery.

Mr. Jacobs stood on the end of the porch with his hands in his pockets. He was looking down at the scene of the crime from last night.

The nerves in Trish's shoulders tingled. "Umm. Hey, Mr. Jacobs. Are you on your way to church?"

"Hey, Trish. Come over here, honey, and look at this," he said with curiosity.

Trish walked over and stood next to him. "Eww!" It was too dark to see last night, but she could see Darlene's accident in the morning light. A faint smell of booze and chili invaded her nose like an allergic reaction.

Because of Darlene's condition last night, Trish thought it would be best to walk Darlene through her basement entrance. She spent the night in Trish's apartment. Darlene would've died if her father saw her sick and drunk. After David convinced Ted to leave,

David was sweet enough to help Trish get Darlene in the house. Poor guy didn't even get a goodbye kiss for his efforts.

"Uh huh, what do you think that is?" he asked as he fidgeted with the brim of his tan wool cap.

"Looks like a big dog with diarrhea to me," Trish said and quickly walked up to the porch with her bags.

"You know, I bet that boy up the street let that Rottweiler out in the middle of the night again. What in God's name does he feed that dog?"

Trish's eyes widened. "I don't know, but it looks like a lot of it."

Mr. Jacobs shook his head in disapproval. "I'll shovel it up when I get back from church."

Trish shook her head. "Okay, Mr. Jacobs. Drive safe." She quickly went in the house.

****

Trish prepared her hangover remedy as she thought about David. She wondered what he was doing today. Was he thinking about her, too? With the blender going and her deep in thought, Trish didn't notice Darlene staggering into the living room.

"Will you please shut that thing off?" she asked with just an edge of nastiness.

Trish jumped and cut the blender off.

Darlene exhaled. "Thank you." She was wearing one of Trish's nightshirts. Her short, thick blonde hair stood up like a porcupine hair. She stumbled towards the couch and plopped down.

Trish couldn't help but smirk. "I have to say, you look like hell."

"I feel like hell. I feel like I died, went to hell, and came back," she complained.

Trish bit back laughter. She poured her remedy into a tall white cup, picked up a plate of croissants, and then tucked a glass of orange juice under her arm. She picked up her remedy with her free hand and walked to the sofa.

She handed the glass to Darlene. "Here. It will make you feel better."

Darlene turned her nose up at the red liquid. "What is it?"

"I call it the Hangover Recovery."

Darlene took the glass. Trish sat the plate of croissants on the coffee table and held her juice as she sat down next to Darlene.

Darlene sipped the remedy. She frowned at the taste. "Eww, what's in this?"

"Can't tell you that. Hold your nose and drink it."

"No way."

"You want to feel better, right? So, it's either this or what some other people do."

"What's the other thing?"

"Drink more alcohol."

"Ugh," Darlene groaned and held her nose for a healthy swallow of the remedy. "I'm sorry I ruined your evening."

"You didn't ruin anything. It was great until the 'brawl for all' and that wasn't your fault."

"How do you know?"

"I know you," Trish said and grabbed a croissant.

"So, tell me what happened between you and David

last night."

"Not until you tell me what happened after I left the club."

"Well, we ate. Phillip went to the bathroom - leaving me and Teddy alone. Ted said he was sorry that I saw what I saw. I asked him why he shamelessly flirted with me two weeks ago if he didn't like me. He said, he does like me, but he likes other women too; and if I was more experienced, I would know that, but he likes my innocence. That's what makes me so attractive to him."

Trish frowned. "What the hell did that mean?"

"I don't know, but I didn't like it," Darlene said and took another sip of her drink.

"It's like an insult and a compliment in one package. Teddy is usually so smooth. A goofy smooth, but usually a ladies' man nonetheless."

"Yeah, well, I told him that he didn't have to worry about hurting my feelings anymore because I was done. He tried to sweet talk me, but I wasn't having it."

"Sounds like you put your foot down," Trish said and bit into her croissant.

"Phillip came back to the table. I asked him if he wanted to dance. He said yes, and so we slow danced. We were...enjoying each other. Phillip was rubbing my back. He gave me a kiss on my forehead. I guess he remembered himself because he asked if he was making me uncomfortable. I said no. It felt nice. Next thing I knew, Teddy was grabbing Phillip's arm. I told him to keep his hands to himself, and Phillip told Ted to mind his own business." Darlene finished the foul-tasting remedy. "I figured it was time to go home, so I asked Phillip to drive me home. We went back to the booth to get my purse, and Ted was hot on our heels. Teddy said I wasn't leaving with Phillip, and he grabbed my wrist. Not hard, but I still didn't like it. This was the part where I caused trouble."

Trish was intrigued. "What did you do?"

"I grabbed a glass of water that was on the table and I threw it in his face. He let me go then. I think he got distracted by the ice that went down his shirt."

After all these years, Trish was finally rubbing off on Darlene. Trish smirked because it sounded like something she would do. "I bet." She took another bite of her croissant.

"Barry came over and asked what was going on. I apologized for the scene and told Barry that Phillip was taking me home. Barry said that was fine and told us to have a good night. Teddy tried to stop us from leaving, but Barry stopped him. Barry must have kept Teddy busy for a few minutes because we didn't see him again until we were leaving the parking lot. He was standing outside the doors looking like a wild man with a wet shirt. Phillip laughed." Darlene smiled. "Then, I laughed when Phillip blew his horn at him."

Trish chuckled. "Oh boy, I bet Teddy was hot. I don't think any man or woman has made a fool of him before." Trish took a sip of orange juice.

"Phillip asked me if was up for a little fun. I said maybe. Long story short, we ended up at a drag race."

"Come again?"

"We were only there for thirty minutes. These guys got Phillip to agree to a quick race. I was in the passenger seat. Phillip won the race and three hundred dollars. We hugged. Phillip picked me up and twirled me around. The race was the best part of the night."

"Let me guess this part. You two didn't know that Teddy caught up with you at the drag race."

"Yes, but we didn't know that until we got home. Phillip helped me out of the car and next thing I know a SUV pulled up- really fast. Teddy jumped out of the SUV cussing at Phillip for racing while I was in the car and driving like a madman on the way home. They traded a couple of insults, but the last one I remembered was Phillip calling Ted a sexually addled brain adolescent. That's when Teddy grabbed him."

"And that's when David and I-"

"Yep. I guess the ride didn't agree with my stomach. Oh no," Darlene said with a horrified look. "I threw up next to the porch. Daddy will see it when he goes to church."

"Relax. He thinks a dog did it. I got your back, girl."

"How did you convince him of that?"

"Not sure. I think I got lucky that it was brown and something your dad had never seen before. Luckily, he doesn't have any sense of smell because it sure didn't smell like dog poop."

Darlene's facial features relaxed.

"Teddy could have handled it better, but I understand his concern. Riding shotgun in a drag race was dangerous. Phillip could have wrecked. You could have been hurt or killed."

"I know, but I felt so free- so alive. Now, tell me what happened with David," Darlene said softly.

"He took me to a twenty-four-hour diner. On the way there, he told me that his father used to take him there when he and Teddy were kids. David is a regular there. The owner and his wife were nice. While we were there David told me about the blonde bombshell. Her name is Heather Young. She and David were engaged while he was living in New York."

Darlene's mouth dropped open. "You're kidding? I didn't know he was engaged before."

Trish continued to tell Darlene about Heather and the sordid details of what happened in New York.

****

Darlene went upstairs to take a shower before her father came home. While Trish was upstairs with Darlene, David called. He called to check on Darlene. Trish assured him she was fine and told him about her conversation with Mr. Jacobs. David got a kick out of it. They didn't talk long because David was expected at his parents' house. He also said he wanted to keep his promise to her about giving her time and space to think.

Trish lay on the couch in her apartment daydreaming about David. Her face warmed as she thought about his mouth and hands on her body. The memory of his honey words played through her mind. She really had grown fond of him. Then, an ache gripped her. Trish realized she missed him. Throwing her hands up in frustration, she wondered why she asked David for space. Was she crazy? Darlene was right; he was smart, mature, responsible, loyal, and a damn good attorney. What Darlene didn't know was that David was sexy, a great kisser, and he liked to take his time when- her eyes closed as she fantasized about him removing her clothes, caressing her body, and making her thighs wet with his kiss. A smile slowly spread across her lips.

"Hey, beautiful dreamer," Darlene said, interrupting Trish's thoughts.

Trish opened her eyes to Darlene staring at her. "Why are you standing over me like a serial killer?

Darlene smiled and sat down in the recliner. She wore a pink sweat suit. "It's nice to see you in love. Makes your face glow."

"I'm not in love." Was she?

"Don't deny it. I've been watching you and David. You two have fallen in love."

"You read too many romance novels."

"You can lie to me, but don't lie to yourself."

Trish's curiosity got the best of her. She asked, "What makes you say I'm in love?"

"Well, like I said, your face is glowing, your mind wanders- like it did just now and at The Clover Club, and your eyes light up when David is around, no matter how much you try to keep a straight face."

Trish contemplated what Darlene said. "I see. What makes you think he's in love with me?"

"David can't keep his hands off you, he undresses you with his eyes, and he goes nuts when he doesn't know where you are. Oh, and he follows you. Somehow he always ends up where you are."

Trish frowned. "Most people would call that stalking."

Darlene let out a small laugh. "Well, there are a lot of ladies out there that would love to have a stalker like him."

"I don't know. I don't know if I'm in love with him.

I know that I have grown to like him a lot. Perhaps we're on the rebound," Trish said with worry. "We've hated each other for years, then out of the blue he's kissing all over me and I...well...I don't discourage him."

"Are you sure you two hated each other? Sometimes people use aggression to cover up their true feelings."

Trish sat up and looked at Darlene. "You took a psych class last semester, didn't you?"

"No, I took it in undergrad, thank you very much, but it is true."

"Well, David did admit to me that he always found me attractive. I guess I have to admit that he's the tall, dark, and handsome type, but once again. It's just physical."

"And, once again, opposites attract. But, then again-"

"What?"

"David can be a bit of a hot head when it comes to something or someone he really cares about, like you. You're both passionate, and neither one of you backs down from a challenge."

"I don't know." Trish shook her head. "I need to think about this some more. Let's talk about something else. I see that you're feeling better."

"Yes, your nasty drink helped a lot. I also took some aspirin. By the way, Phillip called while I was upstairs. He asked me out for New Year's Eve."

Trish's eyebrows arched up. "Interesting. What did you say?"

"I accepted. He has tickets to the ECTV New Year's Eve ball."

"Do they televise the ball? I can't remember."

"No. Hey, you should come, too."

"Are you nuts? Last time I heard, those tickets cost seventy-five dollars a piece."

"One hundred, now. The price went up four years ago."

Chapter 27

Monday afternoon, Ted burst into David's office with the grace of a rhino. He dropped a large manila envelope on David's desk and plopped down in the chair across from it.

"Good morning to you, too," David said and twisted his mouth. He picked up the envelope. "What's this?"

"A little something from my connections in L.A. Our hunch paid off about Robert Jameson," Ted answered.

David opened the envelope and pulled the pictures out. The first picture was of Robert receiving oral sex from a man with blonde hair. It appeared they were in a luxury hotel room. David had seen pictures of defendants and plaintiffs in explicit situations before, but this was the first time they'd been of gay sex. "Whoa!"

"Yeah, that first one is a bit of a shocker," Ted said plainly.

David flipped to the next picture. It was of Robert having sex with a redheaded female. "I see. He is bisexual."

Ted shook his head.

David flipped to the last picture. It was Robert again with two blonde women. It appears that they were fondling his chest. "Is that a straw up Robert's nose?"

"Yep," Ted said flatly.

"Do we know who these people are? Where were these taken?"

"Prostitutes at a whore house in L.A. The place is clean, high class, and discreet. From what I understand, the madam has strict rules about patrons and her workers using protection. Either way, Trish got tested for STDs before she left L.A. She's clean. My contact says that people can get anything or anyone there as long as they pay the price. The date and times of Robert's ehm...appointments were stamped in the corner by the camera."

David looked up at him. "Wait. How do you know Trish got tested for STDs?"

"She told me."

David's brown eyes widened. "Don't tell me you showed her these."

"Of course, I showed them to her."

David looked up to the ceiling. "You idiot! How could you show her these? How did she take it? Is she all right?"

"Calm down, David. She had a right to know, and she's fine. Hell, she's better than fine. When I showed her those pictures I thought she was going to laugh herself to death. After she got her wind back, Trish said she was glad she got tested for STDs a week after her and Robert split. If she hadn't, she would have freaked out over the pictures. She never suspected that Robert was into, let's say, advanced sexual activities with multiple people."

David exhaled with relief that Trish wasn't upset by photographs. Robert Jameson was a fool to let Trish go. All the money and sex in the world were not worth giving her up. "Very nicely put, I must say. How did your contact get such clear pictures? They're so good I would swear he was in the room with them."

"I don't know, and I don't want to know. Unfortunately, I couldn't get any physical evidence concerning Jameson's cocaine use."

"It's fine. I think this is more than enough leverage to negotiate a better settlement. I don't think Robert wants his future bride to find out about his extracurricular activities. Even if she did know, I don't think they want this coming out in a courtroom."

"Don't suppose they do. Now, for the fun part, do you want me to go ahead and call my contact and ask him to send a copy of these pictures to Jameson's attorney; courtesy of you, of course?"

"Absolutely. I want this divorce finalized as soon as possible," David said and stood up. He grabbed a legal pad and a folder.

Ted's eyebrow arched up. "Oh? How much progress did you make with Trish the other night?" Ted inquired.

"After the call. I'll give you some privacy. I have to go over some things with Mrs. Hinkle anyway," David said and started to leave the room.

Ted stood up and walked to David's phone.

Five minutes later, David entered his office and closed the door.

"It's done, little brother," Ted said. "Jameson's lawyer should get your-" Ted made quotations marks with his fingers. "Confidential information by the end of the day."

David clicked the button for the intercom, "Mrs. Hinkle?"

"Yes, David," she answered.

"Call Jason Clinton of Maxwell Law Firm. Tell his secretary to expect a confidential envelope from us by the end of the day concerning the Jameson case."

"Yes, sir."

"Thanks." David sat down in his office chair.

"So? What's the temperature of the Trish Truman situation?" Ted asked flatly.

"Warm, I think," David said with hope. "I got the chance to tell her about Heather. She was very understanding. Now, I'm trying to give her some space, but at the same time I'm trying to express my serious interest in her."

Ted shook his head. "Yeah, I saw the roses. Very classy."

"Thank you. I can't help but notice your somber mood. Surely, you're not still brooding over Saturday night."

Ted started pacing back and forth. "Yes, I tried calling Darlene three times yesterday. First two times no one picked up, and the third time Trish answered and said Darlene was taking a shower."

"Well, I'm sure she had a hangover."

"When Trish reported to work this morning I asked if she told Darlene that I called."

"What did Trish say?"

"Trish said that she told Darlene that I called, and Darlene called me the scum of the earth and that she hopes she never sees me or hears from me again. Trish made it clear that any type of contact with Darlene right now would be met with aggression."

"Ouch," David said. "Well, it's probably for the best. You weren't serious about her. She isn't the good time type."

"I know that. I just feel like well…..what Darlene said, scum. I didn't mean to hurt her feelings. I really didn't. Usually if a woman is mad at me I can charm my way out of it. But, I don't think it's going to happen this time. I guess my ego can't handle the fact that a woman – hell, any woman - hates my guts. Oh well, I'm sure I'll be over it by Christmas."

David shook his head. "Another thing, you never told me why you were about to fight Phillip."

Ted stopped pacing and perched himself on David's desk. He proceeded to tell David the events that led up to the roughhousing.

****

A couple of days later, Trish was typing up reports for Teddy when the phone rang.

"Shaw Investigations," she answered.

"Hey, beautiful," David greeted.

"Well, hello, sir. What can I help you with today?"

The last time Trish talked to David it was Sunday afternoon. He called to check on Darlene. On her first day, a dozen of red roses were delivered. The card said, *I'm giving you time and space like you asked. This is my way of letting you know that I am thinking of you- a lot.*

"Personally, I have the urge to speak with the sexiest woman in Clary."

Trish giggled.

David chuckled. "Okay. We have to be serious now. This is a professional call."

Trish cleared her throat. "Yes, Mr. Shaw. How can I help you?"

"I have news concerning your divorce case, Ms. Truman. I would like to discuss this with you in person. Can you meet me at my office?"

Trish wanted to do a somersault. "Is today too soon? I can swing by around 11:30. I need to run some errands. I'll just add you to my to-do list."

"See you at 11:30, Ms. Truman."

"All right, Mr. Shaw. Goodbye."

"Goodbye, beautiful," he said and hung up.

Trish smiled when she hung up the phone.

******

David felt foolish because he was as giddy as a schoolboy. Trish was due to arrive any minute.

Trish walked through the front door. "Greetings, Mr. Shaw." she said as she approached him.

"Ms. Truman." He nodded. "Please step into my office."

They walked into David's office. He closed the door behind him and quickly stepped closer to her. "Can I you kiss now?"

Trish placed her hand on her chest like an offended Southern belle and dropped her mouth open. "Why Mr.

Shaw, that wouldn't be professional behavior. I strongly suggest that we greet each other with a handshake."

David twisted his mouth. "Ha. No thanks. I'll wait."

They both smiled and walked to the desk. Trish sat down in a chair and David sat on the desk in front of her.

"Where's Mrs. Hinkle?"

"She had a dental appointment. She also had some errands to run. I don't expect her back until two.

"So, Mr. Shaw, what did you need to see me about?"

"As you know, the P.I. I hired came up with additional information concerning your soon-to-be ex-husband."

"Yes."

"I relayed the information to your husband's attorney, and I took the liberty of renegotiating the original terms. Your husband agreed to them - rather quickly."

Trish gave him a quizzical look. "Do you mean you got me a bigger settlement?"

"I do," David reached behind him and grabbed a typed list. "As soon as you sign the divorce papers, and after they are filed, of course, you will receive the following settlement: eight million dollars in cash, five hundred thousand dollars in stocks, an apartment building that brings in one hundred and twenty thousand dollars a year located in Los Angles, and a three-bedroom beach house in the Bahamas," he finished proudly.

Trish's mouth dropped open. "Are you serious?"

"All you have to do is sign the papers," David said and reached behind him again for the divorce papers.

Trish stood up. David handed her the papers and a

pen from his front pocket. She placed the papers on the desk.

"Sign on the second page," he said.

She did so without hesitation.

"Flip to page four and initial," David said.

She did.

"And sign the last page."

Which she did.

David smiled and handed her the list of assets. "The list of assets you can keep for your records until I can mail you a copy of-"

Trish quickly threw her arms around David's neck and gave him a kiss on his mouth. She broke the kiss just as quickly as she started it.

He looked down into her eyes. "You know this is breaking professional conduct."

"Yes, I do." she admitted and smiled. She started to move her hands away.

David caught her by the waist. "Oh no, too late to correct yourself now."

Trish smiled. "I suppose it is."

They came together in a searing kiss. Trish dropped the papers she was holding. David tugged at her white cotton coat. "Take it off," he demanded against her lips.

She shrugged out of the coat and let it drop on the floor. His hands quickly unbuttoned her purple silk blouse, revealing her black bra. Trish loosened his tie and started unbuttoning his shirt. She rubbed his muscular chest as David started pushing things off the desk and onto the floor.

David hiked her up on the desk that was now bare for the exception of his computer. She swung her legs on the desk and parted them, and David climbed onto the desk. He was on his knees in the space between her legs. She reached for his black belt and unfastened it. David thrust both hands in her hair. He watched her as she unbuttoned and unzipped his pants. Trish shoved her hands down the back of his pants, caressing his buttocks. David groaned as he slowly leaned down to signal her to lie flat. Trish kept her soft hands in his pants.

He took her hot, welcoming mouth again, and she moaned against his lips. David lapped at her mouth- then started laying kisses down her cheek, stopping at her neck. He kissed and sucked at the sensitive part between her neck and shoulder.

Her right hand squeezed his buttocks as she let out a soft moan. "Oh God, is this really happening?"

"Hmmm," he murmured as he continued to kiss her neck. One hand moved down to her breast. David cupped it and applied pressure.

"Oh, David. Are you sure it isn't too soon?"

He lifted his head and looked down at her. Her eyes were half closed, and her lipstick was smeared. "It's not soon enough. I dream about you in my arms every night," he said and kissed her. "I lie awake at night wishing you were there to hold- to kiss." He kissed her again, but this time it lasted a moment longer. He pulled away and said, "And to make love to you."

They came together in a kiss full of want and need.

The door swung open. "David! Shit!" Ted exclaimed at the sight of them.

Trish gasped and closed her blouse, holding it closed with her hands.

David stood on his knees staring dead at Ted.

David's face grew red with frustration. "Somebody better be sick or dead, Teddy. If not, get out."

Ted looked down. "I'm sorry. You- you know I'm not a pussy blocker. The world would be a better place if everyone had sex on the regular."

Trish rolled her eyes.

"Ted! What do you want?" David said.

"I need you to come with me to the police station …right now," Ted said and walked in the room without looking at them.

David climbed off the desk. Trish immediately got up and turned her back to button her blouse.

"Why?"

"Mom got arrested," he said flatly as he surveyed the floor full of files, papers, paper clips, pens, and pencils.

"Mom? Our Mom?"

"Uh, yeah. Why do you think I came in here like a wild man? She's been trying to call you. Your service didn't know where you were, so Mom ended up calling me," Ted said as he stared at the phone that was on its side on the floor.

David remembered that he told Mrs. Hinkle to forward the phone to the service, so he wouldn't be disturbed while she was gone. "What did she get arrested for? Maxing out her credit card?" David asked with disbelief.

"She got accused of…shoplifting." Ted said.

David and Trish's eyes baulked.

"From what I understand, from her frantic ranting, she was at the mall. A boutique was having some sort of thirty percent off sale. She went to the counter, paid for her items, and started to leave the store. What Mom didn't know was that a bra was hanging on her purse. It must have snagged on her bag as she walked through the aisles at some point. She headed for the exit and the alarm went off. Before she knew it, a sales clerk grabbed her and yelled for mall security."

"Where's Dad?" David asked with a shocked look on his face. He tucked his shirt in and adjusted his pants.

Ted finally looked up at them. "He's working at the hospital today - and besides, Mom needs a lawyer not a doctor."

"Unbelievable," David said and started buttoning up his shirt.

"You better hurry, David. You don't want her spending the night in lockup," Trish said softly, picking up her coat.

"Tell me you can get her out today, David. Judging how she sounded on the phone she's freaking out already. And Dad will blow a gasket if she has to spend the night with hookers, drug addicts, and who knows who else."

David looked up and let out a long, frustrated breath.

Chapter 28

It was Christmas Eve and Trish felt empty. She loved the decorations of Christmas time, but she hated the feeling she was experiencing. Even though Mr. Jacobs and Darlene were like family, she was lonely. This was the first time in nine years she would spend Christmas as a single woman. Trish found herself thinking about her parents and grandparents. Her mother loved Christmas time, and her grandmother would give out free coffee on Christmas Eve and Christmas Day at her restaurant. Trish blamed herself for her mood. She never should have gone to the cemetery that morning of all mornings to put flowers on her loved ones' graves.

All the constants in her life were gone. She was thankful for the Jacobs, but it wasn't the same. They were the true father-daughter tag team. Trish was the adopted divorcee orphan. For the last two days, she had put on a brave and happy face in public, yet inside- pain, loneliness, and sadness filled her heart. She began to wonder if the people in her life loved her for her. Did they really know her?

Tears filled her eyes as she lay on her back on the

couch in her apartment. Her knees hung over the armrest, letting her feet dangle off the side. A red candle burned on the kitchen island, and she watched the flame flicker on the candle. Her cell phone rang.

She reached over to the coffee table to pick it up. "Hello," she answered in a monotone.

"Trish?" David said with a quizzical tone.

"Hey, David. What's up?" she said, struggling to sound normal.

"What's wrong? You sound weird."

"Maybe because I am a little weird," she joked.

"Ha. Are you busy?"

"Not really. I'm just hanging out in my apartment. Why?"

"I called to invite you to my parents' house tonight. Everyone is here, and some folks here are dying to see you again."

"What folks?" Trish asked with suspension.

"If you come over here, your questions will be answered."

"I can't. I'm really...tired. Maybe I can catch up with you and your family tomorrow."

"Uh huh. Where's Darlene and Mr. Jacobs?"

"Darlene went to the community center. She's helping out with the children's Christmas program. Mr. Jacobs went to hang out with his buddies for some Christmas male bonding or something. After all that, Darlene and Mr. Jacobs are going to meet at church for the Christmas service."

"Are you going to the service?"

"No."

"You're depressed, aren't you?"

"No," she said defensively. "I'm just worn out. This has been...the busiest holiday season I have had in a couple of years."

"It's not like you to turn down social activities."

"Well, maybe you don't know me as well as you thought."

"What does that mean?"

"Nothing. It was a statement. I need downtime like everyone else. I don't always act like I'm hyped up on caffeine."

"I don't think you're always hyped on caffeine. You're awfully defensive tonight. You're upset and depressed."

"I am not."

"The holidays can be hard on some people. You know what helps?"

"No, but I'm sure you're going to tell me."

"Being around people that care about you."

"David, I'm tired."

"Who's the grouch now?"

She let out a groan.

He chuckled. "Come on, sweetheart. Everyone's dying to see you."

"My plan tonight is to fall asleep on my friendly living room couch. Really, I'll catch up with you tomorrow."

The line went quiet.

"David?"

"Trish," a woman said. "This is Elizabeth Shaw."

Trish was shocked that David's mother was on the phone. "Oh, Mrs. Shaw. How are you?" Trish struggled to sit up on the couch.

"Not good. I hear you don't want to come to my party tonight."

"Well…I- I appreciate the invitation. I just don't want to impose."

"You won't be imposing. We heard you moved back to Clary, and we are dying to see you. So, you bring your little tooshie over here PDQ. The address is 3030 Nicholas Lane, Claremont Estates. It's a brown brick two-story house with white Christmas lights."

"Yes, I know the address, but, Mrs. Shaw, I-"

"But, nothing. I won't take no for an answer. If you won't come on your own, I'll send Richard to fetch you."

The last thing Trish wanted was to go to a Christmas party and for Dr. Shaw to leave his own party to come pick her up. "That won't be necessary. I'll be over in forty minutes."

"Good. See you when you get here," Mrs. Shaw said and hung up.

Trish flipped her phone closed. "Damn, I don't remember her being so pushy." She let out an exasperated breath and got off the couch.

****

Trish freshened up and put on an ivory sweater and matching stirrup pants. Knowing she had to put on a performance of Christmas cheer, she also donned her Santa Clause hat. Since the Shaws lived in one of the most prosperous areas of town, Trish pulled out her fox fur. Just like her mother, she wasn't going to let a bunch of rich folks show up a downtown girl.

Luckily, she had a habit of buying one or two extra gift baskets for Christmas – just in case she forgot to get someone a gift. There were two rolls of beef sausage, one block of Swiss cheese, one block of cheddar cheese, two packs of gourmet crackers, and a jar of cheese spread in the basket. She grabbed a bottle of Chardonnay from her kitchen cabinet.

She totted the items as she walked the two blocks to the Shaw house. That was the closest she could park. Apparently, everyone in the neighborhood was having a party.

Trish stomped past the luxury cars as she complained and cursed into the night. "The last thing I want to be doing is carrying this crap in high heeled boots for forty blocks. Christmas my ass. Damn, damn, damn."

"Now that's not a good attitude or nice language to use on Christmas Eve," a male voice said.

The voice came from the walkway in front of someone's house. Trish looked over to see a tall man dressed in full Santa Clause garb. "Well, I be damned, Santa."

"Ho, ho, ho. What has a pretty girl like you got to be mad about on Christmas Eve?"

"I'm cold and grouchy. What are you doing on the sidewalk? Aren't you supposed to be riding in your sleigh delivering toys?" she asked with a hint of sarcasm.

"The reindeer needed a break. Now, what has you so riled up, young lady?" he asked as he walked to her- still spouting his Santa voice.

Trish turned her nose up at him. "Do you really care? You don't even know me. And why would I tell my problems to some stranger?"

"Well, I'm not a complete stranger. I'm known all around the world. I care about all children no matter how old they get."

She twisted her mouth and thought for a moment. Sometimes it was better to talk to strangers. You usually don't see them again. "It's Christmas, and I have no one. Everyone I have ever loved or loved me is either dead or gone."

Santa's eyes grew concerned. "Dead? Gone?"

Trish swayed back and forth for a moment. "Yes. See, my divorce just became final. Don't get me wrong, I'm glad to be rid of my husband - he turned into a cheating money-grabbing jerk - but we were married for nine years. He was the first and only serious boyfriend I ever had, my childhood sweetheart, my first love. I sacrificed so much so he could become a doctor. I even sold my grandmother's restaurant to help pay for his education. After my parents died, he was the only person I had left. He left me for some old lady with money," she spat out in a high-pitched voice.

"I see. What about your parents?"

"My mother died first. She was hit by a drunk driver," Trish said sadly.

"Oh, I'm so sorry. It's hard to lose a loved one unexpectedly."

"I just turned eighteen. My father died a couple years later. Complications with pneumonia, but I think he died of a broken heart. He wasn't the same after Mom died. I never should have left him. I...I...was going to

Clary University. I wanted to be close to home, but Robert, my now ex-husband, got into medical school in L.A. He asked me to marry him and come with him. He even asked my father's permission. My father agreed, I dropped out of college, married Robert at the courthouse, and went to L.A. My father said he was happy for me, but he would miss me. God knows, if I- if I knew he was going to die two years later, I would've insisted he come with us," Trish said as she fought back tears. She took a couple of deep breaths to get herself under control and continued. "My grandmother died of old age. She left me her restaurant. She knew Dad didn't want it. He loved construction and landscaping. That's what he did. He owned his own construction business. He said it was his dream."

Santa's eyes crinkled like he was smiling. "Your father wanted you to live your life. All fathers want their little girls to be happy. And at that time, that's what made you happy. Don't feel guilty about his death. He wouldn't want that."

"Oh, I know, I think. I guess I was asking for a dose of reality when I went to the cemetery this morning."

"You went to the cemetery on Christmas Eve?"

"I know. Crazy right? But, I kept putting it off since I moved back to Clary. I put flowers on my parents' and grandparents' graves. I never knew my grandfather. He died a couple of months before I was born."

"Surely, you have friends," Santa said with concern.

"I do. I have my girl, Darlene. We've been best friends since we were little- because our fathers were best friends, you see. Her dad is my godfather. They treat me like family, but it's not the same. Sometimes, I feel out of place. It isn't anything that they do. I don't know what it is."

"Loved ones are missed the most around the holidays. It's natural. But, the best way to honor loved ones who are gone is to be happy and live the best life you can. Also, you have to remember the people who are still in your life care about you very much."

Trish smiled. "Yes, and I care about them. I'd kill for Darlene and Mr. Jacobs."

Santa ho-ho-hoed. "Hopefully, it won't come to that. And as far as your ex-husband goes, I'll make sure he'll get two truckloads of coal this Christmas."

Trish smiled again. "I would take great joy in that. But, I think Robert might already be gnawing at the bit."

"Oh?"

"Yes, my lawyer, who by the way, I am convinced is the best lawyer in the city and no one knows it; really nailed him. He got me a bigger settlement than I originally asked for. I can't imagine Robert was happy about it."

"Sounds like you got your Christmas gift early this year. That's something to be grateful for. And sounds like your ex deserved to be knocked down a peg in the wallet."

Trish was grinning from ear to ear now. "Yes. I am grateful, and now that you mention it, it does seem like I took some steam out of Robert's stride." She giggled and Santa chuckled.

"I think you got the last laugh and will continue to have it as long as you keep your spirits bright and be open to new possibilities."

Trish smiled. "Yeah. My life could be worse."

"That's right."

"I never thought I would say this as an adult, but thanks, Santa."

"Ho, ho, ho," he said joyfully.

Trish laughed.

"Where are you heading, pretty one?"

"I'm going to the Shaw party."

"That's my next stop. Is it okay if Santa walks with you there?"

"Of course," Trish said.

"Why don't you let me carry that basket for you? I promise I let you have the credit," he said and stretched his hands out.

"Thank you," she said and handed it to him.

They started walking up the sidewalk.

"Do you do this every year? Come to this neighborhood."

"I've gone door to door every year on Christmas Eve for thirteen years in this neighborhood. If I didn't show up, everyone would be disappointed. Especially, the little boys and girls."

"It's sweet that you take time out of your own life to do that." Trish said.

"I'm Santa. It's my job to spread Christmas cheer."

Trish shook her head and smiled.

"The lawyer you bragged about...that helped you with your divorce, what is his name?"

"David Shaw. He is brilliant. Truly, if you have any legal problems go to him. His office is downtown."

"Yes, good-looking young man. I know where his office is. I stop by the toy store a few blocks away every year to say hello to the good boys and girls in there."

"One time I saw him in court and he was, well, magnificent. Brilliant. Very charismatic and he goes the full mile for his clients."

"Sounds like he comes highly recommended. It also sounds like you're fond of the young man."

Trish let out a bit of a squeal. "If I tell you, will you promise not to repeat what I said at the party when we get there?"

"I promise. Santa can keep a secret, I assure you."

"I am fond of him. I'm afraid I might be too fond of him. It's strange and scary. I just got divorced you know. I don't think I should like a man this much so quickly."

"Ho, ho, ho. Love comes along when you least expect it. You have to be brave enough to accept it when it does."

"I didn't say I was in love with him."

"Maybe you are and don't know it or don't want to admit it to me. However, if you're not now, you will be very soon. I've known the Shaw boys since they were little. They're pretty tenacious when it comes to something they want."

Trish giggled as she remembered one of David's steamy kisses. "Tell me about it."

Santa chuckled. "That was definitely a loaded comment. Are you going to tell Santa more?"

Trish smirked. "Oh, Santa, you know a lady doesn't talk about such things."

"Oh boy."

They both laughed.

"I...I could be...you know...falling for him. I find myself thinking about him a lot lately. I don't know how he feels about me though."

"By the way you speak of him, he is a smart young man. With that being said I'm sure he adores you and thinks of you as often as you think of him."

Trish smiled. "David did admit the other day that he thinks of me often."

Santa shook his head. "Now see, love can bloom during Christmas."

"Oh, I don't know, maybe," she shyly replied.

"Looks like we're here," Santa said.

Trish looked at the large two-story house that was decorated in white lights. "Oh, yes, and remember this is our secret."

"I won't say a word," he said and put his gloved finger on his lips and winked at her.

They smiled as they walked up to the house and climbed the three steps up the porch. Trish pressed the doorbell. It played a Christmas chime. Trish admired the wreath that was on the door.

"Wow, Mrs. Shaw really is into Christmas. I haven't seen David's parents since I was sixteen. I wonder how much they've changed."

Before Santa could say anything, the door opened. Elizabeth Shaw stood at five-foot-six wearing a long green dress with long sleeves. It lightly hung from her slender body, and her dark hair was in a French braid. For a woman in her mid-fifties, she barely had any wrinkles. Her pale skin was flawless.

"Merry Christmas, Mrs. Shaw," Trish said.

"Trish? I haven't seen you since you were a teenager. You were pretty back then, but you're prettier now," Mrs. Shaw said with a bright smile.

"Thank you. These are for you." Trish turned her

body to indicate the items they were carrying. "Oh, I hope you don't mind that I brought a friend."

"Ho, ho, ho," Santa said.

Mrs. Shaw giggled. "Not at all. Hi, Santa," she said in a high voice and waved her hand.

"Hello, have you've been a good girl this year?"

"Oh, yes," she said a bit seductively.

"Good, because I have a special gift for you."

"Oh," Mrs. Shaw said and giggled with excitement.

Trish fought the urge to turn her nose up. She couldn't believe Mrs. Shaw was flirting with Santa Claus right in front of her.

A girl with blonde hair in a ponytail, who looked she was around fourteen, approached them.

"Kelly, this is Trish. She's a friend of your cousins," Mrs. Shaw said.

"Which ones?" Kelly asked.

"Teddy and David," Mrs. Shaw answered. "Trish, this is my great-niece, Kelly."

"Hi," Trish said.

"Hi, I like your coat. You look bad to the bone. Is it real?"

"Kelly, it's not polite to ask such a thing," Mrs. Shaw whispered loudly.

"It's okay. No, it's not. I don't like hurting animals," Trish answered.

"Nice," Kelly said and nodded her head with approval.

"Kelly, take these things into the kitchen, please," Mrs. Shaw said and gestured towards the wine and gift basket that Trish and Santa were carrying.

Kelly took the items and said, "See you guys later,"

and left the foyer.

Trish found it strange that the girl didn't acknowledge Santa.

"Please come in," Mrs. Shaw said.

Trish and Santa stepped into the foyer. Mrs. Shaw closed the door. Santa helped Trish take her coat off. Mrs. Shaw took it and hung it up in a closet. They walked out of the foyer and into the living room. There were people sprinkled in every corner and seat.

Teddy sat on the edge of the sofa holding a beer mug. He had on a Santa hat and a white turtleneck. He stood up when he saw Trish. "Hey, Trish, you finally made it inside. I saw you two from the window. What were you and Dad talking about?" he asked as he walked over to them.

Trish blinked. *Dad? Seriously?* Mrs. Shaw wasn't a freak with a Santa fetish. She was flirting with her husband. No wonder Kelly didn't acknowledge Santa, she knew it was her uncle coming to his own house. Then, her face fell and she froze. Here she was thinking that she was talking to a perfect stranger, who she didn't think she would see again after tonight and it wasn't. Trish threw a fit, had a pity-party, and bared her soul to David's father.

Trish literally and utterly wanted to die right then and there. Then, she remembered that David's father was a doctor and would probably revive her, so it was no use dying.

"Are you all right?" Teddy asked.

"I think your father did his Santa impression for Trish. It appears she didn't figure out who she was really talking to - until now."

"Oh God," Trish mumbled, barely moving her lips.

"Should I get your medical bag? Trish looks like she's about to pass out," Teddy joked.

"No, but she could probably use a drink to warm her up," Dr. Shaw said.

"Yes, get her a drink and take her to David. He's been waiting for her." Mrs. Shaw looked at Trish who still had shock on her face. "Oh don't worry, dear. Whatever you told Santa will stay between him and you."

Trish brought her hand to her forehead.

Teddy was amused by her reaction. "Dad, I'll pay you $100 if you tell me what she said."

"I'll pay you $200 to drop it," Dr. Shaw said as he took off his beard.

"I'll collect my check at the end of the night," Teddy joked.

Chapter 29

David drank his scotch as he listened to Uncle Edgar brag about all the fish he caught in July. He saw Ted walk into the den from the corner of his eye and then approach him.

"I sensed you needed saving when you didn't come back into the living room," Ted said.

"Saving from what? I'm telling some damn good stories, boy," Uncle Edgar said as he rubbed his belly. "Ain't that right, David?"

"Yes, sir," David said.

"Your girl has arrived. I would have brought her to you, but she got caught in a conversation in the kitchen with Daisy, Melanie, and Marcus. They were a year ahead of her in high school. They're catching up."

"Girl? What girl? You got a girl? You didn't mention a girl." Uncle Edgar slurred.

"He probably didn't have a chance. Take a breath, Uncle Edgar. Let your alcohol digest," Ted said.

"I have to go, Uncle Edgar," David said with a smile.

"I want to hear more about the *womens*," he slurred.

"Ted, will fill you in on all the *womens* you want to know about," David said.

"Thanks," Ted said sarcastically.

David quickly left them. He weaved around friends and family to the living room.

"Hey, David, have you tried this caviar? It's delicious," Fran said.

"Earlier, it's good," he replied as he was trying to get to the kitchen.

"Marvelous," Fran said and put a cracker with caviar in her mouth.

"This is some tree you have here!" Katie said in her Brooklyn accent. She was looking up and down at the Christmas tree next to the window.

"Thank you." His mother beamed proudly.

David finally walked through the swinging door of the kitchen. He noticed Trish stood in a small circle with Marcus, Melanie, and Daisy. He approached them.

"Hey," David said and put his arm around Trish's shoulder. "Mom did the trick, huh?"

"Yeah, but I'm glad I came. Thanks for inviting me," Trish said with a big smile.

Marcus, Daisy, and Melanie went silent. Their faces were blank.

"What's wrong with you guys?" Trish asked.

"I..um….what?" Daisy stuttered.

"I must be drunk," Melanie said.

"I think we're all seeing the same thing because I'm the designated driver," Marcus said and scratched his short afro. "Unless this punch is spiked."

"What are you talking about?" David asked.

"Are you serious with that question?" Daisy asked

with a perplexed look.

"The last time we knew you two were mortal enemies," Marcus stated.

"I think the term mortal enemies is a bit strong," David said.

"Are you kidding me?" Melanie said with amusement.

"Yeah, remember the fourth of July when Trish beat David up?" Daisy asked.

"I wasn't there, but I heard about it. Everyone was talking about it at school," Melanie said with amusement.

"She didn't beat me up," David said.

"That's right. Trish didn't beat David up," Marcus said.

"Thank you," David said.

"She whooped his ass," Marcus said and started laughing.

Daisy and Melanie smirked. David wasn't amused at all.

Trish smirked. "That was years ago. We're cool, now. I even worked in David's office for a couple weeks."

"What!" the threesome said.

"Why is this so hard for you guys to believe?" David asked.

"I don't think you two realize or remember how your mutual animosity looked to the outside world," Marcus said and sipped his punch. "When you put your arm on Trish's shoulder I was bracing myself. I thought Trish was going to break it off."

"I have no intention of doing that, so you guys won't

see a fight this evening," Trish stated.

"Damn, would have made this Christmas party memorable," Daisy said.

"Yeah, no fair. I missed the first one years ago. I always hoped to see the rematch," Melanie joked.

David looked up to the ceiling.

The back door opened. Bobby, who attended high school with David, walked in. A light trail of smoke hung around him. He closed the door and pulled his stocking cap off his bald head, and then he looked up at the group. He gawked at Trish and David. His dark skin almost turned gray. "What the hell is this?"

"Haven't you heard? Trish and David are best buddies now," Daisy announced.

"Shit," Bobby said. He put the stocking cap back on his head. He also grabbed an open wine bottle from the table.

Bobby turned back towards the door.

"You just came back from a smoke," Marcus stated.

"Who cares, this is one of the signs of the apocalypse. I'm going to enjoy myself while I can," Bobby said and walked back out the door.

Everyone laughed.

****

Trish stood alone next to the Christmas tree. David got caught in a conversation with an older gentleman concerning probate laws. Dr. Shaw walked up to her. He had taken off his beard, but still wore the Santa suit and hat. "Are you having a good time?"

"Yes, I am."

"Good. Glad to see you in good spirits."

"By the way, that trick you played on me was not nice," Trish said.

"It wasn't a trick. I was in character. I can't break character while I'm out. What if a child saw me?" he asked with a not-so-innocent smile.

Trish leaned her head back and examined his face. "I see where he gets it from."

"Excuse me?"

"David can be rather incorrigible sometimes. I see he gets it from you," Trish said and shook her head.

He chuckled. "If that's the worst you can say about the boy, then I did a good job. Elizabeth was right. I don't divulge what people tell Santa."

Trish looked down. "I know. It's just...I'm sorry you saw me have a fit out there. I thought I was alone."

He smiled. "I'm a doctor; I've seen and heard people say and do worse. At least you didn't beat my son up again."

"Dr. Shaw."

"Just kidding, Trish. But, just like so many years ago, you two have become the talk of the party."

"Oh, boy," she said somberly.

He smiled again. "It's not that bad. Just some folks that know you two's history are a little stunned. Bobby finally came back inside. I think it got too cold for him. I'm happy for the distraction. At least everyone isn't talking about Elizabeth being arrested."

"Oh, I almost forgot. What happened with that?" Trish asked.

"By the time I found out about it, the charges were

dropped. David said the ADA had bigger fish to fry. I think it had more to do with what Ted told me."

"What was that?"

"Ted told me David threatened to sue the store for so much money that it would have to close. He even played with the idea of suing the mall, too. It was enough to scare the store owner, who knows that Elizabeth shops there often, to drop the charges." Dr. Shaw chuckled. "You're right, my son is a remarkable attorney."

David walked up to them. "Why are you two in a huddle?"

"We're not in a huddle," Dr. Shaw said. "How did you get away from Jackson?"

"Uncle Edgar called him over to tell him a fishing story," David said with a smile.

Dr. Shaw shook his head.

"Trish, Trish," Mrs. Shaw called out a foot or two away. "Come over here. I want you to meet my sister."

"I catch up with you guys later," Trish said and walked towards Mrs. Shaw.

****

"So, what do you think?" David asked.

"I think she's a nice girl. You seem to enjoy her," Dad said.

"But?"

"No buts, I like her - a lot. I just want you to be sure about what you want. That girl has had a lot of losses and disappointments in her short life. She doesn't deserve any more pain."

David looked at his father closely. "You sound concerned for her. Ted said he saw Trish talking to Santa outside. What did she say?"

"Now, son, you know-"

"I do. Just thought I give it a try."

"When or if she wants to tell you, she will," Dad said.

David's eyebrow rose.

Later in the evening, Trish and David sat on the brown leather sofa in the den. A couple of people milled around the room talking.

"Once again, thank you for a lovely evening," Trish said.

"You're very welcome," David said. "You're not about to leave are you?"

"I think I should soon. They were predicting a snow shower tonight."

David shook his head. "So, what did you and Mom talk about after you met my aunt?"

Trish smiled. "Just party talk. Nothing serious."

"Hmm, and what did you and my father talk about?"

"He told me that you got the charges dropped for your mom," she said and sipped her wine.

"I'll rephrase. What were you talking to Santa about?"

"Um, the holidays?"

"Trish."

"We were. Mostly."

"Care to elaborate?"

"Maybe another time," she said and looked down in her glass of wine. "What are your plans for Christmas Day?"

David thought for a moment. He decided to let her have her way in changing the subject, for now. "I'm spending the night here. In the morning, we'll have breakfast and open presents. In the afternoon, I'll go with Mom for the house to house Christmas cheer tradition in this neighborhood - it's my turn. Ted did it last year. We'll have a formal family dinner, and then we're all going to a concert at Claryfield Hall."

"Wow, sounds like a packed day."

"What sounds like a packed day?" Mrs. Shaw asked as she walked to them. She sat down next to David.

"Our family Christmas activities," David answered.

"Oh, yes. I am so excited for tomorrow. Trish, why don't you join us for dinner and the concert?"

"Oh, I can't. I promised Darlene I would do Christmas Day with her."

"Well, bring her along and her father, too. Dear man, James Jacobs, he's been our financial advisor for years. Made us a pretty penny."

"I don't think Darlene will go for that, and I wouldn't dare impose on an intimate family gathering."

"You are not an imposition, young lady, so get that out of your head. I like having you around. Especially tonight. You were a delicious distraction from that ordeal I went through a few days ago. Ted said you knew about it."

"Um, was that a compliment?" Trish asked.

"It was, and it was also a thank you," Mrs. Shaw replied.

"And thank you for inviting me, but I really should go, it is getting late, and I believe the weatherman is right about snow showers tonight."

"All right. Thanks for letting me push you around a little bit tonight," Mrs. Shaw said and smiled.

Trish smiled too. "Sure."

"I'll walk you to your car," David said and patted Trish's knee.

Mrs. Shaw grinned at them.

Chapter 30

Trish woke up to Darlene singing Jingle Bells in her bedroom. "Oh, for goodness sakes!" Trish groaned and turned over.

The clock said 8:30. "I need to get a lock put on that upstairs' door. Aren't you a little old to act like an excited kid on Christmas morning?"

"It's not my fault you stayed out all night with David," Darlene chimed as she twirled around the room.

"I wasn't out all night. I was home by 10:30. It just started snowing. You guys were in bed already. *And* – I was at a Christmas party."

"With David," Darlene teased and plopped down on the bed next to Trish.

"Yes. Mrs. Shaw insisted I come to her party. However, I am glad that I went. I had fun."

"And you got to see David," Darlene chimed.

"Yes. Okay, it was great to spend Christmas Eve with David."

"Tell me all about it. Did he steal a kiss while you were there? He seems to have a habit of that. Who was at the party?"

"Later," Trish groaned as she sat up. "I'll tell you later. Grab that envelope on my dresser before I forget about it."

Darlene hopped up and went to the dresser. She picked up the envelope with the green bow on it. "What is this?"

"Your Christmas gift."

"Your gift to me is under the tree upstairs."

"This is another one. I didn't want you to open it in front of your dad."

Darlene opened the envelope. She pulled out a piece of paper and read it aloud. "A one-hundred-dollar gift certificate to Debra's Lingerie."

"Yes, use it," Trish said and ran her hand through her hair to separate the tangles.

"You know better than anybody that I don't have use for lingerie. Who do I have to wear it for?" Darlene pouted.

"Yourself. Get some things that you can wear under your clothes. Even though no one will see them, you'll know it's there. A woman has more confidence when she is wearing something sexy under her clothes. If anything, it'll give those granny panties of yours a break."

Darlene shook her head. "For you I'll try."

"Good."

"Now, get dressed so we can have breakfast and open gifts. The parade starts at 11:30, and I want a good spot."

"Ugh, Darlene, I really don't want to stand in three inches of snow and twenty-degree weather to watch that cheesy parade. I can't believe we liked it when we were kids," Trish said with a frown.

"It's not cheesy anymore. Not since ECTV started sponsoring it. They televise it."

"Oh goodie," Trish said as she dragged herself out of bed.

******

After Trish, Mr. Jacobs, and Darlene came back from the Christmas Parade, Trish fell asleep on the sofa upstairs. She woke up to Mr. Jacobs loudly snoring in the chair. She twisted her mouth in aggravation as she looked over at him. He had woken her up from a tantalizing dream about David.

In the dream, she was lying on her back on a bed. Her hair sprawled across a pillow. She watched him as he took his shirt and tie off. As he was unbuckling his pants, she heard snorting sounds, that's when she opened her eyes and her dream ended.

It made sense that she dreamed of David since she was thinking about him before she fell asleep. She even thought of him during the Christmas parade - which she had to admit wasn't that bad. She looked at her watch, it was two o'clock. David should be going house to house with his mother by now. Trish cursed herself for not taking Mrs. Shaw up on her invitation for dinner. She wanted to spend time with David; to learn more about him and his family. A woman shouldn't be separated from the man she loved at Christmas. It was practically sacrilegious. Her eyes widened. Love.

She slowly sat up. "Oh, my God," she said as she

swung her legs to the floor.

Mr. Jacobs snorted a few times and continued snoring.

"I'm…I'm..in love with David," she whispered.

Now that she knew this, Trish wondered what she was going to do about it. She couldn't tell him. What if he didn't feel the same? She'd be humiliated. At the same time, she couldn't keep it a secret forever. Darlene had picked up on Trish's feelings before she had. "Oh boy," she whispered and stood up.

Darlene wouldn't tell, yet other people could figure it out. It would be written all over her face eventually. She would have to be careful. If she spent more time with David, maybe his attraction to her would grow into love.

She thought of the dream she just had. With a little luck, it could become reality. She wanted him. Today. Tonight. Now. She walked to the desk next to the stairs and dug into her purse. She pulled out her cell phone and address book. Trish walked up the stairs and stopped on the landing. She turned and sat down at the top of the stairs.

She quickly opened the address book. Trish found the number she wanted and opened her phone. She dialed and prayed as it rang that he'd pick up.

****

Ted was watching TV with his father, Uncle Edgar, and Kelly, when his cell phone rang. He dug in his pants pocket and answered it. "This is Shaw."

"Teddy, it's Trish. Are you alone?" She sounded a bit desperate, and she was whispering.

"Uh, hold on a minute," Teddy said and took the phone away from his ear. He stood up and started walking away.

"Where are you going?" Uncle Edgar asked.

"I need some privacy," Ted said.

"Yeah, Teddy can't talk to his girlfriend with us listening," Kelly said with a smirk.

Ted smirked back at her and winked. He left the living room and went upstairs. Ted quickly went into his childhood bedroom and closed the door. "You still there?"

"Yes."

"What's up, Trish?" he asked as his muscles tensed. Was she in some sort of trouble?

"I know this is short notice, but I need your help with a project," she said shyly.

Ted cocked his eyebrow up. "Project? What is it?"

"First, how upset would your mother be if David missed the Christmas evening activities?"

A slow smile spread across Ted's face. His muscles relaxed. He sat down on the bed. "Oh, I'm sure she'll be fine with it if it was for a good reason," Ted said with playfulness in his voice.

"Good. Here's what I want to do."

Chapter 31

He lounged in an armchair next to the window. David was having a drink as he tried reading a book about international law. It wasn't working. He couldn't keep his mind off Trish. He wondered what she was doing. Did she get what she wanted for Christmas? He thought about the gift he had bought her. It was at his apartment. He didn't have the nerve to give it to her because he thought it might frighten her. David didn't want to scare her off because he expressed too much too soon. The gift was pretty expensive.

David looked up when the phone rang. His mother answered it.

David looked back down at his book. He heard his mother talking, but he wasn't really paying attention until she called his name.

"David, it's Ted. He needs your help," his mother said with a straight face.

David quickly closed his book and stood up. He strode to his mother and took the phone from her.

"Ted," David said.

"David, you're not going to believe this. I stepped

out for a couple hours, you know, to visit one of my lady friends. On my way back, a weird sound started coming from the engine. By the time I pulled over the car completely died on me!"

"You just got that SUV." David said with astonishment.

"I know! Luckily, I was only a few blocks away from your apartment. I walked there and let myself in with the spare key you gave me. I hope that was all right. I couldn't stay in the car I would have frozen to death."

"It's fine. I'm glad you were so close."

"You mind picking me up. Mom will have a fit if I miss Christmas dinner."

"Sure, I'm leaving now."

"Great, maybe we can share a quiet drink here before we head back. I already have a head start on you."

"Figures. See you in fifteen minutes," David said and hung up. He looked at his mother who had a wide-eyed look.

"He told you he broke down?" David asked.

She shook her head.

"Don't worry, Mom. I'm going to pick him up now, and we'll both be back in time for Christmas dinner. He kissed his mother on the forehead and left the living room."

****

Elizabeth watched her son leave the room as a slow smile spread across her face. Richard came up behind her and wrapped his arms around her waist. "Is everything all right? David went out of here in a hurry."

"Everything is wonderful. Our son thinks he's picking his brother up because his car broke down, but it didn't. David is going to get a surprise when he gets to his destination."

"Oh? And what is the surprise?"

"The best Christmas gift he's gotten in a long time."

****

David was thankful that the plow trunks had done a good job clearing the roads. He was able to get to his apartment building within normal time. He knew Ted was knocking the drinks back because he sounded pretty angry about his car. Not that David blamed him. He just bought it last year.

David walked to his front door and tried the knob before he used his key. It was locked, so David pulled out his key and opened it. He walked in and closed the door behind him. David started to take his coat off. "Ted?" he called.

David threw his coat on the couch as he smelled food coming from the kitchen. He walked towards the smell. "What are you cooking, Ted? You know Mom's got a four-course meal she's been dying to serve all month," he said as he walked into an empty kitchen.

David's eyebrow arched. He looked at the table. There were fresh rolls and a casserole dish with macaroni and cheese. Then, he looked over to the counter. There was a white crockpot. He walked over to it and lifted the lid. It was a roast with carrots and potatoes around it. David slowly put the lid back and turned around. "What is going on?" he mumbled.

Walking out of the kitchen he called Ted's name again. He thought he heard a female giggling - from his bedroom. David turned. His bedroom door was slightly open, and a faint light shined throw the crack.

He strode to the bedroom. "Ted, if you got a woman in here, I'm going to-" He stopped when he pushed the door open.

Trish was propped up against a couple of pillows on his bed. Her right leg was crossed over her left. She wore a red teddy and her fox fur coat draped off her shoulders. Her makeup was flawless, and her hair was curled at the ends – grazing her shoulders. One arm was propped up against a pillow beside her. The other arm lay across her stomach. Trish had a big smile on her face. She raised her hand and waved hello as her fingers moved back and forth. The covers were pulled down to the end of the bed. The room was lit with one white candle on the dresser across the room and another white candle that was on the table a few feet away.

His lips parted and his mouth watered. It was everything he could do to not drop to his knees.

****

He just stood there gaping at her. Had she gone too far? She did enter his home without his permission and set up camp. "I hope you don't mind that I made myself…comfortable while I waited for you," she said and started fingering the pillow next to her.

"No," he whispered. "I don't mind at all. How... how... did you-"

"Get in? Teddy let me in."

"He knew," David stuttered.

"Yes. I wanted to see you, but I wanted it to be a surprise. I called Teddy, and he was very helpful," she said nervously.

David took a few steps towards her. "Remind me to thank him."

Her face beamed. She was afraid he was angry. "Are you hungry? The pot roast needs to cook for another hour, but there are strawberries on the nightstand. That should be a good appetizer."

He was next to the bed, now. David didn't take his eyes off of her. His eyes darkened as he loosened his tie. "Actually, I'm more interested in dessert." David sat down next to her on the bed. He reached up and caressed the side of her face, and she leaned into his palm.

"This isn't a dream is it? You're in my apartment... in my bed... wearing next to nothing."

"No, it's not a dream. I'm here," she whispered.

He leaned in and kissed her softly. She heard him kick off his shoes. He deepened the kiss as he climbed on the bed with her. She rolled over on top off him. David placed his hands on her upper arms and pushed down the fur sleeves to her wrists. She pulled her hands out of them and threw the coat away from the bed.

Their lips parted. Trish untangled the loose knot in David's tie, and as their faces brushed against each other, she started to unbutton his white shirt. His chest rose and fell as she completed the task. David sat up as she smoothed her hands over his chest, pushing the shirt off his shoulders. David whipped the shirt the rest of the way off as Trish scooted down. She unbuckled his belt. He hissed when her hand brushed against the bulge in his pants as she unbuttoned and unzipped his dark gray pants. She started pulling at the waist of his pants. Helping her, he lifted his hips.

Trish pulled his pants down to his ankles and past his feet and then removed his black socks. Before she could take in his masculine form, David sat up and grabbed her by the shoulders. He pulled her back on top of him. His lips took hers. Sucking and licking, laying claim with his tongue. Trish allowed it for a moment, and then pulled her head away.

"What's wrong?" he asked dazed and confused.

She smiled. "Nothing. I- I…just want you to let me have my way for a couple of minutes. Lay down," she whispered and gently pressed his shoulders.

David did what she asked as she softly kissed his chest, letting the tip of her tongue graze his skin. He rubbed her shoulders as Trish kissed her way down to his erection. Taking his magnificent erection in her hand, she stroked it slowly. She softly kissed the tip as she stroked. Then, her tongue sensually licked around the tip. David groaned as his head fell back on the pillows.

The sound of his pleasure warmed her heart and thighs. She wanted nothing more than to please him – to make him feel like he was floating on a cloud. She sat up and shimmed her bountiful breasts outside of the teddy. When she laid back down, she took his organ into her mouth. Her breasts grazed his legs. He groaned again. Her head moved up and down as her tongue licked his shaft. David's breathing was deep and ragged.   She stopped sucking. Trish gently took him in her hand again and guided the tip of him across her nipple. A shot of pleasure rushed through her as her nipple grew taunt. Trish sucked in a breath. She did the same movement on the other nipple.

"Mmmm. I think you've had your way long enough," he said in a ragged breath.

She placed his erection between her breasts and stroked his shaft. "Why? Aren't you enjoying yourself?" she asked with a wide-eyed innocence.

David smiled. "Yes, but I don't want it to end this way."

"This way is nice, I promise," she said as she continued to stroke.

He sat up and grabbed her shoulders. He smirked. "Another time. For right now, I want to do something better than nice." David took a hold of her waist and pulled her up on top of him. He rolled her over on her back with ease.

He quickly pulled the red teddy off of her and stood on his knees. David's eyes traveled up her body. "You're so beautiful," he whispered.

Trish shyly turned her head. "Oh, David."

He lay down on top of her. "Look at me, sweetheart."

She turned her head.

"You are the most beautiful thing that has come into my life." He gave her a quick kiss and moved away.

Before she could wonder why he was moving away from her, the question was quickly answered when he parted her legs. Without hesitation, David dove his face into her womanhood. She gasped. He kissed and licked her button. He inserted his middle finger inside her core as he continued his kiss on her nub.

Trish placed one hand on her chest as her breath caught. David continued his seduction in her center. It felt like it went on forever. The teasing was torture. She couldn't stand it anymore.

"David, please. Make love to me, now, please," she groaned.

He slowly raised his head and pulled his finger out of her wetness. David slowly crawled on top of her. "Oh, sweetheart, how can I refuse? Especially, since I've wanted you to say that to me for weeks." He positioned himself between her legs.

David placed one hand on the side of her face as his other hand reached between them. He guided his erection down her soft wetness. She let out a whimper. David found the entry point. Trish inhaled with anticipation. In one depth move, he entered her. She released the breath she was holding. David pushed in a little deeper, and Trish placed her hands on his back. Her hips wiggled with demand. He responded by slowly moving in and out of her.

Her eyes fluttered closed as the sensations below eased the repression she held onto for weeks. Then, David stopped. Her eyes flew opened. He was looking at her. His eyes were dark, and his breath was unsteady. Then, he started pumping again - never taking his eyes away from hers. Every time she started to close her eyes, David would stop.

She met his movements as he went in and out of her. After a few minutes, he gathered Trish into his arms and pulled her off the bed without breaking their connection.

David rested her in his lap. She maneuvered her calves to rest under the back of her thighs. David started bouncing on his knees. He was so deep inside her that she thought was going to explode into a million pieces. Trish tightened her grip around him. Her breath quickening with each pump. Their bodies were mashed together like a Greek statue of two lovers.

Trish's hand slid to the back of his neck – into his thick dark hair. She let out a long moan. "Oh, yes," she whispered in his ear.

Sweat glistened on their bodies. She was moaning more now. Trish felt her body warm as the pleasure of David inside her started traveling up her waist to her chest.

David tightened his arm around her waist. His other hand grabbed her bottom and gave it a little squeeze. She moaned louder.

"That's right, take it….take it all," David said huskily.

She felt her body about to release. The words I love you popped in her head. She bit his shoulder to keep from saying it aloud. David's body trembled. Her cries of pleasure were muffled against his shoulder. His pelvis shoved into her as he moaned her name.

They quietly held each other as their breathing slowed. David lifted her up and laid her down on the bed. He rested on top of her- nuzzling his head between her breasts. Their breathing was slow and deep.

After a few minutes, David lightly kissed the side of her breast. "You're incredible," he said."

Trish smiled. "Me? What about you? I was trying to keep up with you," she breathed.

David let out a chuckle and raised his head. "Are you all right? Do you need anything?"

Trish smiled at him. She never known a man quite like David. He was so considerate and sweet. She thought of her girlfriends' husbands in L.A., they all complained about how their husbands would just roll over after sex and fell asleep. No cuddling and no talking. Even her own husband did that. Not David, not only was he holding her, he asked if she needed anything.

"Oh...I," she stuttered.

He sat up a little more. "What is it? What do you need?"

"I'm thirsty. I was going to reach over for a drink. I have sparkling wine on ice on the nightstand."

David started to roll over to the other side of the bed.

"David, I could have-"

"I want to," he said with a smile. He stood up and looked at the nightstand.

Trish felt a chill. She sat up and pulled the blankets up from the end of the bed, covering herself as David opened the sparkling wine. He poured it into a glass and took a sip. "This is pretty good. Did you get it at that gourmet store downtown?" he asked and gave her the glass.

"Yes. They were having a tasting that day. I bought a couple of bottles of it," she said and took a drink of it.

David walked to the dresser and pulled out a pair of black pajama bottoms. He put them on and walked back to the nightstand. Trish had finished her drink and moved closer to the nightstand.

"Another?"

Trish smiled. "Yes, please. I'm really thirsty."

He smiled and took the glass from her. He filled it up again and gave it to her.

"Thank you. Aren't you going to have some?"

David grabbed a strawberry out of the bowl next to the wine. "I had some scotch earlier. Don't want to mix," he said and bit into the strawberry. He sat down on the edge of the bed and offered Trish a bite of the strawberry. She took a little bite and giggled.

He smiled. "So, what is that box next to the strawberries?"

"That's your Christmas gift. I had the urge to get you one, but wasn't sure if I was going to give it to you."

"You already gave me a gift. You," he said and gave her a smooch on the cheek.

"Well, I guess you're getting two. Open it."

David turned and picked up the box. He removed the lid and pulled back the tissue paper. It was a gold tie clip. "Wow, thanks."

"That's gold."

"Yes, it will go well with the gold cufflinks Ted gave me for Christmas; or should I say you bought me for Christmas."

"I didn't-"

"Don't try to cover for him. For six years he has bought me a tie for Christmas. I also know he hates to shop. He gets a sexy young assistant and wham everyone gets good gifts for Christmas. It wasn't that hard to figure it out," he said with a smirk.

"Okay, you caught me. Did your mom like the crystal punch bowl?"

"She loved it, and Dad loved the monogrammed

scarf."

"Good," she said with a smile.

He smiled back. "I'm glad you brought food. I didn't have anything in the refrigerator."

"You're telling me. I opened your fridge and I saw a carton of milk that expired a month ago and a few cobwebs."

He laughed. "I'll comp to the milk, but there are no cobwebs."

"It's bad. I actually shrieked. I heard an echo," she said and laughed.

He laughed, too. "I'm glad you brought something. I think I worked up an appetite." David put his hand on her knee.

"I think I did, too. I'll go fix us a plate."

"No, you stay there looking beautiful. I'll get us food. After all, you cooked." David gave her a long kiss and stood up.

Chapter 32

When David returned with a tray, Trish had put her teddy back on. She also put on his white dress shirt over it. She sat up in the bed. Her hair was lightly tousled and looked as soft as feathers.

"Well, what do we have here?" she asked cheerfully.

David sat the tray over her lap and carefully sat down on the edge of the bed- looking at her. "It appears to be Darlene's macaroni and cheese, rolls, and roast with potatoes and carrots; thanks to a lovely woman."

Trish smiled. "And other things, two glasses of water and a gift box."

"I got you something too, but I was too much of a coward to give it to you."

Trish tilted her head to the side. "You're a lot of things, David Shaw, but a coward is not one of them." She grabbed the box as David grabbed a fork.

She opened the gift box, inside was a black jewelry box. Trish slid it out and opened it. A tennis bracelet with rubies and diamonds sparkled at her. "Oh, David."

"You like it?" he asked.

"I love it, but it looks like it cost a lot."

He smirked. "Don't worry. Business has picked up, and I think it is only going to get better. Ever since you showed up, I've had lady luck on my side."

"Aw." She swooned and put the bracelet on. "Thank you so much."

They spent the next thirty minutes feeding each other and talking about what they did earlier that day. They curled up in bed – holding each other.

"Where do we go from here?" Trish asked.

David smiled. "We'll do what other couples do. Go out to lunch, dinner; make wild passionate love until we can't see straight."

Trish giggled. "That sounds good to me."

"Good. But, there is something I need to know."

"What's that?"

"What did you tell Santa on Christmas Eve?"

"David, what does that matter now?"

"You were depressed that night when I called. Even though you're fine now. It bothers me that you were hurting, and I didn't know what it was. I didn't know how to fix it."

She raised her head from his shoulder and looked down at him. "I- I went to the cemetery that morning. I put flowers on my parents' and grandparents' graves."

David furrowed his brow. "You went by yourself?"

"Yeah."

"Why didn't Darlene go with you? You could have called me. I would have gone with you."

"I had to do it alone. I kept putting it off for so long. I'm glad I went, but it made me think about things. I realized that I was alone. Other than a cousin in New Jersey I haven't seen or heard from since I was eighteen,

I'm the last living Truman. Between that and my divorce being final, I got a little down. Santa just reminded me how blessed I truly am."

David hugged her tight against him. "You're not alone. You have me now. And if something is wrong or you feel….depressed, I want to know about it, okay?"

Trish gave him a small smile. "Okay." She rested her head back on his shoulder, and he caressed her back as they fell asleep.

****

Trish woke up at midnight. She slowly slipped out of David's light hold and got out of bed. She picked up the strawberries, wine, and the glasses and left the room. She went into the kitchen and washed dishes and cleaned up.

She was walking back into the living room when her cell phone rang. Trish quickly went to her purse. She didn't want the noise to wake David up. She opened her phone. "Hello?" she whispered.

"I have been calling and calling. Where are you?" Darlene asked.

"I'm at David's. You knew where I was going. You made the macaroni and cheese."

"Yes, but you didn't say anything about staying out all night."

Trish plopped down on the couch. "Sorry, Mom."

"Well, Daddy did say that I was worried for nothing. He went to bed two hours ago. I was just surprised. You were so adamant about having time and space to think. I didn't think you'd- you know."

"No, I don't know," Trish teased.

Darlene exhaled. "You know. Go all the way."

Trish stifled a laugh at the out of date phrase. "I have to admit, I hoped it would happen. I would have felt pretty humiliated if David rejected me with what I had on when he came home."

"Oh my! I want details," Darlene said.

The bedroom door opened, and David emerged. He walked to the sofa and sat down next to her. Trish mouthed, *it's Darlene*. He smiled and wrapped his arms around her waist."

"Trish?"

"Yeah, I can't talk about that now."

"Why?"

"David is up and-"

"Oh, okay, tell him I said hi."

Trish chuckled as David started nibbling at her free ear. "Darlene says hi."

"Hi, Darlene," he said and continued to suckle on Trish's earlobe.

"He said-"

"I heard him. Ask him if you two are girlfriend-boyfriend now. You better be after tonight."

Trish smiled. "Darlene wants to know if we are girlfriend and boyfriend, now."

"Yes," he said and started kissing her neck.

Trish giggled. "He said yes," she whispered.

"Good. I'm going back to bed. You two have a good night. I assume you'll be home tomorrow."

"Yes, I'll be home tomorrow," Trish said with a smile because David found that sensitive spot on her neck.

"Okay, bye," Darlene said and hung up.

Trish closed her phone. "You are bad. Doing that while I'm on the phone."

David looked up. "I couldn't help myself. Let's go back to bed."

"You know, I'm not tired."

"Who said anything about sleeping?" he asked with a wicked smile.

****

The next morning, David and Trish lay on the sofa watching TV when the phone rang.

"Ugh. Ignore it. It'll stop," David said.

"What if it's your family? Maybe they are checking on you," she reasoned and sat up.

David sat up. He reached for the phone and answered it. "Hello."

"Hey, David. I'm dying to know - how did things go last night?"

"Ted, I can't talk-"

"It's okay. Talk to him. I'm going to take a shower," Trish said and stood up.

"David?"

David watched Trish go into the bathroom. "Yeah, I'm here,"

"Oh, is Trish still there?"

"Yeah, but it's okay. She went to take a shower."

"Well, I guess that's the answer to my question. I hope you're not mad at me for lying to you."

"Don't worry about it. The best Christmas gift you ever arranged for me," David said with a smile.

"Great, so is she going to spend the day with you?"

"If I've got anything to say about it, yes," David said. "Why?"

"Mom wants to have brunch with all of us and Trish, if possible."

"Oh, is Mom mad about last night?"

Ted laughed. "Mad? No way. She knew all about it. I told her that Trish had a surprise dinner arranged for you and Mom was ecstatic."

"Sounds like Mom likes her."

"Yeah, so brunch? Can you two make it or not?"

"I'll ask Trish."

"Brunch is scheduled for one. If you can't make it, please call Mom."

"I will."

"I got to go. Bye."

"Bye," David said and hung up.

David heard the water running in the shower. He started thinking about shower beads hitting Trish's bare skin, and Trish holding a bar of soap as she ran it over her shoulders. David smiled and went to the bathroom.

He quietly opened the door and closed it. David dropped his pajama bottoms as he looked at the shower curtain. He strode to the tub and pulled the curtain back. "Hey, good lookin'."

She gasped. "David! You nearly scared the life out of me. I didn't even hear you come in."

He stepped in behind her. "Sorry, I decided I needed to shower, too," he said with a smile. Her hair was in a loose bun.

"I see," she said with a smile. She was holding a bar of soap. "If you promise not to get my hair wet I'll help you… shower."

"Deal. I would love your help."

She flashed her perfectly white teeth as she lathered the soap in her hand. "Let me get behind you."

They traded places. The water beat on his chest. David leaned his head under the sprinkles as Trish rubbed soap on his back. Her soft hands massaged his shoulders. He took his head out of the water and ran his hands through his dark hair, shaking away the loose water.

"Oh. Easy, Mr. Splash Man," she teased and smoothed soap down his backside.

David turned around to face her as the water beat on his back. The steam from the water surrounded them. Trish rubbed one soapy hand over the top of his chest. David reached for the bar of soap in her other hand. She let him have it.

He ran the bar down her back as she rubbed his chest. They came together in a kiss. His erection grew. It rubbed against her stomach.

He groaned against her lips. "Turn around, sweetheart," he said in deep voice.

She slowly turned around.

David lathered the soap between his hands and placed it on the soap holder. He reached around her and cupped her breasts. She leaned against him. Soap suds lathered on her bosom as he squeezed and rubbed. Her breath caught when he flicked her nipples with his thumbs.

Her nipples toughened with arousal. He continued to

flick them as Trish's breathing quickened. Her head pressed against his wet chest.

"Oh, you've done it now. You got my hair wet," she said raggedly.

A sly smile crossed his lips. "It's not wet. It's damp," he said huskily.

She chuckled. "Do you ever stop being a lawyer?"

"I'm afraid it's in my blood. Now, bend over Ms. Truman."

Trish leaned down.

"Move up a little and brace your hands against the wall, please."

As she did it she asked, "Am I being frisked?"

He couldn't help laughing. "Yes, spread your legs, please."

She did as she looked over her shoulder.

David stepped to her. He took himself in hand and moved his erection around her sex. He found what he wanted and pushed in. She let out a moan. She was tight and wet. He slowly moved in and out of her. He reached around and cupped her breasts as Trish started to meet his movements.

"You're so… passionate, and you feel so good," he groaned.

After a few minutes of him pumping inside, her walls tightened. She lifted her head and started making light moaning sounds, almost like a purring. He moved one hand from her breast and slid it down the front of her stomach. He kept working south until he reached her soft black hair. He worked his middle finger between her folds to rub her clitoris. He thrust deeper into her and he rubbed.

"David!" she cried and grabbed his hand below. "It's too much." She let out a moan.

He kept tickling her button and quickened his deep thrusting. "Oooh, it doesn't feel good?"

"Uh, it does, but-" she stopped as her legs trembled, and loud moaning replaced her protest. Her moaning shuddered through him, and he had no choice but to allow the release. David pushed and stilled in her as she cried out his name – twice. Her knees buckled. David felt her slipping and caught her by the waist with one arm. He slowly guided them both down in the tub. He loosened his grip on her after they were safely settled. The steam from the shower kept them warm as they caught their breath.

Trish leaned her back against his chest.

"We better pull ourselves together and get dressed," David breathed.

"Hmm?"

"We're having brunch with my family at one, sweetheart."

Chapter 33

A few days later, David and Mrs. Hinkle were going over a list of tasks. "On a personal note, I would like for you to send a bouquet of flowers to Trish- at her home."

Mrs. Hinkle smiled. "What do you want the card to say?"

"Say, I am looking forward to New Year's Eve."

Mrs. Hinkle made a note on her pad. "Anything else?"

"No."

"What are you two going to do for the New Year?"

"I'm taking her to the ECTV ball."

"Oh, you're going to make use of the tickets Mr. Manley gave you. He was so grateful that you won the custody suit for his son that he dropped the tickets off personally. Handsome man."

"Mrs. Hinkle," David teased.

She chuckled. "I still got my sight young David. But, I'm afraid I'm a tad too old for Mr. Manley. A man who owns his own TV station and is a millionaire usually dates young women- way younger."

David shrugged. "Anything can happen."

She smiled. "I understand why *you* feel that way."

"Hello?" a woman's voice said from the reception.

David's muscles tighten because he recognized the voice.

Heather Young appeared in the doorway wearing a brown leather skirt, a white turtleneck, and a long white fur coat.

Mrs. Hinkle stood up. "Good morning, may I help you?"

"Good morning, hon," she said sweetly. "I was hoping to get a minute or two with David."

Mrs. Hinkle looked at David whose face had turned to stone. "It's okay, Mrs. Hinkle. Close the door on your way out."

"Yes, sir," Mrs. Hinkle said and started to walk out of the room.

"Thanks, hon. And that color is adorable on you."

Mrs. Hinkle stopped. "Thank you, miss?"

"Young. Heather Young."

"Thank you, Ms. Young," Mrs. Hinkle said politely. She closed the door when she left the room.

David leaned back in his chair. "I thought you went back to New York."

Heather walked over to the desk. "I did. I came back." She sat down in one of the chairs and crossed her legs.

"Why?"

"You know why, sugar. I don't give up that easily. We had something special before, and we can again, but this time it will be better."

David straightened in his chair. "I made it clear to you that I've moved on. There's nothing to fight for."

"Oh? Where's Patricia? Obviously, it didn't work out."

"Her position was temporary. My regular secretary was on medical leave."

"So, you don't see her anymore?" Heather fished.

David started to become irritated. "Whether I do or I don't is none of your concern and has no barring in my decision regarding going back to you."

A slow smile spread across her lips as she shook her head up and down. "You're dating her. Is her divorce final, yet?"

"Heather, that is none of your business."

"Oh, I forgot. You protect your clients' privacy no matter how innocent the information is. No big deal. I can find out myself some other way, if I want. It can't be that hard to find out gossip in a city this small."

"Heather, don't you go near her," he said practically through gritted teeth.

"Relax. I won't have, too. She's smart enough to see the light on her own, soon enough."

"What do you mean?"

Heather rolled her eyes. "Oh come on, David. Surely, you don't think you have a future with her. Yes, she's very pretty and sexy, even smart, but that doesn't change the fact that she's black. You two grew up in totally different cultures. And the biggest obstacle will be your career. Some clients look down their noses at interracial couples. How could you consider being seen with her on your arm at public functions?" she asked with snobbishness.

A slight shade of red rose in his jaws. "Get out of my office and take your bigoted attitude with you."

"I resent that! I'm not a bigot. I'm a realist. I'm not unreasonable, David. I don't mind you sleeping with her every once in a while - just be discrete. If you and Patricia are comfortable, I would like to join you. Like I said, she is extremely desirable."

David wanted to throw Heather and the chair she was sitting in through the window. "If you were a man, I'd break your neck for that." He wasn't sharing Trish with anyone - man or woman - especially Heather. This woman was insane.

"You're blowing this completely out of proportion. When did you become so sensitive?"

Mrs. Hinkle burst into the office. "Mrs. Young, it's time for you to leave."

David's eyebrow arched up. He glanced down at the phone. The intercom was on.

Heather stood up. "Who are you to order me anywhere?'

"A woman. You see, he's a gentleman. He wouldn't dare manhandle a woman – even one as vile as you. However, I don't have that problem."

Heather laughed. "An old frail thing like you? Please."

Mrs. Hinkle marched to Heather and slapped her across the face.

David's eyes widened as Heather's head was rocked to the side.

"Now tell me, how old and frail was that?" Mrs. Hinkle asked with controlled anger.

David whirled around the desk at lightning speed.

"Why you old bat!" Heather was about to strike Mrs. Hinkle back when David grabbed her arm.

"Get out of here, now," he said in a deep voice.

Heather was incredulous. She glared at David. "You're going to let her get away with doing this to me? To me! Fire her, David!" she demanded in a high shrill.

"Fire her? I'm thinking about giving her a raise," he said and let go of her arm. "Leave. And if you come near me or anyone associated with me ever again, I'll file a restraining order. That won't look good to your high society friends in New York. And you better believe I'll make sure they'll hear about it."

"Damn you! You'll regret the day you ever laid eyes on me, David Shaw," she said with venom and started heading to the door.

"I've regretted laying eyes on you for the past two years!" he yelled in her direction.

She twirled around staring daggers at him. After a moment, she left without another word. When the front door slammed, Mrs. Hinkle said, "She is unbelievable."

"Yes, I know that now," David said and ran his hand through his hair.

Chapter 34

New Year's was a time of resolutions, hope, and a fresh start. That was David's attitude walking into the New Year's Eve ECTV Ball with Trish on his arm.

David's parents reserved a table. Trish, Darlene, Phillip, and the Shaws were talking and drinking.

"Isn't this wonderful?" Mrs. Shaw said. "I just wish Teddy would have come along."

"Now, dear, you know Teddy would rather be dead than attend a ball," Dr. Shaw said and patted her hand.

"Oh, I know, but family should be together on the holidays. What if he's all alone?" Mrs. Shaw asked sadly.

"I doubt that he's alone, Mrs. Shaw. Your son is very....sociable," Darlene said and gulped her drink like she was swallowing a bitter pill.

"Uh, I'm sure Ted is fine. He mentioned he was going by The Clover Club. That's more his speed," David chimed in.

Benjamin Manley Sr. approached the table. "Happy New Year," he greeted with a smile.

"Happy New Year," they all replied back.

"Thank you for coming, Dr. Shaw, Mrs. Shaw. And thank you for paying for a table. Did you know that fifty percent of the proceeds will be donated to the hospital?"

"No we didn't, but that's good to know," Dr. Shaw said. "ECTVs contribution is very much appreciated."

"Good. David, how have you been?"

"I've been great and thanks for the tickets. Have you met our guests?"

"Well, I remember Ms. Truman. How are you?"

"I'm fine, thank you," Trish said happily.

"And who are these good-looking people with you?" Mr. Manley asked and looked at Phillip and Darlene.

"I'm Phillip Dunn and this is Darlene Jacobs," he said and stood to shake Mr. Manley's hand.

"Nice to meet you both. Are you enjoying the party?"

"Very much so," Phillip said and sat back down.

"Oh, yes. It's so wonderful and glamorous," Darlene beamed.

Mr. Manley smiled at her. "I'm glad you're having fun. Ms. Truman would you like to dance?"

"Oh ye-" she stopped and looked at David.

"It's okay," he said with a smile. He looked up at Mr. Manley. "Just bring her back."

"I will," he said with a smile and offered Trish his hand.

She took it, and they walked quietly to the dance floor. He held her hand and put one around her waist. Trish placed her free hand on his shoulder.

"I take it from the exchange that you and David had that you two are seeing each other."

She smiled and shyly glanced down. "Yes."

"You two look happy."

"We are."

"Good. I knew he was smart. He scooped you right up. I wish I was quicker on the draw," he teased.

She chuckled. "Oh, Mr. Manley. I'm sure you have women beating down your door."

"Yes. Millionaires usually call them golddiggers."

Trish smiled at his honesty. "Surely, not all."

"Maybe not. It takes time to weed through the bushes to find the diamond in the rough."

"I was happy to hear that your son won his custody case."

"The whole family was ecstatic. The little one got to spend Christmas with us. My whole family is grateful to David."

"That's wonderful. Have you considered using David's services in the future?"

"I have. Actually, my lawyer for the station is about to retire."

"Sounds like you have him on retainer."

"I do. I have considered a number of candidates who could possibly replace him."

"I see. And you're considering David as one of them?"

"Yes, but I'd like to know more about his experience as a lawyer. He only opened a practiced two years ago."

"He practiced law in New York for a couple of years. I can't remember how many. Perhaps you should set up an appointment with him. Ask him questions, like a job interview - if you don't mind me saying."

Mr. Manley smiled. "A woman who stands by her man."

Trish smiled shyly again. "I didn't mean to be pushy. I…please don't let my lack of-"

"You weren't pushy. Just a woman in love."

She didn't bother to deny it. It was written all over her face. The whole room probably knew she was totally and hopelessly in love.

"That's very considerate of you."

****

It was two minutes before midnight. Trish stopped dancing with David to run and get them two glasses of champagne. Waiters were passing out party hats and noisemakers. He planned to tell Trish that he loved her tonight. He thought New Years was the perfect time. A whole new year- a whole new him. David loved her, and he didn't care what anyone thought about it.

Not that he totally believed Heather was right about his career being affected if he was in an interracial relationship. However, he knew bigotry still existed. As far as he was concerned, those people could burn in hell. It was almost 1995, for crying out loud.

He snapped out of his thoughts when he heard the crowd counting down. He looked around for Trish. She was wearing a red dress that showed off her lovely shoulders.

"Five, four, three, two, one -Happy New Year!" the partygoers yelled.

Auld Lang Syne started to play, and streamers and balloons fell from the ceiling. A hand was on his shoulder. Thinking it was Trish, David turned around with a smile.

It was Heather. Before he could react, Heather grabbed the back of his neck and pulled him in for a kiss. Heather's lips pressed against his. The tip of her tongue poked at the opening of his mouth; urging him to participate. He grabbed her arms and pushed her away. "What the hell are you doing?" he asked.

"Just getting in one last kiss, sugar," she yelled over the crowd.

As he wiped away her red lipstick with his hand, David spotted Trish a foot away. She stared at them with her mouth open. She had on a black party hat. When she realized David saw her, Trish dropped the champagne glasses. She turned and disappeared into the crowd.

"Uh oh," Heather said and started laughing.

David brushed past Heather into the crowd.

****

Trish rushed back to the table and grabbed her handbag and wrap. She went through a side door that led outside. She ran into the garden area of the ballroom. Pain shot through the balls of her feet, so she stopped to remove her heels. She carried them in her hand as she ran a half circle to the front the building. She stopped running and begun to walk when she saw a row of limos and town cars along the sidewalk of the building.

She began to shiver uncontrollably because of the cold as the feet of her stockings were damp from running in the snow. Tears of hurt and anger ran down her face.

She was getting close to the building entrance.

The doorman must have seen her from the lobby, because he came running out the glass and brass lined doors and jogged to her on the sidewalk. "Miss. Miss. Are you all right? What happened to you?"

She sucked in a breath and spoke in a broken sob, "No, I'm not all right. I'm a fool. I just want to get out of here."

"There are cabs on standby - our way of preventing drunk driving during an event. I'll be happy to walk you to one."

Trish started putting her shoes back on. "No. Just tell me where they are. I can get there on my own."

"Please. Let me at least run and get one for you. I'll have him pull up to the entrance. That way you don't have to walk anymore."

Trish nodded her head in agreement.

******

"Mom, are you sure you didn't see her leave?" David asked her frantically.

"I'm positive," she said.

"Maybe you should check the ladies room again?" his father suggested to his mother.

"I checked twice."

"She could have lifted her feet up in the stall," his father said.

"Or went to another bathroom in the building," David said as he frantically looked around the crowded ballroom.

Darlene and Phillip approached them. "Thank, God," Darlene said like she was out of breath. "I thought we'd never get to you in this crowd."

"Yeah, is it me or did the people multiply instantly after midnight?" Phillip said.

"Have you guys seen, Trish?" David asked.

"That's why we were trying to get to you," Darlene said struggling to catch her breath. "We saw the whole thing from the balcony," she said as she tilted her head upwards and to the left. "Trish ran outside through the back door."

David was about to go to the back door when Phillip grabbed his arm. "Wait, she's not out there anymore."

David's eyes were wild. "Then where did she go?"

Phillip let go of David's arm. "We went outside. By the time we got to the front door, a cab drove by with her in the back. We called after the cab, but it just kept going."

"She must be going home," David said.

"You better go then, son. This shouldn't wait until the morning," his father said.

David nodded to his father and left. He rushed through the crowd as fast as he could. Once he got his coat from the clerk, he burst outside.

"You have your ticket, sir," the doorman asked.

"I didn't use valet, but did you see a woman in a long red dress get into a cab?"

"Yes, sir. I put her in the cab myself."

"Did she say where she was going?

"She mumbled something about going home."

"Thanks," David said and ran across the parking lot. He could see his breath in the cold. After another minute of jogging, he finally reached his car. When he started digging in his pocket for his keys a sharp pain hit him in the back of the head. He grabbed the spot where the pain came from.

His vision became blurred. Then, a cloth was slammed over his nose and mouth. Chloroform! He tried to fight the effects, but he blacked out within moments.

Chapter 35

Trish lay in her bed with tears streaming down her face. When she got home, Trish tore her dress off and crawled under the covers. She didn't even bother to wash the tear-stained makeup off her face. She had almost cried herself to sleep until she heard Darlene shouting her name. Trish remained silent hoping that Darlene would go away. She should have gone to a hotel for the night.

"Trish," Darlene said and she rushed into the bedroom. "Oh, Trish," she moaned as she climbed in the bed next to her. "Look at me."

Trish didn't move.

"Trish, things didn't happen the way you think. Phillip and I saw the whole thing from the balcony. Didn't David explain that to you?"

Trish remained silent.

"You wouldn't let him?"

"No one came and what is there to explain?"

"I don't understand. When we told David you left the ball he was coming after you. Are you saying he didn't show up?"

"Yes," Trish spat out.

"Well, Daddy is in bed and if you came straight down here you wouldn't have heard him knock. Then again, he could have come to your back entrance."

"Darlene, no one has come by the house since I've been here. And what is there to explain. I know what it was all about now."

"What are you talking about?"

Trish finally sat up and turned to Darlene to look at her. Darlene's eyebrows rose at the sight of Trish's runny mascara and smeared lipstick. "It was a game to him, Darlene. In L.A., I heard dozens of stories of divorce attorneys seducing their female clients. It's a sport for them. Take all you can get from the sleaze bag husband, get a hefty fee, and some pussy on the side."

Darlene's mouth dropped open. "I don't believe that. This is not L.A."

"No, but David was a New York attorney. You don't think they do the same thing up there?"

"Trish, if you would have seen him after you ran off tonight-"

"He had to make it look good, Darlene. He doesn't want to look like a sleaze bag in front of his parents and potential clients."

"Something must have happened to him. Where is he? He should have been here by now."

"Yeah, something happened all right. He got what he wanted and now he's going to move on with the woman he loves."

"Trish-"

"Darlene, I don't want to talk about this anymore and I mean it!" Trish shouted. "Now, will you please leave me the hell alone?"

"All right. All right," Darlene said and scrambled off the bed. She left the bedroom.

****

Darlene entered the living room, and Phillip stood up when she came in. "Well? Is everything okay?"

Darlene shook her head. "Something is terribly wrong. Trish is extremely upset, and she said David never arrived."

"Maybe he decided to come by in the morning. Or he tried to knock and nobody answered. Your father is upstairs, and if Trish went straight to her flat, no one would have heard him knocking."

Darlene put her hands on her hips and shook her head. "You know as well as I do that David is crazy about her, so he wouldn't have gone home to wait for in the morning. And as far as no one hearing David knocking, he would have woken the whole neighborhood if he had to. You saw how frantic he was."

"Yes, he was distraught," Phillip said and put his hands in his coat pocket.

Darlene rushed to the phone.

"Who are you calling at this hour?" Phillip asked.

"The police. I'm going to report David missing. I've got a bad feeling. I could be wrong, but it's better to be safe than sorry."

****

The next morning Trish showered, got dressed, and packed. She decided to go to the Bahamas. After all, she had a vacation home there now. Her plan was to get some sun, confirm information with the caretakers, and figure out what she was going to do for the rest of her life. She got the keys along with the paperwork for her settlement a few days ago. She wrote a check to David for the rest of his fee that day, but he wouldn't take it. Actually, he tore it up.

As she wrote another check for the rest of his fee, a voice that sounded like her father, popped in her head. *If that boy didn't care about you, he would have taken your money.*

"It was an act to sucker me in," she mumbled as she tore the check from the book. She stuck it in an envelope addressed to David's office to the attention of Mrs. Hinkle. After all, it's not like he didn't earn it.

She picked up her cell phone. Trish called the airport to confirm her eight o'clock flight and connecting flights. After she hung up, she grabbed her purse, carry-on, and suitcase and headed up the stairs.

Trish clumsily entered the living room as Mr. Jacobs was setting a tray on the table. He had six coffee mugs and a pot of coffee on the tray. He looked up at Trish.

"Mr. Jacobs, I'm leaving town for a while. I have an eight o'clock flight. I have some out of town affairs to attend to."

He had a grim look on his face. "It was my call not to wake you. I thought you needed rest before you had to deal with this. Put those bags down, honey. You're not going anywhere."

Panic gripped her body. "Oh God, is it Darlene. Did

something happen to Darlene?"

He shook his head from side to side. "No, she's fine. Sit down, honey. I'll tell you what's going on. I'll pour you some coffee."

"You're scaring me. Tell me what has happened."

At that moment, Darlene and Phillip came through the front door. They stopped when they saw Trish standing there looking petrified.

"Oh, honey, don't worry. We'll find him," she said.

"What the hell are you talking about? What is going on? And why are you two wearing the same clothes that you had on last night?" Trish asked, becoming frantic.

"You haven't told her?" Phillip asked.

"I was about to," Mr. Jacobs said and sat down on the sofa.

"Trish, no one has seen David since the party. He hasn't called anyone, and no one can find him," Phillip said.

"We've called the police several times. They said there were no accidents that fit David or his car's description, and we have to wait twenty-four hours to file a missing persons report. We've been out all night looking for him ourselves since they won't help. That's why we're in the same clothes as last night. We came home to take a break, and I was going to change," Darlene explained.

"Yeah, I've been doing the driving. I haven't been home," Phillip said. "We even stopped by the hospital to see if he was admitted to the emergency room."

Trish blew out a breath of frustration. "That's because he is with Heather- Heather Young. They're probably held up in a hotel room in town. Did you try

The Wingate Hotel?"

"Um, no," Darlene said as she looked at Trish like a deer in headlights.

"He isn't with her," Phillip said with disgust and walked over to the table to fix a cup of coffee. "David isn't going to trade a real lady for a painted hussy like her. Even I give him more credit than that."

"Me, too," Darlene said. "I truly believe something happened to him, Trish. David was on his way to the house last night to explain to you what happened on the dance floor."

"Darlene, you know I love you, and I don't mean any harm when I say this, but you haven't seen, heard, and had the experiences that I have had. There are a lot of guys out there who are good at pulling the knight in shining armor act. Even the most experienced women can be fooled by the best smooth talkers."

"What about me and Phillip?" Mr. Jacobs asked. "I've lived a long time, and I am an experienced financial advisor. I wouldn't have gotten as far as I have if I couldn't read people. I had a talk with David on the night that you and Darlene went to that club. Believe me, he has no desire to be with that woman. He wants you. Phillip travels all over the world, and he's a success in his own right. Once again, he wouldn't be successful if he couldn't read people."

"In the financial world," Trish countered. "And Mr. Jacobs don't you think you're a little bias considering that you like David?"

"I'm not bias. I'm not crazy about either one of the Shaw brothers. Will you listen to what I saw last night?" Phillip asked.

Before Trish could answer, Phillip spoke. "Darlene and I were in the balcony with a couple of other guests. We could see the entire dance floor," he said and sat down with a cup of coffee in his hand. "We saw you and David dancing, you left a couple of minutes before midnight. While you were gone, he waited for you-alone- or so I thought- at first. I noticed the blonde chit in a black dress. She stood out to me because she didn't have a drink or a noisemaker in her hand. She just stood there like she was waiting for something or someone. She was a few feet from David- it didn't appear she noticed him. Matter of fact, it looked like he was looking for you to come back. He didn't notice her. The clock struck twelve, I gave Darlene a hug, and we were blowing our noisemakers as we were looking down on the crowd. I noticed the blonde chit looking about - she stopped when she spotted you making your way through the crowd carrying two champagne glasses." Phillip took a sip of his coffee.

"That's when Phillip pointed Heather out to me," Darlene said and sat down on the sofa next to her father. "As soon as she saw you, she made a B-line straight to David. She waited until you got close enough to see them. She patted him on the shoulder, David turned around, and she laid a big kiss on him."

"Yes, love. The chit set both of you up. No doubt," Phillip said in his thick British accent.

"We saw your heart break right there in the middle of all those people. We saw which way you ran, and we saw David trying to go after you."

"We tried to catch you outside, but you were already riding away in a cab," Phillip said and sipped his coffee again.

Trish thought for a moment. "Okay, let's say David and I were setup. It obviously worked. He didn't come over last night. So, her plan worked to come between us. He has to be with her. Especially, if there were no accidents reported fitting his description and you checked the hospital. He couldn't have just vanished."

Mr. Jacobs poured a cup of coffee. "He could if he got kidnapped."

"Now that's just crazy. Who would kidnap him?" Trish asked as she shook her head.

"Maybe a client who he lost a case for?" Phillip threw out.

"David doesn't lose cases," Trish said. "I think he's at The Wingate Hotel. I really do guys."

There was a pounding at the door.

"Come in," Mr. Jacobs yelled.

Ted whirled into the house closing the door behind him. "Any word?"

"No," Mr. Jacobs answered.

Ted looked terrible. His hair was disheveled, and he hadn't shaved. He had on a green dress shirt, which was wrinkled, his signature black leather coat, and a pair of black jeans. He looked at Trish and her luggage. "Where the hell are you going?"

"I have an eight o'clock flight," she answered plainly.

"Unbelievable! My brother is missing, and the woman he loves packs her bags! Put that crap down, you're not going anywhere!" Ted exclaimed.

"Ted, we just told her. Give her a break. She didn't know," Darlene snapped.

Ted bit his lower lip. He looked down in shame. "I'm sorry. I should have known," he said as he shook his head and looked up at her. "I guess I'm running on empty and I'm…."

Trish shook her head. *Why hasn't David called anyone? He's got everyone worried sick.* "Forget it. I can see how worried you are. Have you tried The Wingate Hotel?"

"Yes, he's not there," Teddy answered.

"Get yourself some coffee, son," Mr. Jacobs said and gestured at the coffee table. "You look exhausted."

Ted walked towards the coffee table and poured himself a cup.

"Ted, did you ask the desk clerk if Heather Young had a room there?" Trish asked.

"Yes. Heather hasn't been there since her last surprise visit to town."

"How do you know he wasn't lying?" Trish asked.

"Because I slipped the desk clerk forty bucks. He better not have been lying," Teddy said and took a big swig from the coffee mug.

"Did you try his apartment?" Trish asked.

"Of course, I did. That was the first place I went when Mom called me," Ted said and topped off his cup.

"Well, there's only one other place I can think of," Trish said calmly.

Chapter 36

Everyone in the room looked at her. You could hear a pin drop. "Where do you think he is Trish?" Mr. Jacobs asked.

"New York City," Trish said.

"New York City," Phillip, Darlene, and Teddy repeated.

"Yes, they could have easily flown or drove last night. Possibly drove. New York is only four to five hours from here."

"They? You think he went to New York with Heather?" Teddy asked.

"Yep," Darlene answered for Trish.

Teddy looked at Darlene and back at Trish. "Are you insane? He didn't go to New York with that tart."

"Why not? It's not that farfetched. She tried to convince David to go back with her before," Trish said.

Teddy rolled his head back to the ceiling and brought it back down to look at her. "Why would David go to New York with her, when he is in love with you?"

"He's not in love with me. I know because he has never said it. David loves Heather. I don't think he ever stopped loving her," Trish said defensively.

A hint of red flashed around Teddy's neck. "Maybe…just maybe he was holding back because you needed time and space to think?" he asked sarcastically.

"There's no reason to get snippy. I'm just trying to come up with a logical explanation as to why-"

"No reason to get snippy! My kid brother is missing, and you're acting like we're playing a game of Clue!"

Darlene's face flushed red. She jumped off the sofa. "Don't you yell at her like that you…you…jackass!"

Ted turned to look at Darlene. He was about to say something when Phillip intervened.

"All right!" Phillip yelled without leaving his seat. "Let's not get overheated."

"It's not going to help David if we all start turning on each other," Mr. Jacobs reasoned. "Ted, I seriously suggest you take a couple of deep breaths before you say another word. Trish, if David went to New York he would have called someone by now. His parents, his brother. No one has heard from him, honey."

"Love makes people do things they don't normally do," Trish said barely above a whisper. She should know. Trish left her hometown for her first husband and threw herself at her divorce attorney, who she hated as a child, just a couple of weeks ago.

"No matter what state of mind David was in, he wouldn't leave town without letting someone know. My mother is about to have a nervous breakdown, and my father has rung his hands so much it's a wonder his skin isn't raw," Ted said.

Trish frowned. For the first time, she actually considered that he vanished without a trace. Where could he be?

The phone rang.

"See!" Trish exclaimed.

"See what, love?" Phillip asked with confusion. Everyone else in the room looked at her.

She dropped her luggage and power walked to the phone. "I bet you twenty dollars that is the Dear Jane phone call," Trish said. Actually, she hoped it was. She would rather believe that he left her for another woman, than something happening to him.

"You're in denial now," Ted mumbled.

Trish picked up the phone. "About time you called, you coward. You got your family worried sick," she answered.

"Um, I think you got me mistaken for someone else, miss," the woman said.

"Oh," Trish said with slight embarrassed. "I'm sorry."

"It's fine, miss. My name is Annie, I'm a nurse at Clary Memorial Hospital," she said.

Trish's fingers tingled. She was wrong. David was hurt. He was hurt and alone and here she was thinking that he was a womanizer and a bastard.

"I'm looking for a woman named Trish Truman."

"Yes, I'm Trish," she said cautiously.

"Good, I finally found someone. I'm calling about Mrs. Ruth Hinkle. She's had a terrible accident."

Trish looked up. Everyone in the room was staring at her. "What happened to her?" Trish asked.

"Her? Heather?" Ted asked.

Trish shook her head.

"She fell down the stairs in her basement. Luckily,

someone found her and called an ambulance, but he didn't leave his name. When the ambulance arrived, her front door was cracked opened. We've tried to contact her sons, but we can't reach them. We also tried calling her employer a...Mr. David Shaw, but we couldn't reach him either," Annie said.

"Her sons are out of town for the New Year. Mr. Shaw is ....not available." Trish said.

"Oh I see. When we told her we couldn't get in touch with her emergency contacts she became agitated again."

"What do you mean again?"

"Last night when she woke up in the emergency room she was hysterical. We couldn't understand what she was saying. The doctor was afraid she might give herself a heart attack -considering the condition she was in -so he sedated her."

"What!" Trish exclaimed. "Was the ER doctor drunk? She's not crazy."

"We had no choice, Ms. Truman. Mrs. Hinkle has a broken hip, a fractured arm, a sprained collarbone, a severe cut to her head, and a serious concussion. She was working herself up into a frenzy."

"Okay, so she got upset again this morning because you couldn't contact anyone on her list?"

"It seems so. I asked her if there was anyone else we could contact she gave me your name and this phone number. She also gave me the name.....Teddy Shaw. However, she could only remember his office number and since it's New Year's Day..."

"His office is closed. It's okay; Teddy is here with me. I'll tell him what has happened."

"Good. Can you get here as soon as possible? I think she will calm down once she sees a familiar face."

"Yes, I'll leave now."

"Good. She's been moved to a private room. It's on the fourth floor, room 406."

"Okay, and thanks for calling," Trish said and hung up. "It's barely seven o'clock and all hell has broken loose."

"What was that about?" Mr. Jacobs asked.

"Sounds like someone is hurt," Darlene commented.

Trish rushed to her pile of bags and grabbed her purse. "It's Mrs. Hinkle. She fell down her basement stairs last night. She's in the hospital all alone and she's scared. She asked for me and Teddy. Her sons are out of town."

"Good Lord!" Mr. Jacobs exclaimed.

"Oh, that poor woman," Darlene said.

"Yeah, some quack sedated her last night like she was a crazy person. I'm sure she was just scared. All they had to do was talk to her," Trish said with disgust as she pulled her coat on.

"Trish, I know she asked for me, but unless she's on death's door-" Teddy said.

"It's okay, I'll just explain that you're busy. I don't want to tell her David is missing; she'll get more upset than what she already is," Trish said as she walked to the door.

"Are you sure you're okay going by yourself?" Darlene asked.

"Yes, I don't know how long I'll be, but if you get any word about David call me on my cell phone."

"Okay," Darlene agreed.

"Hey, Trish," Teddy said and strode to her. "Look, about a few minutes ago…"

"It's okay, Teddy. I understand. I know you love him."

Teddy brought her into his arms. He put his chin on top of her head. "And you love him, even though you never said it," he whispered.

She smiled against his shirt and then brought her gaze up to look at him. "If anybody can find him, it's you. His big brother. I have faith in you, Teddy."

"Thanks," he said with a weak smile.

Chapter 37

Trish slowly walked into room 406 and closed the door behind her. Mrs. Hinkle was propped up on the bed. Her arm was in a cast, she was wearing a clavicle brace, and her head was wrapped in thick bandages. Trish slowly approached the bed and sat down on the stool next to it.

"Mrs. Hinkle. Mrs. Hinkle, It's Trish," she whispered.

Mrs. Hinkle slowly opened her eyes. They were bloodshot and full of fear.

"It's okay, Mrs. Hinkle. I'm here."

She could only mouth her words at first, then she was able to say Trish's name aloud.

"You poor woman. Did they sedate you again? You seem so groggy."

"No, pain medication makes me sleepy. Not important now. Where Teddy?" she asked in broken English.

"He will be here later. Teddy is working on an important case; he couldn't leave at the moment. But, he sends his best, and he'll be here to cheer you up soon."

Mrs. Hinkle squeezed her eyes shut. She let out a whimper that sounded like a wounded animal.

Trish got nervous. "He's coming. I promise."

"No, now. He needs to be here - now," she whispered and opened her eyes. "You need him. David needs him. We all need him. He is the...only one that...can stop-" she stopped talking to wince in pain.

"Stay calm and take your time," Trish said and placed her hand over Mrs. Hinkle's. It was obvious the woman was trying to tell her something. Something important. That idiot doctor. Why didn't they listen to her? What if she was trying to tell them the medications she was allergic to?

Mrs. Hinkle took a deep breath. "Listen, very carefully. I did not fall like they said. I- I was pushed.... down the stairs."

Trish's mouth dropped open. "What? Are you sure?"

"Yes. I...was dressed to leave...the house to go to a party at a friend's house. I walked down the hall," she said and stopped to take a breath. "I heard a nose in...the basement. Loud, never heard before. It was so loud, I thought that my furnace ...broke down...it's old you see."

"Go on," Trish urged.

She took another breath. "I opened the basement door. I thought I saw a ...shadow. I called down...hello. Then, I...was pushed...really hard...from behind." She cried. Fear and tears plagued her eyes. "Tumbled...so long...I thought...I would not stop. Landed on my back, I saw...her....she stood... top of the stairs. Closed my eyes....pretended I was," Mrs. Hinkle sucked in a sob. "Dead."

"Oh God," Trish said as she closed her eyes.

"She spoke….said…let's go. I stayed still. Heard someone…step over me…go up the stairs. Open eyes for a moment, saw large man…not fat…broad…maybe muscular."

"Do you know the woman who pushed you?"

"Young…she-devil," she sputtered out.

Trish wrinkled her nose. "A young she-devil?"

"Nooo…no," Mrs. Hinkle said and took a deep breath. "Heather Young, the...she-devil."

Trish's eyes grew wide like silver dollars. Her mouth went dry. "How do you know it was Heather? You never met her?"

"Did...I did. Came in office…a few days ago. Said terrible things….about you and David…relationship. Slapped her."

Trish was taken aback. "David slapped her?"

"Nooo…I slapped her."

Trish was astonished. Mrs. Hinkle was a sweet soul. Trish never heard of Mrs. Hinkle harming anyone. Heather must have really got under Mrs. Hinkle's skin. "You did?"

Mrs. Hinkle lightly grabbed Trish's hand. "She got angry. Told David…to fire me. He refused. She realized…then…she really didn't have a chance…with him. Threatened…David. Neither one…of us….took it seriously. Came…for me…revenge."

Trish placed her hand on her chest. Her heart pounded so hard that it felt like it was going to come out of her chest. "The nurse told me someone called an ambulance for you, but he wouldn't give the dispatcher his name, and there was no one at your home when the ambulance showed up."

Mrs. Hinkle swallowed. "Must have been my….companion….for the evening. In his youth, he spent time…..in jail. I left the door unlocked….for him to come in. He must have seen me… called for help. Probably didn't stick….around because the cops….might have…been called. He doesn't…like them much."

Trish shook her head with understanding.

"Nurse…can't find David. Where?"

Trish squeezed her eyes shut. She couldn't lie to her. Mrs. Hinkle knew something was wrong since David didn't come with her to the hospital.

Mrs. Hinkle squeezed Trish's hand.

Trish slowly opened her eyes to look at a distraught Mrs. Hinkle.

"David?"

"I don't know where he is. No one does. Teddy, Phillip, and Darlene have been searching for him all night."

Mrs. Hinkle groaned, and then she applied more pressure to Trish's hand. "Find…Teddy, now."

Trish jumped up and grabbed the hospital phone. She dialed Teddy's cell phone number. "Come on, come on," Trish urged the ringtone.

"Shaw," he answered roughly.

"Teddy, you need to get to the hospital, now. Room 406."

"Has Mrs. Hinkle taken a turn for the worst?"

"Her accident wasn't an accident. She was pushed down the stairs in her own house," Trish blurted out.

"What?" he exclaimed. "Who the hell would do that

to her?"

"Heather."

"Heather? I didn't know Mrs. Hinkle knew her."

"Heather came into the office a few days ago. Sounds like Heather, David, and Mrs. Hinkle had it out. Mrs. Hinkle even slapped her."

"Hold on. I'm making a U-turn."

Trish waited.

Teddy came back on the line. "David didn't say a word to me about it."

"He didn't say anything to me either. The way Mrs. Hinkle talked, they didn't take her seriously."

"What do you mean?"

"She came after Mrs. Hinkle out of revenge, and she threatened David for rejecting her. After I get off the phone with you, I'm going to call the police. Mrs. Hinkle should give a statement. She needs to report this."

"No. Let me call them. I know a lieutenant on the force. We went to the academy together. I called him earlier about David, he's been doing an unofficial search for me. At least we have a lead now."

Mrs. Hinkle started groaning Trish's name.

"Hold on, Teddy, I think Mrs. Hinkle is trying to tell me something. What is it, Mrs. Hinkle?"

"No cops. She devil...found out I survived...she'll come. Not safe here. Can't...defend myself."

Trish shook her head. "Teddy. Mrs. Hinkle doesn't want us to call the cops. She's afraid that Heather will find out she survived the fall and try again. It sounds like she meant to kill Mrs. Hinkle. I'm inclined to agree with her. She's totally defenseless."

"Tell her not to worry. I'll get her protection, and tell her I'm on my way."

"I'll be here when you arrive. Mrs. Hinkle shouldn't be left alone now."

Chapter 38

Teddy held and caressed Mrs. Hinkle's hand as she gave a formal statement to the police officer. After she was done, Teddy kissed her hand. He bent his head over the older lady's hand – resting his forehead on her hand. "She'll pay for doing this to you, I promise."

The other cop was a lieutenant. He had long dark hair that was pulled back in a ponytail. He wore a long leather coat and black slacks. "Ms. Truman when was the last time you saw David Shaw?" the lieutenant asked.

"New Year's Eve. It was midnight."

"You mentioned something about going home after the New Year. Did anyone see you leave?"

Teddy looked up at the lieutenant. "Harry."

"Thanks to Mrs. Hinkle's statement the search is official now, Ted. Not saying Ms. Truman did anything to your brother, but I have to be thorough in the report.

"It's fine, Teddy. Yes, there was a doorman who helped me get a cab. Also, Phillip Dunn and Darlene Jacobs saw me walk out the door from the balcony of the ballroom."

"The ECTV Ball?"

"Yes."

"Was anyone home when you got there?"

"Mr. Jacobs was, but he was asleep. I say it was forty minutes until Darlene came home, and she did see me there. We talked for a few minutes, and I went to sleep."

"All right," the lieutenant said.

"Does she need a lawyer, Harry?" Teddy asked sarcastically.

Harry stared at Trish. "Nah. Even if I did suspect her in the case, how could I prove that a little thing like her abducted a big guy like David?"

Mrs. Hinkle whimpered.

"Jesus, Harry," Teddy said. "Your mouth is still like a bull in a China shop."

Harry tipped his head to Mrs. Hinkle. "Beg your, pardon. I didn't mean to upset you any more than you already are, ma'am. The department faxed a picture of Heather Young to hospital security. An officer is on his way to guard your door. An officer will be outside your door until she's caught."

"Thank…you," Mrs. Hinkle said.

Harry tipped his head to Mrs. Hinkle again.

"Now that I'm cleared and security has been set up, what are you doing to find David?" Trish asked.

The lieutenant glanced at Mrs. Hinkle. "Let's go in the hall."

After they filed out in the hallway, Harry addressed them. "What I'm about to say isn't what you're going to want to hear. So, brace yourselves. Even with an APB out on Heather, it's going to be tough finding her or

David. I wouldn't be surprised if the big guy Hinkle mentioned was a pro. We went over the parking lot where David's car was last seen with a fine tooth comb. Nothing unusual. It's like he vanished without a trace."

Trish fought the urge to tear up. "It sounds like you're giving up before you get started," she choked out.

"Not at all. I'm just saying it's going to be tough, and it's going to take time. I got a couple of the boys running a background check on Heather. Hopefully, something will come up that will give us a clue to where she might have taken David and more about the big guy."

Dr. Shaw and Mrs. Shaw approached them.

"What are you two doing here?" Teddy asked.

"Darlene called and told us what happened to Mrs. Hinkle. How is she?" Dr. Shaw asked. "Besides, we couldn't keep sitting at the house. We were going crazy."

"Weak. She has a bad concussion, broken hip, sprang collarbone, and a fractured arm," Trish said.

"Poor thing," Mrs. Shaw said.

"She's lucky that she's alive. She could have broken her neck," Dr. Shaw said.

"I think that was the idea," Harry said.

Dr. Shaw and Mrs. Shaw looked at the lieutenant.

"Mom, Dad, this is Lit. Harry McDonnell."

"And the officer looking at us?" Mrs. Shaw said and nodded her head to the cop next to Mrs. Hinkle's room door.

"That's Officer McKay," Harry answered.

"Are you here about my son? Do you have any leads?" Mrs. Shaw asked with desperation.

"Partly ma'am, you see we came here for Mrs. Hinkle. Apparently, she was pushed down the stairs. She didn't fall like the ER thought she did. We came to take her statement."

"Dear heavens," Mrs. Shaw said.

"Did she know her assailant?" Dr. Shaw asked.

"Harry, let me tell them," Teddy said.

"Sure, I got to get back to the department anyway."

"I'll stop by later," Teddy said.

"All right," Harry said and walked away.

"What is going on, Teddy?" Mrs. Shaw said.

"There's no easy way to say this; Mrs. Hinkle was pushed down the stairs by Heather."

Dr. Shaw's eyes bulged. Mrs. Shaw turned paler than she already was.

"David's Heather?" Dr. Shaw asked with disbelief.

Teddy looked down at Trish.

"Yes," Trish said pressing her lips together.

"I didn't mean-," Dr. Shaw started.

"I know. We're all in shock right now. Any of us can say anything at any given time considering the situation," Trish said.

"Why would Heather hurt Mrs. Hinkle?" Dr. Shaw asked.

"Long story short, Heather snapped when she was in David's office the other day. She and Mrs. Hinkle got into it, and David rejected Heather. She threatened David," Teddy said.

"Do you think Heather did something to David?" Mrs. Shaw asked.

Teddy and Trish couldn't answer her.

"I thought she was done hurting my boy," Dr. Shaw

mumbled.

"Oh God-" Mrs. Shaw started, and her head went backwards. Dr. Shaw grabbed her arms.

"He's okay, Elizabeth. He has to be," Dr. Shaw said with a pained expression.

Trish wondered if Dr. Shaw believed what he said because his face expressed fear, not optimism. "Yes, Heather might have pushed Mrs. Hinkle down the steps, but she wouldn't harm David, I don't think. She did love him at one time. Maybe she just took him somewhere private to talk. Get him to take her back." Trish cringed as soon as she said it, but she would rather think that, than think Heather pushed him down a flight of stairs or worse.

"Perhaps. It's not far-fetched. Maybe Heather got him tied up in a roach motel- trying to talk sense into him or what she thinks is sense," Teddy said.

"I can call all the low budget motels," Trish said.

"Waste of time. Heather would have used an alias - if she has him at a motel," Teddy said.

"Okay, I'll get a picture of Heather and David and go to these motels. A desk clerk might recognize them."

"Trish, honey, it's a long shot, a possibility, yes, but a long shot," Teddy said shaking his head.

Trish couldn't hold it in anymore. "Well, it was a long shot that David and I started dating. It was a long shot that we would ever spend Christmas together. It was a long shot that I would-" Tears started streaming down her face. She couldn't stop them. She sniffed, then frowned. She covered her face with her hands - embarrassed by her lack of self-control. She cursed herself for falling apart in front of David's parents. The last thing they needed was to be more upset by her emotional outburst.

Teddy pulled her into his arms for a hug. He held her as she sobbed. "I was wondering when you were going to breakdown. I knew you weren't made out of stone."

Someone pulled one hand away from her face. It was Mrs. Shaw, she was giving her a handkerchief. Then, Mrs. Shaw hugged her from behind. Dr. Shaw walked up and placed his hand on Teddy's shoulder.

Chapter 39

David held out all night. Not only was his left eye swollen and closed, his lip was split, he had a bloody nose, and he believed he had a cracked rib. The man with brown hair and hazel eyes wanted David to write a note – a suicide note. It was clear what this man was going to do after David wrote the note, so David refused. He'd been tortured ever since.

What David didn't know was who and why. During the times he wasn't threatened or hit, David thought about who was behind this. Past and present clients were happy with his services. He considered that it could be a jealous competitor. Even though most colleagues shook his hand after a case, it didn't mean they were happy that they lost. At the same time, he couldn't fathom a lawyer who would risk his career and going to prison over a professional grudge.

The broad man came waltzing back into the room. "Still here I see."

"Well, it's not like I can stand up and walk to the parking lot of - wherever this is," David stated. His hands were tied behind his back around a pole, and his legs and ankles were tied together in front of him.

The man knelt down to face him eye to eye. "It's simple, you write what I want you to write and this will be painless or you won't experience anymore pain. It will be quick. Capeesh?"

David met his stare. "I'm not going to make this easy for you or whoever you're working for. So forget it."

The man slowly got up. "You've got an iron will. I'll give you that. No matter how unreasonable." He walked away from David and to a satchel that sat on a folding table. He pulled a canteen from it and walked back to David. He knelt down again and took the lid off.

"What's that?" David asked.

"Water," he answered and offered it to David.

David turned his head.

"Now, you're being prideful."

"How do I know it isn't poisoned? It's obvious you have instructions."

"Watch me." The man took a big swig from the canteen and opened his mouth to show David that he swallowed the liquid.

He offered the canteen again and this time David accepted. Life and hope went down his throat quenching the pain and worry.

The man stood up again. "This is nothing personal you know. It's the job. What I do."

"Before we go on with this, will you give me the courtesy of telling me who your employer is?"

He heard a sliding door open and close from a distance. David heard the sound a couple of times last night.

"Won't have to. I think you two are about to meet."

David couldn't believe his one opened eye when she stalked into the warehouse area. Her hair was in a ponytail that flowed down her back, and she wore blue jeans and a blue sweater. "Heather."

"Damnit, I told you not to hurt him. People aren't going to think David committed suicide with a bloody face. There's even blood on his shirt," she shrieked.

"I don't know why you insisted on him writing a note. I could have shot him and made it look like a suicide in an ally in New York," he said.

"Don, I told you- it's personal. People finding his body isn't enough. I want his memory and reputation questioned and tarnished."

"Personal. That's how people get caught you know. Complicating a simple killing. Look, I don't know what you expected. A guy like him isn't going to be persuaded or bullied into writing a suicide note. I would have told you that if you gave me enough time, but no, you had to have this taken care of immediately."

"If you thought it was such a dumb plan why did you accept the job?"

"You offered double my usual rate. With that being said, where's the other half?"

"I told you when the job is done and unfortunately it is not."

Don came closer to her. He whispered something in her ear.

"That's probably for the best; especially now that David looks like he's been in a brawl," Heather said with a twisted mouth. She walked a few steps closer to David. "It's also a good idea because that ole bat survived."

"What," Don said.

"Yes. Not good news."

"Damnit, I should have checked her pulse before we left," Don said with anger.

"Well, you're safe. She couldn't identify you. Me on the other hand...I am in a lot of trouble."

"What do you mean?"

"She knows it was me. My picture was a late-breaking bulletin on TV. It's rather chilling to see your picture on TVs on display in a store window. They also know David was taken- he just didn't disappear."

"Shit!" Don said and started pacing.

"Yes, shit is a good word to say at this point. I had to put my sunglasses on and my hood over my head. It's a good thing I checked out of that dreadful motel early this morning. I've got wigs in the car, just in case. Glad I stay prepared."

"We need to finish this and get the hell out of this town before they start blocking the roads. We should have put him in the trunk last night and drove over the state line. Found an isolated place there. But no, you just had to play your mind games," Don said as he continued to pace.

"Oh shut up! I'm not a complete amateur."

"Right," Don said sarcastically and headed for the table with the satchel.

"What are you doing?"

Don pulled a gun out of the bag and tucked it in his back pocket. He grabbed the bag and slung it over his shoulders. "I'm getting ready. We need to dump his car and do him."

"Not yet," she said.

"Why not?" Don asked with irritation.

"This is the last time I'm going to see David. I want some time alone with him. Why don't you go out and get us something to eat? They don't know about you, yet."

"You are unbelievable. You had more sense when I met you a couple of years ago, but now…you've lost it."

"Just go, Don. Get some sandwiches or salads or something."

Chapter 40

Teddy drove while Trish rode shotgun - checking a list of motels. Mrs. Shaw remembered that she had a picture of David and Heather together in one of her old photo albums at home. Teddy and Trish stopped by the Shaw house to find it.

"After we check this place, we're going to stop for coffee and food," Teddy said.

"Why? We just got started. We've only check three motels so far."

"Because we're running on empty. I haven't eaten since last night, I'm sure you haven't either, and I need another jolt of caffeine."

"Teddy, you do think David is okay, don't you? I mean, she wouldn't physically harm him, right?"

"I hope you're right about that, but the way Mrs. Hinkle talked about what happened in the office," Teddy said and shook his head. "And we know what happened to her."

"Yes, but Mrs. Hinkle is a stranger to Heather. If she truly loved David at one time....she couldn't bring herself to hurt him."

Teddy pulled into the pothole-filled parking lot of Dale's Motel. "I'm not going to lie to you, Trish. Heather never was a gracious loser. I never thought she would go this far, though. That New Year's kiss that she laid on David - in front of you - is more her style. But, if she has really snapped, and what she did to Mrs. Hinkle proves she has….I don't know what she is truly capable of, now." Teddy parked the SUV and cut the engine off.

Trish took a deep breath.

"You holding up, okay?"

"Yeah, come on," Trish said.

They got out of the car and walked to the office of the motel. Teddy opened the glass door for Trish.

"Happy New Year," the skinny middle-aged clerk in the plaid shirt said.

"Happy New Year," Trish forced out. The last thing she felt was happy.

"My name is Ted, Mr. uhm.."

"Dale. The Dale on the sign."

"Oh, you own this establishment," Ted said.

"Yes, sir," Dale said proudly.

Ted reached into his pocket. "Well, Dale, my colleague and I are looking for these two people." Ted showed Dale the picture of Heather and David.

Dale looked at it. "I've never seen the guy, but the girl, yes."

Trish and Ted looked at each other and then back at the clerk.

"You've seen the woman? When?" Ted asked.

"This morning. She checked out a few hours ago. Sorry you missed her."

"Did she say where she was going?" Trish asked.

"No. Actually she was pretty snooty."

"I bet. Was she with anyone?" Ted asked.

"I don't think so, but I wasn't the one who checked her in. When she checked out she was alone."

"What kind of car was she driving?" Trish asked.

"What room was she staying in?" Ted asked.

"Uh why? Why are you two looking for this woman?" Dale asked.

"This woman is wanted by the police. She pushed an old lady down the stairs last night and we believe she had my brother, the guy in the picture, abducted."

Dale's light brown eyes widened. "You're kidding?"

"I wish," Teddy said with an expressionless face.

"Are you two cops?"

"I'm a P.I. and Trish is my brother's girlfriend."

"We would be grateful for any information you could give us," Trish said.

"I understand, miss. But, I think I should call the police and give a formal statement before I tell you anything else. They probably should do a search of the room."

"You can do that after you talk to us. My brother's life is at stake. He's been missing for almost ten hours," Teddy said as he was getting rattled.

Trish placed her hand on Teddy's arm. "You know the man is right. The police can do forensics on the room. We can't do that. Let him call and we'll just wait here, okay."

Teddy was quiet for a moment. "Okay," he reluctantly said. "Ask for Lit. Harry McDonnell, he's working the case."

****

He called from a pay phone to find out what room Ruth Hinkle was in. Don pretended to be a relative of David's. He told the clerk he wanted to send flowers. She was hesitant to give him the information at first, but Don's flirting got him what he wanted.

Don moved quietly throughout the hospital. He walked past Mrs. Hinkle's room swearing to himself concerning the cop that was posted at the door. The cop barely paid attention to him. He went around the corner and went through a door that said exit. He slowly went down the stairs. No way he could get to Hinkle now, but he realized that it was no big deal. Before he came to the hospital, he confirmed that he was not identified - no way was he going to trust Heather's word.

When Don reached the parking garage he knew he had to cut this cord. No way was he going down for Heather's crazy obsession.

Chapter 41

"What did you do to Mrs. Hinkle?" David asked.

"All I know is she took a bad fall down the stairs," Heather answered with an innocent look, but with an evil glaze in her eyes.

David stared at her. "You pushed her down the stairs!"

Heather looked at him coolly.

"My God, Heather, you hurt Mrs. Hinkle, hired some moke to chloroform me, and drove me out to an abandon warehouse all because I rejected you," David said with astonishment.

Anger flashed in her eyes. "You did more than that. You spat on everything I've done during the past two and half years. I told you that I was with George for us – not just for myself. You couldn't see past your pride to hear me out."

"I did hear you out!"

"You heard what you wanted to hear," she said and pulled a gun out of her purse. She tossed the purse on the floor, holding the gun at her side. "You thought I was lying. I know you did. Did you really think I enjoyed sleeping with that old sweaty windbag? He was disgusting. Some of the things he made me do in bed!" she shouted and shook her head with disgust.

"You didn't have to, Heather. You had a choice to walk away at any time. Or better yet, never got involved with him in the first place," David said gently.

"Yes and no. I explained to you why I got involved with him. In the end, I did walk away – with everything," she said softly.

"He died. If he hadn't have died, you wouldn't have come here."

She gave off a weak smile and slowly shook her head at him. "You really don't have any faith in me at all do you? I loved you, David and I missed you, terribly. And I was sick and tired of *him*. George wasn't you."

No. She didn't. She couldn't. "Heather, did you kill George?"

Heather paused for a moment before looking directly into David's eyes. "Yes." As the affirmation hung in the air, Heather turned and walked away from him. David's stomach curtailed as Heather disappeared into the shadows.

****

Trish sat in a wood chair in the lobby of Dale's Motel listening to Dale and the night desk clerk give their statement to a police officer. After they were finished, she went outside and stood in the crisp, cold air. She walked a few steps away from the door of the office and leaned her back against the brown brick.

Bending her right knee, she placed her foot flat on the wall.

She exhaled. Light smoke signified her warm breath. Trish wondered how she could doubt David. Of course, he wasn't a womanizer. Other than their heated exchanges in the past, he always been a gentlemen. She had never heard of him leading a woman on. Robert's betrayal affected her more than she thought. At the time, Trish didn't bother to confront David and Heather at the ball. She just ran off and labeled him a liar and a cheat. Turning her back and cutting her loses, she didn't try to fight for him or their relationship. She shook her head.

Trish called herself a fool for underestimating Heather. It was obvious that she was a wolf from the moment Trish met her. A woman like that wasn't going to back down when she really wanted something. Trish understood why Heather wanted David back. Yet, Heather had snapped. Perhaps if Heather couldn't have him, no one could.

"Pop, if you can hear me, we could use your help down here. Ma, Gran, feel free to chip in, too. David is in serious trouble. Yes, I know you're shocked like everyone else, but really he's a good man. He doesn't deserve to be taken out by a femme fatal. And well...I love him. It's New Year's Day, we should be curled up on the couch watching cheesy parades on TV. Not separated with one of our lives at stake."

As if someone was standing beside her, she heard a faint female voice. *Get in her head. If she wants to hurt him, she would want privacy. No one in hearing distance.*

"Where would she take him? A place no one could

hear him call for help. No one could hear a gunshot. Somewhere…"

"Somewhere?" Teddy repeated as he and Harry walked up to her.

She didn't acknowledge them. She almost had it. A memory flashed of her, Robert, Marcus, Daisy, and Melanie when she was eighteen. It was winter break. She just finished her first semester of college.

"Trish?" Teddy said uneasily.

On New Year's Eve they drove out to Westback Mill. It had been shut down for three years. Teenagers and college kids would sneak out there to party and make out in their cars. That night, Melanie swiped a bottle of vodka from a restaurant she worked at. They went to the old mill, squeezed through the shackles on the door, and partied like there was no tomorrow or anything called a hangover.

"She's in shock," Harry said.

Teddy took a hold of Trish's wrist. "Trish!"

She trembled out of the memory. "What!"

"What is wrong with you? What were you thinking about?" Teddy said.

"I was thinking if I was Heather, where would I take David."

"I'll bite. Where?" Harry asked.

"Westback Mill."

Harry just looked at her like she lost her mind.

"Trish, that might make since if Heather knew the area, but she doesn't," Teddy said.

"Right," Harry said.

"It's not that hard to find the place. It's huge, old, and it looks abandoned. Besides, didn't the lieutenant suspect she's working with a pro. A professional hitman or mobster would seek out a place like that to do a dirty deed or keep a hostage."

"It's only five miles outside of town. I don't think there's a house within two miles of it." Teddy mumbled.

"We're already on the city border- on the road that takes us right to the mill," Trish said.

"You two can't be serious. It's a long shot," Harry said and shook his head.

"Hey, don't doubt her. One of her long shots paid off all ready. Trish could be on a roll," Teddy said.

"Yeah, what long shot was that?" Harry said.

"Checking motels," she answered flatly.

Harry took a draw of his cigarette. He blew out. "Well, checking out an old sawmill sounds more exciting than hanging out with the boys on the roadblocks they're setting up."

"Roadblocks?" Trish asked.

"Yeah, but I'm not sure what good it will do. Heather checked out of this dump a few hours ago. She could be long gone, so let's hope your long shot pays off....for David's sake," Harry said and looked over to a patrolman. "Hey, Ballstic! You want to go on a wild goose chase?"

Chapter 42

David thought about how he was going to get out of this. Surely, people had figured out he was missing by now. Hopefully, the cops or Mrs. Hinkle made the connection between Heather and his disappearance. If not, hopefully Ted had. Trish was so mad at him, she probably didn't care where he was. Why didn't he tell her he loved her while he had the chance? Now, he might die and the woman he loved was mad at him and didn't know how he felt.

David had a feeling he wasn't far from Clary. This could be the old sawmill outside of town judging by the old machinery in the warehouse. Hopefully, Heather or Don left a clue to this place that the police or Ted could follow. He had to stall for a little longer. An idea popped in his head. It made his stomach churn, but he had no other options. He had to make it good and sincere. Heather slowly walked back into the warehouse- still carrying the gun by her side.

"Where did you go?" he asked with concern.

"There's an old office in the back. I went in there," she said solemnly.

"Heather, I understand."

She slowly looked up at him. "Understand what?"

"Why you did away with George. He was a vile human being."

"Oh, David, he was so sexually depraved. After the first three months of our marriage, he asked me if I was up for playing dress up. Ha....I thought he wanted me to wear a nurse's outfit or a scathing piece of lingerie. Do you know what he wanted me to wear?"

David shook his head.

"He pulled out a pink dress with lace. Told me to put my hair up in pigtails. He even gave me two pink ribbons to tie my hair with. I did, but I felt...sleazy....and strange. When I came out...George was more turned on than I had ever seen him. He instructed me to call him Daddy. I-," she stopped. "I didn't think I could feel sicker than I did that day, but I was wrong. The worst was when he made me wear the dog outfit. I threw up afterwards."

David couldn't help the nausea that showed on his face. George was more of a sick bastard than he thought. He sympathized with Heather, but at the same time, she stayed – she did those things. Heather was living proof that money wasn't worth a person's self-respect or sanity. "I- I'm sorry. I should have fought for you. Let you explain."

A tear ran down her cheek. "After what you walked in on...how could you? After a few weeks, I understood how you felt. That's why I didn't pursue you back then. I tried to live with the life I chose and what it cost me....but I couldn't anymore. It was hard to live with a pervert like George after being with a man like you."

Heather stepped a little closer to him.

"Is it too late for us to start over?" David asked.

"I'm afraid it is."

"Why?"

"David, could you really live with the knowledge that I killed George?"

"Yes. Now that I know what you had to endure, I can. He was sick. Making you dress up like a little girl. God knows when he would have wanted the real thing."

"Yes, I thought about that at the time. I wondered if he ever molested a child. Yet, there were no rumors or proof. It could have been only a matter of time. Indirectly, I saved a child," she said with pouty lips.

"Yes," David said and slowly shook his head. "For that you're a hero." David hated to admit it, but Heather could have saved a child's innocence. Even though, what she did was wrong as well.

"What about Hinkle? Can you forgive me for that?"

David was silent for a moment. "She survived. If she died, then no. But, she's okay. Let's call it a lapse in judgement and not speak of it again."

Heather took another few steps towards him. "Because of what I did, the cops will take me away. I have to leave the country."

"That's fine. I'll come with you. I can't have my Southern belle traveling to Europe alone."

"I have accounts in Switzerland. We'll be set for life. We'll have to get you a fake passport and other papers, of course. That shouldn't be too hard. Don can take care of that for us. I already have fake documents. When the NYPD got suspicious about George's death I had Don set some up for me. I setup the accounts overseas a year ago."

"That's fine. Actually, it's brilliant," he complimented.

She gave off a shy smile. "Thank you, sugar. I...have to know something first." Heather got closer to him and got on her knees. She was now face to face with him.

"What is it, Belle?" he asked sweetly. Hoping that his old pet name for her would soften her resolve.

"Do you still love me?"

"Yes," he said quickly and passionately. Inwardly, he felt like he had heart burn.

"Say it. Say the words, sugar. I need to hear it."

He knew this was crucial. He kept eye contact with her. "I love you."

She threw her arms around his neck. His disgust was replaced with anxiety because she still had the gun in her hand.

****

Harry, Officer Ballstic, Trish, and Teddy walked on the dirt path to Westback Mill. They parked their vehicles a few feet away, just in case they were inside. Harry and Teddy wanted to sneak up on them.

"Lieutenant," Ballstic said.

"What?" Harry said.

"Don't you think that brush and snow over there looks suspicious? You know I'm a hunter."

"Yeah, so?"

"So, I know when brush is set in a certain way. Like

if another hunter sets a trap for large prey," Ballstic said and walked to the large brush.

Harry rolled his eyes. "Just hurry."

Ballstic picked up a couple of branches and wiped away some snow. "It's a car," he announced.

Trish, Teddy, and Harry rushed over. Trish saw the black paint and the beamer logo. "This is David's car."

"Are you sure?" Harry asked.

Teddy knelt down and wiped away more snow and pushed aside a couple of more branches. He revealed the license plate. "Yep, this is David's car."

"Okay, the car is here, but it doesn't mean he still is." Harry scratched his dark stringy hair.

Teddy and Trish gave Harry a dirty look.

"I just don't want you two to get your hopes up," he explained.

They continued walking up the dirt path. They reached the back of the warehouse, and there was a large window that was dirty from the season's elements. The four peeked inside. Trish gasped when she saw Heather holding and kissing a bloodied David on his cheek.

Teddy grabbed Trish's coat sleeve and pulled her down – from the window view. Harry and Ballstic huddled beside them.

"Go a few steps away, use your radio- call for back up," Harry whispered.

Ballstic followed the lieutenant's orders.

"Ted, you and Trish go back to the car and wait," Harry whispered.

"No," Teddy said.

"I'm not going anywhere," Trish whispered.

"You two will just be in harm's way if something

goes wrong."

"I got a gun," Teddy said.

"You're a P.I. not a cop," Harry said.

"I went to the academy, too, remember?" Teddy said.

"What about her?"

"Trish, go back to the car," Teddy said.

"Forget it. I'll stay here even if you two go in," Trish said.

"Not far enough away. If David finds out I had you anywhere close to danger he'd skin me alive. And I wouldn't blame him," Teddy said.

"Shhh. Look," Harry said as he peeked through the window.

Trish and Teddy raised their heads.

Chapter 43

Heather released David. She still had the gun in her hand. "Oh, sugar, everything is going to be all right. Once we're out of this city, we can head for the coast. I have a boat...well, more like a yacht. I know how to drive it, so we won't need a crew."

"That's great. We should leave, now. Time is of the essence," David said.

She nodded her head in agreement.

****

"Lieutenant," Ballstic said as he creeped back up in a squat. "A white sedan pulled up. A big guy with brown hair got out."

The four peeked through the window again.

"He put something in his back pocket. It looked like a gun."

"Damnit, Harry, we can't wait for back up," Teddy whispered with desperation.

****

Heather was untying the ropes behind David's back. He heard her put the gun on the floor behind him. David could feel the tightness relieving in his wrist. His hands had fallen asleep. Don came into the warehouse.

"Good, you're back. Change in plans," Heather said and stopped untying David. She stood up.

"Yes, I know," Don said and pulled a gun out of his rear pocket. He pointed it at Heather "Where's the rest of my money?"

"Oh for Pete's sake. It's in my purse on the floor," Heather said with irritation.

Don kept the gun pointed at Heather as he walked to the purse. He picked it up and opened it with one hand. He glanced inside.

The ropes were loose enough around David's wrists that he was able to slip his hands out.

"See," Heather said and placed her hands on her hips. "Now, put that thing down and help me get him up. I'm taking him with me. We need forged papers for David. I'll pay you another two grand for the forger."

Don tucked Heather's purse under his arm. David was then startled by a loud bang that echoed in the warehouse. He heard Heather scream. Don had a stone cold look on his face. David turned his head towards Heather. She was on the floor. Blood seeped through her sweater from the hole in her chest.

"Why did you shoot her?" David exclaimed.

"Oh please, we both know you didn't want to go anywhere with her," Don said as he pointed the gun at him.

David started pawing for the gun that was behind him without being obvious that his hands were free. "Yeah, but you didn't have to shoot her."

"Are you kidding me? She was crazy. She wasn't like that when I met her a couple of years ago. It's a shame, Heather was a good lay, but I'm not going to let some woman drag me to jail because she was good in bed."

David found the gun. "So, do I get the same?"

"Unfortunately. You've seen my face. Got to do the deed. It's a shame really, you're one tough guy."

"Freeze!" Harry yelled from the back of the warehouse.

Don pointed the gun at Harry, but the lieutenant fired two shots before Don got a round off. Don stumbled backwards from the two rounds to his chest. He fell to the floor.

Harry pulled his radio out of his pocket and called for an ambulance as Teddy and Trish ran from the back of the warehouse. Ballstic appeared from the side entrance.

Teddy untied David's legs and Trish threw her arms around David.

"What are you doing here?" David asked. "You could have gotten hurt."

Trish pulled back an inch from his face. "Nice to see you, too." She hugged him again, and he put his arms around her.

Chapter 44

David opened his eyes, and looking over, he saw Trish sitting next to his bed, reading a magazine.

"Hey, sweetheart," he whispered.

She looked up, smiled, and closed the magazine. "Hey, you dozed off."

"How long was I out? The last thing I remember was riding in the ambulance- with you."

"You passed out in the ambulance. The EMTs said you were exhausted and dehydrated. You got a cracked rib, a split lip, a bump on the back of your head, a broken nose, and a black eye."

David grunted. "Thank you, Dr. Truman."

"That's not all you have."

"Oh, what else?"

"You have a very stubborn lady on your hands that is crazy about you. David, I never should have doubted you New Year's Eve. I should have stayed and talked to you. If I had, this would never have happened."

"Shh, this wasn't your fault. Heather was bound and determined to have me abducted. I'm glad we got separated last night. If we weren't, you could have been hurt or killed."

"About Heather - she didn't make it. She died before they could do surgery to remove the bullet. The doctor said she lost too much blood."

A wave of mixed emotions stirred in him. The Heather he met was fun and vivacious. He loved her, but she died the day he caught her in bed with George Young. The one who came to Clary was manipulative, mean, and dangerous- that one he wouldn't miss.

"Are you okay? It's okay if you feel bad about it. After all, you did love her - once," Trish said.

"Yeah, once. I take it Don is dead, too?"

"You're not going to believe this, but he was wearing a bullet proof vest," Trish said and pressed her lips together.

David sat up. He winced with pain.

"Easy, your rib."

"You're right. I don't believe it."

"He was. He just got the wind knocked out of him. Harry figured it out when he couldn't find blood on Don's shirt. I never seen anyone that was knocked out get cuffs put on him so fast."

"I don't blame Harry. Don didn't mess around. My current condition is proof of that."

She gave off a small smile. "David, before your parents come back in, I want to tell you something."

"No, I need to tell you something. Let me go first. If I said this sooner, you wouldn't have thought I wanted Heather back."

"No, David, I've been thinking-"

"Trish, I think I've earned the right to say what I want to say first," he said with determination.

"This is not the time for us to fight."

"Then, close that beautiful mouth and listen."

"Uh," she breathed out and crossed her arms. She looked at him with a sly smile.

He smiled. "Ready?"

Her smile widened. "Yes."

"I love you," he said.

"And I love you," she admitted with a smile. She kissed him on the cheek. "So, now that we got that out of our systems, what do we do now?"

David leaned his head back on the pillow. He was still looking at her. "Once I'm better, I'm going to take you away on a vacation and make love to you every day and night."

She giggled. "That sounds like heaven."

"So, where would you like to go to find heaven?"

"You know, my attorney got me this beautiful beach house in the Bahamas."

Epilogue

Clary, PA
The Clover Club
May 1995

Trish and David sat in a booth necking when Darlene, Phillip, and Marcus approached them.

"Geez, the newness hasn't worn off, yet?" Phillip asked as he smiled and turned up his nose.

The love birds looked up.

"Tell me about it. You two are just sickening, now," Marcus said.

"Don't mind these two. They've never seen true love before," Darlene said with a smile. "But, it is my going away party. It would be nice if my best friend was free to hang out with me. I'll be gone for the whole summer."

"I'm sorry, Darlene," Trish said with a sorrowful look.

"You two can talk on the phone," David teased.

"Yeah, but we won't be able to see each other when she's here and I'm in Paris," Darlene said.

"At least free her up long enough to tell the rest of

the story," Marcus said. "I missed all the action."

"What action?" Trish asked.

"David's abduction and imprisonment by a mobster," Marcus said. "These two told me everything except what happened to the mobster."

David suppressed the urge to groan. He hoped people would have stopped asking about the ordeal by now.

"He pleaded guilty. Don got ten years for kidnapping, possibility of parole in seven years," Trish said.

"So, did the wife really kill her husband?" Marcus asked.

"Yep, Heather confessed to me while I was tied up. The NYPD said George's son contacted them the day after his father died. But, Heather had George's body cremated the next day. They couldn't do an autopsy," David said and sipped his scotch.

"They couldn't test the ashes for poisons?" Phillip asked.

"Nope. She already spread them in the Hudson River," David answered.

"It's all over now, and David is all right and with the woman he loves. Just like it should be," Darlene said.

"Yes, after all was said and done. Things are exactly the way they should be," David said and looked down at Trish.

She was looking back at him with a smile, and he kissed her forehead.

"Ugh, there they go again," Marcus said as he jerked his head away from the scene as everyone laughed.

Thank you

Thank you for reading my book. I hope you have enjoyed Trish and David's journey.

Olivia Saxton

The Rancher

After saying goodbye to her demanding hotel job, Faith Roberts leaves Miami for a long deserved vacation. Her travels lead her to Texas and into the arms of a lonely rancher who is afraid of love.

With patience and understanding, Faith breaks through Adrian's walls. The happy times doesn't last long when Adrian Matthews and his family are setup to lose the Lone Wolf Ranch and their freedom.

By a twist of fate, Faith gets the upper hand to stop the troubles that has plagued the Matthews family. However, is she putting herself in danger for the rancher she loves?

Warning: This work of fiction has explicit language and graphic sexual scenes.

Garvey's: The Return

After a crushing loss, Jodi Garvey returns to Arizona. Jackie and old college chum, Billy Newman gets Jodi back on her feet. They're also helping Jodi hide a secret that will devastate her former lover, Matt Kirby.

Jodi Garvey left town four months ago, leaving Sheriff Matt Kirby miserable. When he finally decides to move on with the angelic Mindy Pandock, Jodi returns.

It becomes obvious that Jodi is hiding a secret after Matt confronts her at Garvey's during orgy night. Matt won't stop until he finds out what Jodi is hiding. Will they be able to work past the pain that they have caused each other and be together again?

Warning: This work of fiction is romance erotica. It has explicit language and graphic sexual scenes.

Made in the USA
Middletown, DE
26 October 2024